Praise for *Bronco Buster*

"*Bronco Buster* is 'Hammerhead' Jed's most uproarious case yet —and given A.J. Devlin's flair for offbeat characters, hilarious dialogue and no-holds-barred action, that's saying a lot! Jed's adventures were raucous enough with the quirky world of wrestling as a backdrop. Throw in a twist-filled day at the rodeo, and you're saddling up for the wildest ride of the year!"
—Steve Hockensmith, *New York Times* bestselling author of *Holmes on the Range* and *Pride and Prejudice and Zombies*

"If you read only one mystery featuring a banana milkshake-guzzling pro wrestler-turned-P.I. this year, make it *Bronco Buster*. Nobody combines slapstick comedy and hard-boiled crime like A.J. Devlin. And if you want more—you will, after this riotous fourth entry in the hilarious 'Hammerhead' Jed series—go back and read the rest. And then read this one again."
—Andrew Shaffer, *New York Times* bestselling author of *Feel the Bern: A Bernie Sanders Mystery*

"Action-packed, with all the colour and gritty din of a small-time rodeo alive on every page, a sadder, wiser but incurably romantic 'Hammerhead' can't resist the lure of a lurid death, drawing him back to his beloved detective work. Don't even try to resist the whirlwind ride of clues, eccentric characters, and that Devlinesque twisty ending!"
—Iona Whishaw, bestselling award-winning author of the Lane Winslow mystery series

"With *Bronco Buster*, A.J. Devlin proves he's the undisputed champion of hilarious and heartfelt mysteries. A riotous and adrenaline-packed romp full of rodeo clowns, lumberjacks, and murderers, the fourth book in Devlin's award-winning 'Hammerhead' Jed

series had me howling with laughter from the first line and crying by the last."
—S.M. Freedman, award-nominated author of *Blood Atonement* (*Globe and Mail's* Top 100 Best Books of 2022, Crime Writers of Canada's Awards of Excellence Finalist)

"*Bronco Buster* is a wild, outrageous, and edgy mystery-comedy—I absolutely loved it! Jed must contend with rodeo clowns, maddened bulls, desperate hatchet throwers, a Doukhobor cult leader, and a cowgirl who lassoes like Wonder Woman. Studded with witticisms, crackling dialogue, and raucous action, this is Hammerhead's best adventure yet. A must-read!"
—M.H. Callway, award-nominated author of *Snake Oil and Other Tales*

Praise for *Five Moves of Doom*

"The third instalment of the always great 'Hammerhead' Jed series, this one was darker and carried some serious gravitas and got my pulse racing in a way few books can. Full of powerful scenes, this book stayed with me for some time after I read it."
—J.T. Siemens, *Globe and Mail Best Books of 2022*

"Compelling, engrossing, thought provoking, yet still humorous, *Five Moves of Doom* is a brilliant look at what happens when you reach rock bottom. Grab a banana milkshake and be prepared for the ride of a lifetime."
—Kathleen J. Kaminski, *Cozy Up With Kathy*

"*Five Moves of Doom* is pure crime fiction entertainment...the kind of novel we like to point to when we talk about independent publishing and how it feeds vibrant new material into the crime fiction scene."
—*Crime Fiction Lover Blog*

"... will have you laughing out loud."
—June Lorraine Roberts, *Murder in Common*

"Keeps the tension high and the pages turning. In the action scenes both the author and characters shine."
—*ReviewingTheEvidence.com*

"Dirty Harry in the movie *Magnum Force* uttered the words 'A man's got to know his limitations,' and we get a glimpse of what that means in Devlin's superb new book."
—Patrick Whitehurst's Top Reads of 2022

Praise for *Rolling Thunder*

"Devlin's comic caper has a goofy charm and action aplenty."
—*Kirkus Reviews*

"Funny, smart, readable ... Devlin takes his cues from the likes of Carl Hiaasen and builds the suspense along with the craziness. Welcome back, 'Hammerhead' Jed and company."
—Margaret Cannon, *Globe and Mail*

"The follow-up to the Arthur Ellis Award–winning *Cobra Clutch* is another action-packed violent mystery.... readers of the first book will enjoy the humor and outrageous antics."
—Lesa Holstine, *Library Journal*

"*Rolling Thunder* hits all the marks for a PI thriller. Thoroughly recommended. 5 stars."
—M.H. Callway, *Eat This Book*

"Strap on your knee pads and buckle your helmet; it's about to get physical."
—*Strong Sense of Place*

"Devlin utilizes a gut-punch at the end of each chapter. He does this deliciously, so that every chapter starts with a pit in your stomach followed by a smile on your face for the flavour of what's to come. Devlin's work is reminiscent of pulp-fiction —fast-paced thrilling stories with bright covers that are as easy to consume as a DQ banana milkshake, but with a spoonful of modern-day grit."
—Caileigh Broatch, *The Ormsby Review*

"*Rolling Thunder* is wonderful escapist crime fiction. It snakes along like a roller derby skater, and you never quite know who Jed is going to run into next – or whether he'll slip through to the next stage of his adventure or end up bouncing on his backside."
—*Crime Fiction Lover*

"Yeah, this one has everything I love about the genre. Action, laughs, attractive women, mystery. This one proves the first novel was not a one hit wonder. Can't wait for the third book."
—*Sons of Spade*

"It's just so much fun, action-packed and non-stop. If you're looking for a fun, violent mystery, check it out."
—*Lesa's Book Critiques*

"Get yourself ready for another entertaining read with the second 'Hammerhead' Jed Mystery. It's the kind of book we need right now."
—June Lorraine Roberts, *Murder in Common*

"Jed is growing as a person and as a character. His horizons are broadening, he takes his mistakes to heart and tries to learn from them, and he genuinely wants to help people. The general decency of the guy makes you root for him, both inside and outside of the ring."
—*Cozy Up With Kathy*

Praise for *Cobra Clutch*

"Set in Vancouver, BC, this intriguing debut offers a fast-paced, graphically violent mystery that pairs well with Glen Erik Hamilton's Past Crimes. Fans of pro wrestling will appreciate 'Hammerhead' Jed."
—*Library Journal*

"… high-pitched violent action sequences, daring escapes, and a thrilling climax."
—Stephen Knight, *Quill & Quire*

"*Cobra Clutch* masterfully blends humor, mystery, thrills, action, romance, and heart into a hell of a story featuring a lively wrestler-turned-PI hero. The action scenes are intense, the quiet times heartwarming and engaging, and the humor expertly interjected to accentuate characters and breathe realism into the story."
—John M. Murray, *Foreword Reviews*

"*Cobra Clutch* uses humor and gritty realism and includes a former tag-team partner, a kidnapped snake, sleazy promoters, and violence inside and outside the ring."
—*BC BookWorld*

"Pro-wrestlers, scuzzy bikers, a yellow pet python, and a private detective—how does Devlin hold it all together in this gritty page-turning debut novel? With a whole lot of style and a splattering of tongue-in-cheek humour."
—Wendy Hawkin, *The Ottawa Review of Books*

"Now this is what I like. A fast-paced and funny ride with a great new PI."
—*Son of Spade*

"Jed infiltrates the sleazy world of pro-wrestling and grapples with the dangerous Vancouver underworld in this engaging debut thriller, a finalist for the 2019 Lefty Award for Best Debut Mystery."
—*Stop, You're Killing Me!*

"Great fun, with an engaging lead as a reluctant [series] detective. Go buy them."
—Victor Catano, *Across the Board*

"Fans of *Jack Reacher* and 1980s action movies will happily add 'Hammerhead' Jed to their list of favorite heroes."
—*Salisbury Post*

"*Cobra Clutch* is a terrific novel, bringing the seamier side of Vancouver to life, while amusing us with witty dialogue, startling characters and amazing plot twists."
—Susan Hoover, *Reviewing the Evidence*

BRONCO BUSTER

A NEWEST
MYSTERY

Copyright © A.J. Devlin 2024

All rights reserved. The use of any part of this publication — reproduced, transmitted in any form or by any means, electronic, mechanical, recording or otherwise, or stored in a retrieval system — without the prior consent of the publisher is an infringement of copyright law. In the case of photocopying or other reprographic copying of the material, a licence must be obtained from Access Copyright before proceeding.

Library and Archives Canada Cataloguing in Publication

Title: Bronco buster / by A.J. Devlin
Names: Devlin, A. J., author.
Description: Series statement: A "Hammerhead" Jed mystery ; 4
Identifiers: Canadiana (print) 20230580270 | Canadiana (ebook) 20230580319 | ISBN 9781774391020 (softcover) | ISBN 9781774391037 (EPUB)
Subjects: LCGFT: Detective and mystery fiction. | LCGFT: Novels.
Classification: LCC PS8607.E94555 B76 2024 | DDC C813/.6—dc23

NeWest Press wishes to acknowledge that the land on which we operate is Treaty 6 territory and Métis Nation of Alberta Region 4, a traditional meeting ground and home for many Indigenous Peoples, including Cree, Saulteaux, Niitsitapi (Blackfoot), Métis, Dene, and Nakota Sioux, since time immemorial.

NeWest Press expressly prohibits the use of *Bronco Buster* in connection with the development of any software program, including, without limitation, training a machine learning or generative artificial intelligence (AI) system.

Editor for the Press: Merrill Distad
Cover and interior design: Michel Vrana
Cover images: iStockphoto
Author photo: Sean O'Brien

  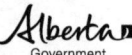 

NeWest Press acknowledges the support of the Canada Council for the Arts, the Government of Alberta through the Ministry of Arts, Culture and Status of Women, and the Edmonton Arts Council for support of our publishing program. We acknowledge the financial support of the Government of Canada through the Canada Book Fund for our publishing activities.

NeWest Press
#201, 8540-109 Street
Edmonton, Alberta T6G 1E6
www.newestpress.com

No bison were harmed in the making of this book.

Printed and bound in Canada

1 2 3 4   27 26 25 24

For Sean O'Brien

Bronco Buster:

[ˈbräNGkō] *mid 19th century: from Spanish, literally 'rough, rude'.*

[/ˈbəstər/] *a person or thing that breaks, destroys, or overpowers something.*

In the Bronco Buster, an opponent is seated against a turnbuckle of the ring while the attacking wrestler jumps in the corner, straddles his or her opponent's body, and bounces up and down on their face and / or chest. Normally treated as having comic or sexual connotations rather than a legitimately painful move.

PROLOGUE
"BLADE JOB"

I was grinding my spandex-covered crotch into my muscular opponent's face when I first heard the blood-curdling scream.

Usually I wore skin-tight, elastic, black pants when grappling in the squared circle, but given the outdoor venue and early summer heat, I had dug up an old pair of black, Speedo-style shorts from my WWE days. They were covered in lightning bolts and had the name "Hammerhead" embroidered in cursive across my ass.

Always looking to expand my repertoire of professional wrestling moves, and knowing I would be performing in front of hundreds of rural rodeo fans who would appreciate a bit of absurdist flair, "Cowboy Cobb" Calhoun had agreed to my request to use a Bronco Buster toward the end of our match to entertain the audience. It was a cringe-worthy, yet crowd pleasing technique, that required me to throw him into a corner turnbuckle, leap on his face, grab the top ropes on either side, and bounce up and down on his smug mug while he appeared to 'suffocate'.

Upon hearing the awful cry, confused spectators switched from cheering to a flurry of nervous chatter, with many trotting off in the direction of the troubling shriek. Not wanting to miss the action, I skipped my usual Five Moves of Doom—a series of in-ring maneuvers which telegraphed an impending victory—yanked "Cowboy Cobb" to his feet, dropped him with my signature Hammerlock DDT, then rolled him up for a quick pin.

Once the referee had slapped the canvas for the third time, I slid out of the ring and followed the people headed toward the source of the screech. It was a matinee performance, so we were grappling in a modest ring located in a smaller section of the open air pro-wrestling pavilion, much closer to the adjacent loggersports area, instead of the large main event showcase for the big Saturday night show. I had also managed to weasel my way out of that booking since I had headlined in the superior squared circle the prior evening. So with "Cowboy Cobb" defeated, I was officially off the clock.

I followed the crowd toward the source of the scream when I noticed my cousin, former IRA operative and legendary pint-pounding pisstank Declan St. James, beside me. This was hardly surprising given his tendency to stir-up trouble when not tending bar and serving brews at The Emerald Shillelagh, my family's Irish pub in downtown Vancouver.

"I gotta feelin' some dosser is up to somethin', Boyo."

I nodded before breaking into a brisk jog with my cousin following suit. We entered the the West Coast Lumberjack competition area of the rodeo, featuring stations for axe throwing, tree climbing, hot saw racing, chair carving, and springboard chops. The commotion took us straight to the log boom pool, front and centre in the loggersports pit.

I didn't recognize the woman standing near the body, but she began hyperventilating while her girlfriend tried to calm her down.

The axe embedded in the sunken dead man's head had been thrown or swung with such force it nearly split the back of the lumberjack's skull in two, no small feat. The long hatchet's handle breached the surface of the water.

But seeing the hulking, denim-clad body submerged with the axe in its cranium near the bottom of the shallow pool was upsetting to say the least. Blood created a circumference of red around the log booms, while the lumberjack's feet and legs bobbed up and down. I took a deep breath and looked around, but all eyes except mine were on the body.

A silence fell across the crowd and we collectively held our breath as a lone log floated directly toward the corpse. The long chunk of wood butted up against the end of the axe handle that was sticking out of the surface of the water. It must have knocked the head of the axe loose, because the next moment there was aquatic movement from below. The double-sided metal blade of the tool-turned-weapon clanged dully against the pool floor, and the corpse buoyed its way to the surface before flipping over and floating face up.

"Jaysus," muttered Declan, as we both recognized the body before us. "That's Jasper. The three o'us just bloody well—I mean—he was our …"

"*Friend*," I managed to say aloud, between gritted teeth.

1:11 P.M.

ONE
"LUMBER MAN DOWN"

The recently renamed Colossal Cloverdale Rodeo and Country Fair was an enlarged and emboldened version of an event held annually in the eponymous southeastern suburb of Greater Vancouver, with its town centre located in the city of Surrey, British Columbia. Although I had been wrestling a lot of late, I had still been hesitant to participate in the exhibition's pro-wrestling extravaganza, set to take place at an outdoor venue that guaranteed a raucous crowd. The last time I had wrestled under such circumstances, I took a hit to my noggin from a nearly full can of Labatt's Blue Lager instead of the usual weakened two-by-four piece of western red cedar I break over my head as part of my victory celebration. You know you're in for a wild time when even a "babyface"—sports entertainment squared circle shorthand for a "good guy" wrestler—is getting beaned in the back of the head by open beers as part of alcoholic projectile friendly fire.

Nevertheless, I relented pretty quickly and agreed to perform, because I welcomed any and all distractions while taking time off as a private investigator to recover from a physically and emotionally bruising case. Once I agreed, my part-time boss at XCCW (X-Treme Canadian Championship Wrestling) was thrilled, although his excitement paled in comparison to Declan's, who began referring to the weekend as the *"mother of all piss-ups."*

Since I had once been a big draw in the WWE, and had returned to local professional wrestling to raise money for a charity for which I cared deeply, I figured it couldn't hurt to show up, forget my troubles, and put on a fun match.

The night before my big matinee bout Declan and I had downed some pints inside the *Colossal Cloverdale Rodeo's* "Longhorn Saloon," a twenty-thousand square-foot pole barn in the middle of the fairgrounds that had been converted into a makeshift pub. We had taken refuge deep within the venue in an effort to find some peace and quiet, and after some pints of ale we found ourselves swapping funny fringe sports stories with a handful of hard-drinking lumberjacks. One man in particular who we befriended—Jasper Adams—was a big ol' stud of a country boy who turned out to be an even bigger professional wrestling fan. He insisted on buying us a round of Guinness. Although I offered thanks from the both of us, my cousin decided to show his gratitude by offering a proper explanation of why the Irish stout is the one and only *"Nectar of the Gods,"* and how anyone who disagrees deserves an *"authentic Celtic knuckle supper."* Jasper seemed bemused and we graciously accepted our new buddy's generosity and company before I shared a few entertaining tales of my time grappling at a pro-wrestling show in Banff, Alberta. Jasper reciprocated with his own recollections of competing in loggersports events in the same Rocky Mountain resort region.

Unfortunately, Jasper's head was now partly sliced in half while his bloody, mutilated corpse floated belly up in a shallow pool next to the thick logs meant for lumberjacks running in place atop them, rather than serving as a scene for a macabre murder.

"Poor bastard never had much o'a chance, did he?"

Declan tossed me a shirt and a towel, and I wiped myself down and covered up my sweaty torso with the most popular and best-selling piece of "Hammerhead" Jed merchandise. It featured a muscular arm and a fist gripping a two-by-four piece of wood being struck by a lightning bolt.

I sighed, feeling my crime-solving compulsions creeping up from within, knowing all too well that I was reaching a point of no return. "Shake?" I asked, hopefully.

Declan handed me a frosty beverage he had already poured from a Dairy Queen cup into a chilled metal tumbler from the portable cooler backpack he wore slung over his shoulder.

"Where's yer usual protein an' creatine an' shite? Cuz I don' think bananas an' ice cream alone qualifies as an ideal recovery drink."

I popped the lid and took a strawless sip of the frosty, DQ treat and licked my lips. "Electrolytes, potassium, and calcium, D," I said smiling. "Everything a post-workout body needs."

Declan flipped a Benson & Hedges cigarette up and in-between his lips, lit it with his Zippo lighter and took a long drag.

"I know ya ain't exactly detectin' much these days, Jed. But we can't let this one go. Jasper was a good fella."

I sighed, knowing my cousin was right. "He was. Whatever his deal was, he didn't deserve this."

"All right, Laddie. Ya know I got yer back. What now?"

I looked away from the grisly scene and took another slurp of my shake.

"I guess it's time to go to work."

TWO
"BANANA GRIND"

The head of the axe had a unique shape. The blade was ground down thinner on the edges and was thicker in the middle, resembling that, of all things, a banana.

Ironically enough, at one point during the previous evening when Declan and I were having beers with Jasper Adams, he talked specifically about the type of outdoorsman equipment that was currently embedded in the back of his skull.

"There are different kinds of grinds, you see," said Jasper, before taking a pull of his bottle of Moosehead Lager.

"Jasper," said my cousin, interrupting as usual. "How in the bloody hell can ya drink that moose piss?" he asked, glaring at the bottle from Canada's oldest independent brewery.

Jasper gave Declan a funny look. I elbowed him, hinting that he should play nice.

"All genuine bushwhackers drink Moosehead."

"Bushwhackers?" asked Declan. "You mean like fellas who like to trim birds' bits south o'the equator?"

"No, Man," said Jasper, before shaking his head and chuckling. "I'm talking about lumberjacks."

"What I want to know is why loggersports, Chopper?" I interjected. "How does someone even get into that?"

Jasper killed what was left of his Moosehead and signaled the bartender for another round. Before he could respond, Declan all but had a fit.

"*Chopper?*" he snapped, incredulously.

"What? You're always saying I call people 'Bub' too much," I replied, in my defence. "I was trying out something new."

"I like it," said Jasper. "And you should see me chop. I make Paul Bunyan look like an amateur."

Jasper leaned forward on the shiny black bar, put aside his empty bottle, and interlaced his fingers. "My grandfather—who helped raise me—was a self-made man. When he was in grade nine, he had to drop out of school and take over his father's job as a tree feller to support his mum and younger brother because a Douglas Fir tipped the wrong way and crushed my great-grandpa to death. After that my Pop-Pop busted his ass, spent years on the green chain before working his way up the foresting biz, all the while getting married and starting a family. The guy basically gave his life to lumber to make sure those he loved always had food on the table and were able to live a decent life."

"Sounds like a grand fella," said Declan.

"And then some. Which is why competitive wood chopping means a hell of a lot more to me than it does to others."

"Must pay well too, yeah?"

Jasper shrugged. "I pick up some scratch here and there from competitions, but I still have to work regular jobs in the mill or drive for days hauling logs to make ends meet. Of course, that's not to say that making a living exclusively from loggersports wouldn't be nice," he said with the slightest of smug smirks. "Hell, that'd even be better than all the love from the Axe Cats."

"What the shite is an '*axe cat?*'"

"You know, 'blade babes.' Like every sport, it attracts groupies."

"Jasper, ya dirty craythur, I think I love ya!"

I nudged Declan to settle down, before asking my new wood-cutting chum a more serious question. "I'm curious about one thing. Why put so much time and effort into loggersports? I mean, if there's not much of a chance of fame and fortune."

Jasper took a big sip of his Moosehead and stifled a belch. "It's fun. I'm damn good at it. But most of all, because I want to honour my gramps. This is the best way I know how."

"I hear you," I said, softly, feeling an instant kinship with the man. I certainly knew it would have made more sense for me to have followed in my father's footsteps and joined the Vancouver Police Department, and that I would have had a leg up as the son of one of the finest ever to wear a VPD badge. Of course, having a childhood obsession with squared-circle action and a mother who encouraged such a passion, kind of threw a monkey wrench into that life trajectory for me. And the fact Declan had an uncle named Darryl "The Barrell" O'Farrell, who was one of the first ever Irish pro-wrestling Heavyweight Champions, didn't help either.

Declan chortled, snapping me out of my wistfulness. I watched as he wiped a phantom tear from his eye and clasped a thunderous hand down on Jasper's meaty trapezius muscles. I figured the abundance of alcohol might finally be catching up with him. "That's bloody beautiful. To yer Chop-Chop Pop Pop!" he said, and we all clinked cans and bottles in a toast.

I shook off the day-old memory and focused on the buoyant body still in front of me. I was pretty sure axes with "banana grinds" didn't just accidently find their way into the back of the heads of lumberjacks. Somebody wanted Jasper dead and they succeeded. Although I hadn't worked as one in a while or even been hired as a PI, I knew that I couldn't help but stick my nose in the case. I had a lot of experience when it came to murders that were committed in athletic subcultures, and by the time the Mounties arrived, sealed off the scene, and dragged their asses until their IDENT unit went to work, the killer could be long gone.

I stared at the corpse as it slowly rotated until it was face down in the water again, all the while standing next to the horrified onlookers. I turned to my cousin.

"We can't leave this rodeo until we find out who did this, D."

"Giddy up, Mate. But where do we start?"

It was a good question. After a moment, I had the perfect answer.

THREE
"JAGGER"

Some people in the crowd who had gathered around the floating corpse gasped when I jumped into the knee-high pool of bloody water. I sloshed my way over to the body, removed the wet workman gloves from the deceased's hands by tugging at the fingertips, then slipped them on. I ignored the chatter from the crowd behind me until I heard a voice holler, "You shouldn't be doing that! It's a crime scene!"

The outburst was quickly followed by a familiar Irish brogue. "Shut yer bloody trap, ya wanker. He's a professional."

Without looking back over my shoulder, I could still tell Declan's scolding had done the trick, and I went about examining the floating remains of Jasper Adams. There was no trauma to his backside or legs, and the tread of his steel-toed, yellow leather, Timberland boots had bits of dirt, sawdust, and wood chips as one would expect.

"Jed!" hollered Declan. I turned around just in time to see him lob a pair of logger goggles at me. I snatched them out of the air, pulled the leather strap back as I slid them over my head, and a moment later the tinted plastic visor gave everything in my field of vision a hint of light yellow.

I held my breath and dunked my head underwater. It was hard to see at first, but there was a thin, silver wire looped around Jasper's neck, which indicated he had been subdued by first being choked before the axe delivered the killing blow. Suddenly slaughter-by-throwing axe didn't seem so likely. It was also clear that the hair-raising holler that had echoed across the fairground couldn't have been the result of Jasper's final death throes, and must have come from the person who found his body.

I climbed out of the pool, whipped my nearly shoulder-length hair back, and sucked in some air before catching my cousin's eye. "There's a wire around his neck," I announced.

"That's a bloody *jagger*!"

I looked at him in confusion and he threw his arms up in the air. "What? I watch SportsNet on the weekends," he said defensively.

The neck wound from the thin wire was seeping blood in the water and it was clear it had been wrenched around poor Jasper's Adam's apple. At the ends of the taut metal cord were two small wooden-ball handles which had given either the murderer—or accomplice?—the leverage to pull hard. As a result, it was difficult to gauge the amount of strength that was used by the strangler. And combined with the clunky axe that now rested on the bottom of the log boom pool, it was also clear that this was not the most efficient of kills.

"Two-man job?" I asked.

Declan leaned forward to offer me a hand.

"Bloody well could be. C'mon, Laddie. Time to scoot."

"There's something else down there," I replied.

I heard the sound of an airhorn being blown and some distant chatter over CB radios.

"Move yer arse, Jed! Security is a comin'!" bellowed Declan.

I ignored the advice and did another otter dive under the water. I used my palms to push away lingering blood until my face was nearly on the bottom of the pool. I took a good look at the shiny object that I had only caught a glimpse of when I first waded into Jasper's final resting place. Lying on the porcelain tile was a broken silver chain interlaced with a simple circular metal washer that belonged more with a nut and bolt than it did at the scene of a crime.

I furrowed my brow as I popped up out of the water. I grasped Declan's hand and he pulled me out onto dry land. I removed the logger goggles and the workman's gloves I had borrowed from Jasper's body, then tossed both items into the shallow pool behind me.

"Dude, *that* is definitely not 'professional,'" muttered the same voice that had chastised me earlier.

I turned around to see a gangly Caucasian guy in a ratty, rainbow-coloured poncho and dreadlocks which looked as if they hadn't been shampooed in months.

"Mind your business, Bub," I replied, but the hemp enthusiast seemed oblivious to my words of warning.

"C'mon, Jed!" snapped Declan.

"Let's go," I replied, as we hurriedly left the crime scene behind us while bustling security guards pushed their way through the lingering crowd toward the scene of our impromptu inspection.

Once we exited the loggersports area we slowed our retreat and began to walk casually, joining the flow of country fair-goers of all ages, shapes, and sizes who were all around us. A can of Harp Lager had magically appeared in Declan's hand while we moved along with the crowd and he had taken three big swigs by the time I finished describing what I had found at the bottom of the pool.

"Ya think he had like some kind o'project goin' in a workshop or somethin'?"

"Maybe. All I know is that a flat washer on a chain seems like an unusual fashion statement jewelry-wise, especially for a seasoned lumberjack."

"Aye, yer not wrong there. Where we headed now, then?"

I replied without hesitation. "To see a clown."

FOUR
"JOKERS WILD"

During our night at the Longhorn Saloon—where Declan and I had stepped up our game by graduating from cans of Guinness to twenty-ounce Imperial draught pints of Red Racer's Extra Special Bitter strong amber ale—the late lumberjack Jasper Adams and I forged a sudden and unlikely bond.

How? By engaging in some good, old-fashioned, booze-induced reminiscing about the lost loves of our lives. Naturally, I shared way too much, especially the regret I felt over how things had been left with Vancouver Police Detective Constable Rya Shepard, my father's police protogé and the only woman who had ever made my heart ache in both good ways and bad.

"She was a really, really, special girl," I said to Jasper, not fully aware of quite how tipsy I had become in the rodeo drinking hole. "And she smelled like lilacs."

"Did you love her?" he asked.

I sighed and killed what remained of my ESB. "Always."

"I hear that. I think you need some more medicine, 'Hammerman'."

"'Hammerhead'."

"What?"

"I'm not a contractor and I don't dance around to nineties pop rap in parachute pants, damn it. It's *'Hammerhead'*."

Declan, with his back to us both while he ogled the many scantily-clad ladies dressed in country and country themed clothing grinding on the dance floor, glanced back over his shoulder and decided to toss his two cents into our conversation.

"Aye, he's speakin' the truth, Mate. Me cuz is too legit to quit."

Jasper liked that one and snorted in laughter so hard foamy white beer suds bubbled out of his nostrils. He wiped his nose on his arm while my cousin leaned closer to me and whispered.

"Besides, lately I think ya should bloody well change yer name to *'Hammered'* Jed."

I shot Declan a dirty look and thumped a fist on my chest. "You can't touch this," I mumbled, slurring my words a little.

"Easy, Boyo. I'm just bustin' yer barse. 'Tis good for ya to blow off some steam after all that shite with yer lady drama."

I nodded begrudgingly, unable to deny the fact that the last big case I worked shattered my self-esteem, nearly left me for dead, and drove a wedge between Rya and me so deep she wouldn't even respond to my texts or phone calls. Despite my best efforts to keep myself distracted, the experience had shaken me to my very core.

Having recovered from his near spit-take, Jasper flagged down our bartender and signaled her for a round of shots of Crown Royal Canadian Whisky.

"Nah, I'm good, Bub," I said.

"C'mon, *'Hammerhead'*! You can't have earned a nickname like that without being able to handle a headache after a boilermaker or two."

I glanced at Declan, a renowned boozer in his own right, who delivered a stinging jab to my deltoid. "He's got ya there, Boyo," he said in solidarity with our new drinking buddy. "Tell Jasper here about yer hot cop angst while I go drain me skin flute at the loo."

I rolled my eyes as he ambled off, but couldn't resist his suggestion. After a few moments I gave in. "Her name is Rya. Wicked smart, funny, and also probably the best member on the VPD since my old man retired from the job." Jasper nodded, "And she's a hottie. More than that. More than beautiful. She … radiates elegance."

If there was an antithesis to elegance, I found it when the busty bartender's cleavage jiggled as she smacked the bottoms of our shot glasses down on the bar, splashing us with droplets of whisky.

"Does your handsome pal here want to make his a 'Dolly Delight,' Jasper?" she asked, smirking and tugging on the big flannel knot of her sleeveless top just above her taut, tanned, and tattooed midsection.

"Maybe next round," replied Jasper. Our server gave me a wink before making herself scarce.

"'Dolly Delight?'" I asked, curiously.

Jasper gave me a pat on the back. "It's when you drink the Crown Royal out of her belly button," he said.

"Guess I missed out."

Jasper chucked. "You have no idea. She's got a deep, lint-free, innie that'll put more wood in your dagger than I chop in a day."

"An adventure for another time," I said, before dropping my whisky shooter into my glass and chugging down the double drink. Jasper didn't miss a beat and did the same. I stifled a burp then continued. "You haven't told me about your heartbreak yet."

Jasper winced. "Kelly Lewis."

"And?"

"Let's just say things didn't end on the best of terms."

"How come?"

"We lived hard … and we loved hard. Part of the rodeo way."

I nodded, knowing all too well what he meant. "Hey, I get it. I used to spend three hundred days a year on the road, moving from one Podunk town to the next, putting on matches like I was an oiled-up, testosterone-charged transient. You click with people quickly when that's your lifestyle."

"Indeed."

"This Kelly was another loggersports athlete I take it?"

Jasper shook his head. "Rodeo clown."

I shrugged my shoulders. "Must have made for some good role play in the bedroom."

"You have no idea."

Like a great white shark smelling blood in the water from nautical miles away, Declan breached the space between our shoulders in seconds, popping his head up and grinning from ear-to-ear. "Did I hear one o'ya dryshites say somethin' about role play?" he asked, excitedly.

"For God's sake, D, if perving out were a superpower you'd be in the goddamn Justice League."

Jasper laughed so hard he nearly fell off of his bar stool. "Sorry, Declan, but he's got you there."

My cousin all but ignored our new pal's remark. "Mmmm…" he moaned, before taking a pull of the fresh pint he had somehow procured in such a short time. "If ya only knew the things I'd get up to with Wonder Woman and her Lasso o'Truth," he said, devilishly.

I shook off Declan's lecherousness and focused my attention back on Jasper. "So, where's this rodeo clown now?"

"Here," he replied, matter-of-factly. "But we're not exactly on speaking terms."

"Why not?"

"It's complicated."

"I hear that."

Jasper sighed deeply and took a big sip of his ale. "I just miss him," he said, wistfully. "More than I ever thought I would."

"*Him*?!?" exclaimed Declan. "Jasper, ya devil, I had no idea ya were fond o'the purple ridgebacks. Settle a bet I have with me mate back home—do ya fellas prefer the one-eyed boys with their shirt sleeves up or Kojak's rollneck?"

I put my elbows on the bar and placed my face in my hands. Even for Declan, this was painfully incorrigible. Jasper delivered a desperate nudge to my side with his elbow. "Jed, what the hell is he talking about?"

"Penises," I replied. "He's talking about circumcised and uncircumcised penises."

I snapped back to the present while we continued along the asphalt away from the lumberjack pit and Jasper Adams's lifeless body. How we had gone from Declan's annoying banter about euphimisms for genitalia to Jasper's head nearly cleaved in half in less than twelve hours was beyond me.

The sun was just beginning to sink from its midday peak. The smell of rawhide, leather, and manure hung in the air like a frothy mist. Declan pounded what was left of his Harp Lager, flattened the can into an aluminum pancake, then tossed the disc away beside him like an ultimate frisbee. I didn't even bother to chastise him for not recycling. Even worse, no one seemed to notice or care about his littering as his refuse quickly found company alongside other empties spread about on the ground.

"You have to admit, D, you kind of made a bit of a spectacle over Jasper being homosexual."

"Bollocks! I was genuinely interested in his opinion. Jaysus, what bloody luck. I finally get meself a gay friend and then some barmy bastard goes all Lizzie Borden on his arse."

The song "Save A Horse, Ride A Cowboy" by Big & Rich pounded over booming speakers in the distance as we reached the eastern entrance to the Stetson Bowl, which was the *Colossal Cloverdale Rodeo and Country Fair's* infamous outdoor stadium. The folks we could see in the five-thousand seat capacity arena were standing shoulder-to-shoulder in the nosebleed section, which combined with the thunderous cheering, made it obvious that the venue was filled to capacity. The Stetson Bowl was sealed off by large wooden gates with spiked tops, as well as a collection of beefy security guards stealthily sipping longneck bottles of beers while on the job, who apparently had not yet been alerted that a murder had taken place nearby.

"Can I help you, Partner?" asked a jacked man wearing a red shirt.

"I hope so," I replied, turning my attention to the backwoods bodybuilder with the word STAFF in white letters stretched so tightly across his chiseled chest I could see his pecs rippling beneath the fabric.

"My name's Jed Ounstead. I'm a private investigator."

Ripplechest eyed me curiously. "Where's your ID?"

I patted around my spandex-clad butt before turning my palms up in the air. "I'm a *pro-wrestler* PI. I don't exactly keep it with me when I'm in the ring."

"No ID, no entrance. And even if you had it, you're no cop so I don't have to let you in."

"Just need a quick word with Kelly Lewis," I said. "He's one of the rodeo clowns."

"Beat it, Bargain Basement Batista."

I exchanged a look with Declan, who despite appearing irritated, had the slightest of smirks starting to form at the corner of his lips.

"Last chance, Bub. We don't want any trouble. And Batista's bald, by the way. This mane may look fall-out-of-bed perfectly tousled, but it requires a conditioner that costs more than you make in a day," I said with a healthy dose of snark, running a hand through my hair which was still damp from the log boom pool.

Ripplechest crossed his arms defiantly. With no other recourse, I gave my cousin the green light he had been so desperately awaiting with the slightest of nods. Declan beamed and took the lead in what was quickly becoming an escalating confrontation.

"Jaysus, yer as dried up as a nun's tit," he sniped.

"What?" snapped Ripplechest.

"Ma liked a few schoops when ya were a bun in the oven, eh?"

"Schoops?"

"Aye. Explains why ya got a bake on ya like a joyrider's front bumper."

"What the fuck are you saying?"

"That ya ain't no Yeats, ya arseweed! Now sod off an' let us save the day then, yeah?"

"Fuck you!" bellowed Ripplechest, who then shoved Declan backwards with one of his meaty paws. The security guard's outburst caused his security pals to suddenly flank him with raised arms and angry glares.

Declan took the aggressive push in stride as he recovered his footing, but I could tell he was pissed off.

"Forget it, D. We'll find another—"

Before I could finish my sentence and in a flash my cousin rammed both of his palms into Ripplechest's musclebound manboobs. "Step aside, ya scut!"

The large man stumbled backwards so hard and fast he nearly fell down. Even his buddies were both stunned by my ripped but sinewy cousin's deceptive strength.

And just like that, once again Declan had gone too far. Ripplechest and his fellow security staff regrouped before all but snarling and charging forward. I leapt between the triggered mob of testosterone and alcohol-charged brawn and my shit-disturber cousin.

"We're leaving!" I announced.

I grabbed Declan by the arm and yanked him away before Ripplechest and his cronies had a chance to process what had just happened or even consider pursuing us.

"You're about as subtle as a Samoan drop," I lamented.

"Ya bloody well let me off the leash, Mate."

"I guess I did," I huffed, "but the clock is ticking. Jasper is dead. If we want to dig up any answers ourselves, we need to act fast before the Mounties show up and shut things down."

"Aye, yer right. Sorry, Mate. Me buzz got the best o'me. I'll behave."

"That's all well and good," I said, after we had put some distance between us, the Stetson Bowl, and Ripplechest and company. I slowed to a stop and my cousin and I looked at each other amidst the steady stream of rodeo fans walking in both directions to and from sales kiosks, food trucks, and events. "But you just burned our one chance to get into the arena. How the hell am I supposed to talk to Kelly now?"

Declan scratched his head and we both stood there stumped for an answer. A moment later, the yokel universe threw us a bone. A big-bellied rodeo clown walked by right in front of us, clutching a six-pack of canned Molson Canadian in one blue-gloved hand and a giant cone of pink cotton candy in the other.

"How do ya feel about a wee bit o'face paint?"

FIVE
"MR. DRESSUP"

It was a struggle to match Declan's pace as he sprinted ahead in pursuit of the paunchy clown. I hustled after them both as they moved away from the fairgrounds and into a sparsely wooded glen, which was a little further east behind the Stetson Bowl. Part of the modest patch of nature was being used as a temporary parking lot for all kinds of rodeo-related vehicles and animal trailers.

Strength wasn't the only thing deceptive about my cousin—he was also fast as lightning. I lost sight of him when he disappeared behind a mobile caravan hitched to a late-eighties, white, rusted Cadillac Sentinel that was one rooftop siren and *Ghostbusters* logo away from doubling as a neglected Ectomobile.

There was a loud thump before the curved green and silver trailer wobbled back and forth on its ramshackle wheels. By the time I rounded the rear of the mobile domicile myself it had stopped rocking. The door was ajar. Aside from burnt yellow grass and a wooded area that was filled with clusters of budding but still leafless trees with dry and cracked branches, there was nothing else nearby save for the raucous rodeo arena, which left the air pungent with the musty scent of sawdust and sweat. The crowd roared in the distance and an air horn blasted, indicating what I assumed was another cowboy clamoring to stay atop a bucking beast of some sort. When I opened the door to the trailer seven seconds later the fans let out a collective sigh, confirming I was correct about the type of rustic challenge that was taking place yonder.

I stopped dead in my tracks upon entering the mobile home. Declan stood behind the now unconscious portly clown, his tattered denim overalls pulled down to his ankles, revealing nothing but a pair of red-striped, tighty-whitey underpants and an abundance of damp leg hair sticking to his thick thighs. The jester's flab was still jiggling as his bulbous upper body lay supine on the floor.

"You know, you could have tied one of his colourful handkerchiefs to the door handle if you wanted some privacy."

"Piss off, ya eejit. Help me strip down this fat bastard already."

"Why?"

"So one of us can go undercover in order to chat with Jasper's joy-boy."

My cousin's impromptu plan began to make sense, but I was reluctant to aid him in violating the rodeo clown any further.

"Did you really need to knock him out?" I asked.

"All I did was put his plump arse in a gentle sleeper hold," he said defensively. "Nodded off like a baby. And the clock's tickin', remember? Your words."

"How'd you know it was the right clown?"

Declan scratched his head. "I guess I kind o'figured Jasper liked 'em fit."

"Maybe we should let this one go, D."

"Bollocks."

I accepted my fate and we began to undress the unconscious entertainer.

Minutes later Declan had gagged the unconscious man with some duct tape he found in a cupboard and was using a roll of twine to bind his ankles and his wrists behind his back.

"Go on, then," said Declan. "Start puttin' all o'that shite on." He nodded toward the double XL clothing and oversized clown shoes that were lumped in a pile at the fat man's feet.

"Why the hell do *I* have to be the one to dress up like a clown?" I protested.

"Cuz it'd take three o'me to fill them dungarees up! Get on it for shite's sake!"

I begrudgingly slipped the denim overalls and ruff-collared yellow shirt over top of my pro-wrestling spandex Speedo-style tights and matching T-shirt I was wearing. Once I had unlaced my glossy, black vinyl, pro-wrestling boots and slipped on the unconscious harlequin's colourful polka-dot shoes, which fortunately were a close fit, I fastened the suspender straps and found myself face-to-face with a grinning Declan holding a makeup kit.

"Now for the fun part."

I cursed loudly before parking my ass in a nearby chair, wincing slightly. I had forgotten how performing a Bronco Buster in a humid environment led to instant chafing in one's groin. I sighed as Declan went about caking up my face with aplomb, humming Ol' Blue Eyes' song "Send In The Clowns."

I tried my best to stifle my laughter but it was a losing battle, and before I knew it, both Declan and I were cackling.

"You're a real son of a bitch, you know that?" I said, still chuckling.

"Aye."

Moments later Declan secured a rainbow-coloured wig on my head, patted me on the shoulders, and gave me a big thumbs up. "Perfect," he declared.

I was a couple steps down out of the trailer when he halted me. "Don't forget this!"

Time slowed as I turned around, only to find him holding up an oversized bright red foam nose.

"No."

"Ya gonna let some poor bloke get gored over yer misplaced pride?"

I gritted my teeth so hard I was almost certain a filling popped out. I snatched the red nose out of his hands and secured it to my snout.

"How do I look?" I asked, instantly regretting the question.

"Like an anabolic Ronald McDonald and Ernie Coombs had a love child," he said, triumphantly.

And with that I went about infiltrating a jam-packed rodeo stadium in the hopes of attracting the attention of a fellow clown instead of one raging, horned beast.

SIX
"SNORTY"

I've had many hot-tempered aggressors attack me before.

One time, when competing during WWE's *Survivor Series*—where I was revealed to be a last-minute surprise addition to Team SMACKDOWN—I made a rookie mistake. I didn't pull my punch after receiving a hot tag, and accidently broke Pietro "Punch Buggy" Patrick's nose with my fist.

Punch Buggy, a wily and seasoned ring general, did not take kindly to a white-hot mid-card babyface (and quickly rising to the main event scene), who was super *over* with the audience, messing up his mangled mug. The guy was already so battered it was hard to tell that his facial features had been affected at all, except for the gushing blood of course.

It was instantly clear to the other eight pro wrestlers in the traditional, five-on-five match, not to mention the seventeen-thousand fans in attendance, that Punch Buggy had been caught off guard by the legit injury and immediately gave in to rage. He charged at me with a fury the likes of which I had never seen, and had it not been for my agility and decision to dive aside he might have clotheslined me hard enough to cause decapitation.

I knew in an instant that our planned spots were out the window, so to maintain the order of elimination that had been pre-determined, I slid between Punch Buggy's legs and rolled him up in a small package, by holding his tights—usually a heel's move—in order to secure a legit three count.

If Punch Buggy was mad beforehand, it was nothing compared to the post-pin fury that spewed out of him after being eliminated. He was so incensed that security had no choice but to pounce on him and forcibly remove him from the ring, while he cussed up a storm so virulent the event should have been upgraded from a PG rating to R.

I thought I'd never again see such a blazing rage in the eyes of an opponent. Of course, that was before I decided to go off half-cocked, dressed up as a rodeo clown trying to lure a frenzied bull away from a cowboy who had just been bucked off the brute.

Although not quite as spry as I used to be, I was still able to lead the animal toward its chute before leaping aside at the last moment. The bull tried to stop its charge a split-second too late, and in a flash the metal gate slammed shut and the fierce creature was safely secured.

The rodeo crowd cheered my efforts, and the other clown in the dust bowl of the arena gave me an approving nod before hustling over to me.

"Nice moves. You must be the new guy, eh? Hell of a way to make an intro."

"Thanks," I said, as the crowd simmered down after the action. "Jed Ounstead," I said, before offering a hand. The other clown stuck out a slim hand and shook mine. "Kelly Lewis."

BINGO, I thought.

"You wanna grab a cold one after this or something?" I asked. "I'm still new to this whole scene and I'd love the chance to pick the brain of a pro like—"

My efforts to cozy up to Jasper Adams's former lover were cut short when a deafening horn blasted and the gates to another chute opened. The rider hooted and hollered, causing me to wince and pray that I wasn't in fact hearing what I was hearing.

The crowd roared to life and it felt like I was moving in slow motion when I turned to face a bucking beast so large it could have doubled as the "Charging Bull" of Wall Street sculpture had it been bronzed.

"*Éire go, Deo, ya rat-arsed bastards!*" screamed Declan at the frenzied spectators, which translated to "*Ireland is forever!*"

The rest of his war cry was pretty self-explanatory.

Everyone in attendance went wild with applause. If the shock at seeing my drunken cousin, complete with a cowboy hat (an item of which I had no idea how or where he had procured) riding a bull caught me off guard, I processed it pretty quickly, because before I knew it both Kelly and I were flanking my buzzed blood brother as he rode the big bull surprisingly well. Buck as it might, the horned monster couldn't shake Declan, whose lean and muscular body remained loosey-goosey with each jerky movement. He clutched the bull rope on the saddle like a lifeline, and once he hit eight seconds on the beast's back the audience erupted with more raucous cheering.

But Declan got greedy and tried to celebrate his accomplishment with a sip of the tallboy of Harp Lager he hoisted in his free hand, the beer splashing out of the can with each buck of the bull. That was all the angry animal needed to toss him from the saddle like a pilot launched from the cockpit of a crashing fighter jet.

"Bollocks!" he yelped, as he flew backwards. Intoxicated as he may have been, I knew Declan would be all right, especially when he tossed his can of beer and tucked himself into a ball before tumbling safely to one knee.

Lewis and I exchanged a quick and knowing look. The livid bovine turned to face us, and snorted dime-sized balls of snot from its snout. Perhaps it was my red-foam clown's nose, but the creature seemed only to have eyes for me. It charged with the collective fury of a dozen of its brethren running through the streets of Pamplona. Try as I might to dodge, there was no escape. In a split-second I went from trying to avoid the beast to accepting the fact it was going to get me—the only question was how badly would I be gored?

Rather than wait for him to reach me, I charged right back, and leapt on his head, trying to thread the needle between the massive horns. Surprised, the brute jutted up its giant noggin just as both my feet landed on it. I flew so high off the ground I felt like Michael Jordan taking flight from the free throw line.

I almost smiled as I floated through the air, although it was impossible to tell with the goofy red lipstick that caked my face in a perpetual grin. I found myself getting caught up in the moment, threw out my limbs at all angles, and did a starfish pose which thrilled the crowd. My red foam nose flew off as wind whooshed past my face. I landed on my feet, then performed a few forward rolls on the soft sawdust and dirt.

"Yee-haw!" yelled Kelly Lewis, while waving around a neon-coloured handkerchief. The bull caught sight of the colourful distraction and started toward my new in-arena ally. And I'll be damned if Lewis didn't manage to time it perfectly, dodging the brute as it unwittingly made a beeline toward the waiting pen. I don't think I had ever heard a more lovely sound than the metal gate clanging shut, and immediately exhaled a forceful breath that I didn't even realize I had been holding in for what felt like minutes.

Declan scrambled to his feet and hopped over the gate of an empty chute, only to be greeted by the prickly voice of a stableman who hollered *"Who are you? Where the hell is Lenny? And why the fuck are you wearing his hat?"*

I figured Lenny may have been sent off to dreamland the same way Declan dispatched our clown friend whose clothes I now wore. I also assumed that my cousin had accosted, then replaced, a bull rider because he couldn't resist the opportunity to cross another thing off of what he called his "eclectic"—and I called "insane"—ever expanding bucket list. I left Declan to sort out whatever mischief he had caused by playing rodeo cowboy and turned my attention to Lewis.

A buzzer blared and an announcer bellowed over the P.A. system that the bull riding had concluded and it was time for intermission. Jasper Adams's ex and I shared a smirk.

"What was that you said about a beer?" he asked, wiping perspiration off his forehead with the back of a gloved hand.

"That the first round is on me. Although considering you just saved my ass, let's make that plural."

He nodded approvingly. Of course had I known what was going to happen next, I would not have been so generous.

SEVEN
"FLANK STRAP"

I grabbed a six-pack of subzero, chilled, take-away brews from the Longhorn Saloon AKA the last place I had seen Jasper alive. Say what you will about rodeo fans, but they don't even bat an eye when a fully costumed clown walks by with an arm full of booze.

I rendezvoused with Kelly Lewis behind the Stetson Bowl, a mere hundred yards from the mobile home of the rodeo performer whose clothes I had stolen. I found it distressing being so close to the scene of the assault, no matter how 'gentle' my cousin assured me he had been. I had no idea how hard Declan choked the poor bastard, but if it was sufficient to ensure that the jester would remain unconscious, I finally had the chance to question Jasper's ex.

I handed Lewis a beer and took a seat on a tree stump across from his lawn chair while he roasted a couple of marshmallows on a long, two-pronged, stainless steel fork. He held them over a small bonfire.

"S'more?" he asked, using his other hand to retrieve some graham wafers and a Neilson's Jersey Milk chocolate bar out of the duffel bag beside him.

"I'm good, thanks," I replied.

He held up his beer and I leaned forward, reaching across the open flame so we could clink bottles.

"To not being gored," he said.

"To not being gored."

We took big sips and reclined in our seats. "That last rider was fucking bananas," said Lewis. "Never seen that guy before. And hoisting a brewski with his free hand to boot," he said, chuckling. "I'm not sure if I just witnessed a maniac or a trailblazer in action."

I wiped the sweat from the back of my neck and tried not to lick my chops like a Pavlovian dog upon hearing the mention of my favourite fruit while anticipation of a frosty banana milkshake tiptoed across my taste buds. "No doubt. I think that guy is from Ireland," I said, feigning ignorance.

Lewis shrugged. "Worse ways to spend a Saturday afternoon."

"I'll drink to that, Bub."

We sipped our brews in silence as I tried to figure out how to smoothly segue the conversation. After a few moments, I gave up and went for it.

"Look, Kelly—I need to be straight with you about something."

"Shoot."

"I'm not a rodeo clown."

Lewis took a big pull from his frosty longneck bottle of suds. "Hey, Man. I know."

"You do?"

"Hell, yeah. Felt like a fraud myself for at least a year on the circuit. But if you pay your dues, in time you'll build up your confidence."

"That's not exactly what I meant—"

"Just don't ever mistake confidence for crazy like that Irishman did," he said, shaking his head while referring to Declan. "I've never seen a beast buck so hard. That wacko must have pulled the flank strap extra tight."

I leaned back on my dry and cracked lodgepole pine stump stool and sipped my beer. Lewis scraped globs of melted marshmallow off of his spit and onto a graham wafer, then topped it with a gooey chocolate bar and squished the sweet sandwich flat with another graham cracker. He took a messy bite and stoked the little bonfire with his stainless steel skewer.

"Flank strap?" I asked, curious what Lewis was referring to.

Lewis slurped the chewy confection of melted gelatin, cocoa, and crumbs off of his lips. "Right, you're new. A "flank strap" is rodeo slang for the sheepskin-lined rope tied around the bull's lower torso near its hind legs. Drives the poor bastards batshit."

I nodded impatiently, frustrated that I was getting nowhere. "My name is Jed Ounstead. I'm a private investigator. And I just recently became fast friends with Jasper Adams."

Lewis stopped chewing and stared at me. "What?" he said, his mouth full of dessert. "But you were—we just corralled a bull together, Man!"

"I know. But I needed to talk with you ASAP and security wouldn't let me in without a little creative deception."

"Why the hell not?" he snapped, quickly growing antagonistic.

I scratched an itch on my cheekbone above my trimmed beard. I felt the makeup cake under my fingernails. I wiped the residue on the oversized overalls I was wearing. "It's kind of a long story. And it's not really worth the time trying to explain it," I said.

Lewis considered my words as he laid his skewer down on the grass and dirt in front of him. He kept his suspicious eyes laser focused on me, despite sliding a cellphone out of his pocket. He stole a glance at his device and tapped the screen quickly a few times before returning his gaze to me.

"You're in cahoots with that Irish jackass, aren't you? I knew there was something off about that whole gong show."

"That was my cousin and his ill-conceived attempt to cause a distraction so I could get you alone to chat."

"This is weird," Lewis said, chomping down the last of his s'more and chasing it with another sip of his beer. "And if it's about Jasper, then I sure as hell have nothing to say."

"Look, I know you guys were lovers. I just need to know what went down between you two. Why the bad blood?"

"What did he say?" he asked anxiously.

"Just that you guys had a good thing going there for a while."

Somehow that cut through Lewis's defenses. "Jasper said that?" he asked, softly.

"Yeah."

"And you believed him?"

"Let's just say the reason we bonded was because we were drowning our sorrows while commiserating over lost loves. I didn't know him well, but I can tell you that I question a lot of people in my line of work. I have no doubt he was being genuine."

Lewis's eyes welled up ever-so-slightly with the formation of tears. He sniffed quickly and cleared his throat.

"I can't believe he hired a PI."

"He didn't. I took it upon myself to track you down after …" I trailed off, catching myself from revealing Jasper's fate. Lewis seemed like he had nothing to hide so far, but for all I knew he had been playing me from the start.

"After what?"

I bit my tongue, unsure of how to proceed. Turned out it didn't matter, because before I could even muster a response, I felt something slink around my neck and tighten so snuggly I was certain my Adam's apple was being crushed.

My hands snaked out behind my head, only to find two giant muscular arms that felt thicker than the tree stump stool

I was sitting on pulling a leather band so taught I started to see dancing stars in my field of vision.

An ice-cold demeanor spread across Lewis's face. He looked over my shoulder at someone while I flailed wildly, my fingers desperately trying to pull the leather belt away from my throat.

Lewis nodded. My garrotte grew even tighter around my neck, and I slid forward off of the tree stump stool and onto my knees. Lewis slowly crouched down in front of me, until we were eye-to-eye, despite my vision beginning to blur.

"Flank strap," he muttered by way of explanation as I succumbed to the strangulation.

Then my world went dark.

EIGHT
"FREIGHT TRAINED"

I'm not sure what brought me to consciousness first—the splashing sound of piss hitting a metal dumpster or the acidic scent of urine wafting up my nostrils. I groaned as I sat up, groggily looking at an emaciated, malnourished pit bull who stared right back at me as he finished piddling. His patchy and unkempt fur sporadically covered the mixed breed's irritated pink skin underneath, and I slowly extended a hand. The stray pooch lowered his leg and approached cautiously, then gave my fingertips a sniff before looking upwards at the dumpster it had just whizzed on and whimpering. I followed the animal's point of view and saw the object of its affection, a half-eaten footlong frankfurter that was sticking out of its foil pouch and dangling above while pinched between the edge of a garbage bin and the receptacle's large plastic lid. I eased myself to my feet despite feeling lightheaded and retrieved the hot dog. The hungry little hobo, which weighed at least thirty pounds but probably should have tipped the scales at fifty, yipped and wagged his tail excitedly. I pulled the weiner free of its wrapping and offered it to my new friend, who snatched it out of my hand and made a hasty retreat down the grungy alley in which I had just awoken. Rows of overstuffed dumpsters lined the narrow passage, which was a single lane wedged in-between a narrow greenbelt of trees and the two-storey rear cement wall of the back of a run-down building. The rotting refuse roasting in the blazing sun in the fetid backstreet was so rank the pooch's stinky pee seemed like a distant memory. I watched as the dog trotted off happily, and found myself envious that the little guy had something to be pleased about.

I, on the other hand, did not.

My neck throbbed and I winced as my fingertips touched my traumatized trachea, alarmed at how hoarse my voice was when I uttered a curse word. I coughed and cleared my throat, then let fly a string of profanity, relieved when the voice I heard sounded somewhat like me.

What the hell had just happened? One minute I'm about to tell Kelly Lewis about Jasper's murder, and then next thing I know I'm nearly decapitated by a flank strap held by arms so beefy they could have made Hulk Hogan's twenty-four-inch pythons look like pipe cleaners.

Did Kelly Lewis already know Jasper's fate when I spoke with him over beers and s'mores? Or had he just been toying with me? I thought he seemed genuinely clueless until pulling off a heel turn that was frostier than my favourite frozen treat.

I licked my lips at the thought of a Dairy Queen banana milkshake, certain that a single sip would not only soothe my sore throat, but be the magic cure-all I needed to muster through the humiliating sneak attack that had caught me completely by surprise.

How had Lewis done it? He clearly knew my attacker and had enlisted his help to take me out. But why? I flashed back to our fireside chat and remembered what must have been him sending a quick text on his cellphone. Things took a turn the moment I confessed my credentials as a private investigator, although he had mistakenly—and very quickly—assumed Jasper had hired my services. That was telling. Yet here I was, alone in a foul passageway while country music blared and rodeo fans cheered in the distance, with nothing but the funk of hot garbage and gasoline from nearby rumbling food truck generators to keep me company.

I started down the tight passageway and walked a couple hundred meters before it curved around a bend, and I found myself in a small gravel parking lot. I walked past several groups of tailgaters crushing beers, catching their collective gazes and causing snickers as they stared at me. I couldn't figure out why I was such an attraction until I saw my haggard and clownish reflection in the tinted rear window of a mud-splashed Chevy Silverado. My red-and-white clown makeup was streaked across my face worse than the dark brown dirt on the exterior of the vehicle, and I did my best to ignore the taunts as I hung my head and continued my walk of shame as a beaten-down Bozo.

I was pretty sure things couldn't get any worse until I heard a silky-smooth voice call out my name.

"Jed?"

I slowed my stride ever so slightly and squinted my eyes shut in a futile attempt to wish away what I just heard as a figment of my imagination.

"JED!" the voice boomed, this time with certainty.

I stopped in my tracks and turned around, like a death row inmate facing the family members of the victims who had turned out to witness his demise.

Her hair was shorter and pulled back into a tight ponytail, but the tips of her blonde locks were still dyed blue-and-red. Although she lacked the DC Comics, anti-hero, Harley Quinn style that inspired her undead roller derby persona "Amazombie," she remained as stunning as ever.

I cursed my luck. Given my appearance, if ever there was a time for her to resemble a demented jester's on-again-off-again girlfriend, now would have been it.

"Hi there," I grumbled to my ex-girlfriend Stephanie Danielson, AKA Stormy Daze, walking briskly toward me in a white tank-top, blue denim cut-off shorts, and a pair of tan wedge sandals that accentuated her long and athletic legs.

She chortled as she took a good look at me, before recovering politely and taking a sip of her lime-flavoured, White Claw hard seltzer. She pulled an unopened can from her back pocket and offered it to me.

"You look like you could use a drink."

I nodded meekly, accepted the beverage, popped the top, and chugged back half of the ice-cold can. It tasted especially delicious as I continued roasting from the heat while wearing my ramshackle clown costume, although a moment later I winced again as the combo of the citrus libation and my still sore throat stung worse than if I had stuck my tongue into a hornet's nest.

"Jesus, Jed, it's an alco-pop, not a shot of Jägermeister."

"Yeah," I said, coughing. "Windpipe's a little tender."

Stormy nodded understandingly as I successfully passed off my strangulation as a peril of professional wrestling. "I heard XCCW was working this event. Wasn't sure if you'd be in the squared circle or not."

"Would you have come to my match if you had been?"

Stormy sighed, and I realized too late that I had just squandered whatever spring in her step and goodwill she brought with her to see me.

"Look, Jed ... after the way we left things—"

"How are the girls?" I asked, cutting her off and referring to her derby squad better known as the Split-Lip Sallies.

She perked up again, grateful I had sidestepped the emotional baggage between us. "They're good. We're off to a hell of a start to the season. Even picked up a new pivot blocker this year named 'Flux InCapacitator.' That girl's a beast."

"Great Scott!" I exclaimed, and we both shared a much-needed tension-relieving chuckle over my low-hanging fruit *Back To The Future* reference. Our shared obsession with eighties and nineties pop culture was just one of the many reasons we had been so great together, but even a smile and another swig of White Claw couldn't make the wistfulness I felt disappear.

"So, what's the deal here?" she asked, nodding toward my attire. "You ditch the 'Hammerhead' schtick for some kind of hardbody Doink the Clown gimmick?"

I nearly blushed that despite looking like a rainbow-splattered buffoon she could still tell I had shed some body fat and added some muscle to my already sizeable frame since the last time we had seen each other.

"Something like that," I replied. "But this—" I said, motioning to my ludicrous attire, "—this is sort of a one-off."

Stormy nodded and took another sip of her cooler. The playful banter was painstakingly replaced by an awkward silence.

"Listen, Stormy, I just wanted to say that, uh …"

"That I look great too?" she asked.

I smiled genuinely for the first time in what had felt like forever. "Yeah. You do. You really do."

She smirked and shrugged playfully. For just a moment I felt a crackle of our old electricity. "You want to join us?" she asked, motioning to a group of friends I didn't recognize who were all gathered around the rear of a pink convertible RAV4.

"I would, but Declan's running around here somewhere and—"

"Say no more," she said, laughing and putting up a hand. "Good grief, I can only imagine what he's up to at a place like this."

"You and me both."

Stormy hesitated, then leaned forward and hugged me tightly. "Take care, Jed."

"You too."

She kissed me quickly on the cheek before spinning around and jogging off, and I did my best to bottle up the array of emotions that swirled inside of me since I had first heard her call my name.

What the hell was I even doing? Jasper was just a day's-old drinking buddy after all, not a friend or a client. I didn't owe him anything. He may have been murdered, but why was I sticking my nose into something the Surrey RCMP were more than equipped to handle? Who was I to get involved? Sure, I may have been a PI who had cracked some big cases, but I was out of practice and there was no reason for me to shoehorn myself into an investigation that didn't require my assistance. Was I so desperate for a fresh ear to whine to after being served a double-whammy heartbreak by being dumped by Stormy and then ghosted by Rya? Or was I simply trying to distract myself from the loneliness that accompanied the loss of a once fledgling love triangle, one I had probably taken for granted and wasn't even willing to admit to myself was a thing until now?

The answer was a resounding yes, of course, which made me feel like Charlie Brown if the sad sack got rejected by the Little Red-Haired Girl. I pushed aside any thought other than that my pro-wrestling match had been mediocre at best and had gone bust the minute a murder ruined the finish. I swore that once I changed my clothes and grabbed my gear, I would get as far away from this godforsaken country fair as fast as possible.

If I was going to feel sorry for myself, then I figured I could lick my wounds from the comfort of my Coal Harbour townhouse. Besides, what the hell did I expect to accomplish by running around a rodeo trying to distract myself from my own despair? Maybe it was time for me to quit the delusion that I wasn't hurting inside and move on with my life by officially returning to the Ounstead & Son Investigations office and seeing whatever cases my old man had for me. I was grateful to the crusty old son of a gun that he had given me some time and space and only now found myself able to admit that I needed the break. I had spent the last eight months taking on so many indy pro-wrestling bookings in the Pacific Northwest and across Canada in addition to my ongoing work with XCCW I could scarcely be described as a part-timer anymore. The truth was I hadn't logged so many hours in the squared circle since leaving WWE right as my career had started blowing up a few years back. It was time for me to admit that I had taken a sabbatical from investigative work since my merciless throwdown with an underground, mixed martial arts club, led by the biggest badass I had ever encountered, a beast of a man who nearly managed to put me down for the count—permanently. Nevertheless, despite my spectacular failure after so suddenly returning to sleuthing, I couldn't deny that the thrill of the hunt for Jasper's killer had left me feeling reinvigorated.

I resumed my march toward the southern entrance gate to the *Colossal Cloverdale Rodeo and Country Fair*, kicking up dirt with my clown shoes as I trudged around the neighbouring Elements Casino racetrack being used for overflow parking. A few kids making the same trek would point me out and snicker, and their parents were sure to keep a safe distance, despite the fact we were all headed in the same direction. Nevertheless I found myself walking more briskly than before and with a bit less melancholy thanks to my unexpected, embarrassing, yet also enjoyable encounter with my former lover. As I reached the turnstiles a teenage Staff supervisor in a maroon shirt scurried over to me so quickly his stringy black hair flapped in the air behind him.

"Jesus Christ, Bruh! You look like you just got butt-fucked and bukkaked by the Joker!"

Nothing classier than rodeo folk, I thought to myself, grimacing at the crude remark. I then decided to cut the kid some slack because, compared to me in my current state, he may as well have been an etiquette coach at Buckingham Palace.

"You can't be out here like this," he blurted out urgently, looking over his shoulder as he quickly escorted me through the gates. "If my boss sees you, he's gonna shit a brick."

"South side locker room," I said, and the Gen Z staffer nodded and led the way. A minute later we reached the side entrance to the small, multipurpose complex where I had geared up earlier before my big match against "Cowboy Cobb" Calhoun. I nodded my appreciation to my escort and tried to open the door, but it was locked.

"Son of a bitch," lamented the kid, fumbling with a ring of keys that was attached to his chunky leather belt by a zip cord. "I don't have the key."

I sighed and resigned myself to my fate of never-ending stares by throngs of people passing by in all directions. Maroon Shirt banged on the door with his fist.

"Somebody open up, goddamn it!" he hollered. There was no response or rescue from the other side of the door. "Keep knocking," he ordered, before standing behind me and puffing out his chest, doing his best to shield me with his lanky, ectomorphic frame. I followed his instructions and continued to rap on the door, but to no avail.

BEEP! BEEP!

Tires squealed as a shiny, black, four-wheeled Rascal Scooter swerved to a stop in front of us, and given the velocity with which the electric mobility machine had been moving, it must have been zipping along at its top speed.

Seated on the lap of a slightly blue-tinted, white-haired octogenarian was none other than Declan. He slung his portable cooler backpack over his shoulder as he hopped off the older lady and onto the concrete. He wasn't but a step away from the scooter when its driver honked the horn again, but this time much more aggressively than the little squawks she had given upon arrival.

"Don't you dare leave without givin' me some sugar, Decals!" she crowed.

My cousin sighed and turned back to his geriatric chauffeur. "You're bloody insatiable, ya know that, Flo?"

The old woman smirked and Declan laid a sloppy kiss on her that created such a loud lip-smacking sound it was all I could do not to wince.

A few moments later he pulled back and spread his hands. "Satisfied?"

Flo furrowed her brow as she adjusted her upper dentures, which had loosened from Declan's smooch.

"Jaysus, slap some Poligrip on them chompers," he chastised.

"You're the one who made me scrape it off," she replied gruffly, before slamming a foot down on the motor vehicle and riding off into the crowd of people walking by.

Declan walked toward me only to find me shaking my head. "What?" he snapped.

"You're flying low, D."

My cousin checked his tattered acid-washed, denim shorts before quickly doing up the zipper without an ounce of shame. The maroon-shirted Gen Z staffer just stared at the scene before him with his mouth agape.

"Ya look right banjaxed," said Declan, upon taking one look at me. "What the hell happened?"

"I'll tell you on the drive home," I replied, before turning my attention to Maroon Shirt. "Can you get us in here or what? I need my bag."

The poor kid looked back and forth between the both of us, still so slack-jawed a baby sparrow could have flown into his open trap and nested. Relief washed over him when he spotted a fellow maroon-shirted staffer walking nearby.

"Tina!" he yelled, desperately. "You got keys for this door?"

Tina nodded and trotted over. Moments later my cousin followed behind me as we made our way past a line of rusted yellow lockers that made it feel like a locker room at Degrassi High.

Declan lit a Benson & Hedges cigarette and took a drag as if there weren't a large NO SMOKING sign on the wall, but since we were alone, no one bothered us. He unzipped his backpack, pulled out my wrestling boots, then tossed them to me.

"I doubled back to that fat bastard's trailer an' snagged these for ya since I know what a fussy wee bitch ya can be 'bout'em," he said.

"Thanks. Was he okay?"

"Well, he wasn't there, so I figure he managed to drag his arse off to a buffet or somthin'."

I folded over my most valuable pieces of ring gear and tucked them under my arm. "Thanks, D. And these are custom-made, for the record."

Declan took a seat on a bench, whipped out his iPhone, and started scrolling through photos with a satisfied smirk on his face. I opened my combination padlock, retrieved my duffel, stuffed my prized grappling footwear into the bottom of the bag, then dug around inside until I found my toiletry kit. I peeled off my soiled and stolen clown clothes, stripped naked, slung a towel over my shoulder, and slipped my feet into a pair of purple rubber Undertaker "Deadman" flip-flops.

"Ya ever try one o'those Ensures?" asked Declan.

"What?"

"Them nutritional shakes blue-hairs drink to keep their bingo wings taut."

"No."

"Ya should," he chastised, savouring another drag of his cigarette almost as much as the eyeful of Flo that was on his six-point-seven-inch smartphone screen. He then used his thumb to double-tap and zoom in on a particular image, and I caught a glimpse of what could only have been a geriatric white bouffant before averting my eyes.

"Me an' that ol' bird chugged a couple an' chased'em with some pints," he continued. "Bloody delicious they are, an' packed full o'protein, just the way ya like."

"I think I'll stick with dairy and whey, thanks."

Declan shrugged. "Yer loss, Mate, cuz I swear they're like a Red Bull for yer willy."

I sighed, exasperated with my cousin's never-ending lewdness, especially after the day I just had. "I'm just gonna clean up and then we can head out."

"They make a banana flavour," he called after me, and it stopped me in my tracks long enough for me to lick my lips. I shook off the thought, lassoed my tingling taste buds, and hit the showers.

I kept the temperature tepid at best as I rinsed off my body, letting the cold water soak my head and cascade down my back. I scrubbed the clown makeup off of my face and it mixed with bits of dirt, dust, and even a clump of marshmallow that washed out of my hair and down my legs before circling the drain near my feet. After about five minutes I cranked up the heat and let the spray pulsate against my aching muscles which felt almost like a massage. Once I had dried off, I returned to my locker and unzipped my grappling gear bag. I slid into my neon Ultimate Warrior boxer briefs and black cargo shorts, then laced up a pair of banana-yellow, low-rise, Converse Chuck Taylors, sans socks. However, when I searched for my short-sleeved burgundy button-down baseball jersey, it was nowhere to be found. Instead, the only shirt I had was the prototype mock up for the latest "Hammerhead" Jed pro-wrestling tee on which XCCW owner Grasby had asked me to collaborate.

"Shit," I muttered to myself, before holding up the charcoal grey garment and taking a closer look at it under the lighting.

The shirt looked good, and I was happy with the off-white, solid, Princetown font I had selected. I also couldn't help but smirk at the new catchphrase I was considering adopting as part of my marketing.

DO NOT GO GENTLE—the immortal words from Dylan Thomas's famous poem that now felt intrinsic to me—were written in an arc across the chest above my usual logo of a two-by-four piece of western red cedar with a bolt of lightning crackling through the wood. Beneath that was the moniker by which I was known as both a wrestler and a private investigator.

With no other choice than to go bare-chested, I sighed and slid on the top, despite how cringey wearing a shirt with my own name on it made me feel. The material was also made from a stretchy cotton-polyester blend, and while the sleeves clung tightly to my biceps and triceps making them feel more pronounced, the breathable fabric fit nicely over my pecs and torso for such a sweltering day at a country fair rodeo.

All in all, it was a damn fine shirt.

"That's bloody brilliant!" crowed my cousin.

I glanced over my shoulder and saw Declan standing there proudly, with his hands on his hips.

"I love the shite on the back," he said, referring to the graphic and additional text I had forgotten was there.

"I don't want to talk about it," I said curtly, before I watched him shrug and turn back around, sticking his butt up in the air as he hunched over a locker that was across the bench seating between us. He was up to something.

I craned my neck to see that while I was in the shower, he had dipped into my gear bag and retrieved my trusty lock-picking kit out of the small leather belt sheath I sometimes wore on my hip when working as a PI. Some sleuth I turned out to be. I was so preoccupied with my own thoughts I hadn't even noticed it was missing while getting dressed.

"What the hell are you doing?" I asked.

"This was Jasper's locker, yeah?"

"So?" I said, sprinkling a quarter-sized amount of hair-styling powder into my hands before running them through my slightly damp mop.

"So, let's bloody well see what he had in here before we Hassellhop our way out o'here."

As if refusing to let our lumberjack drinking buddy rest in peace wasn't enough, invoking the memory of his former furry fetish gal pal's late bunny 'David Hasselhop' and using the poor animal's name as a verb was the last straw.

"Jasper is dead, D. Hasn't he suffered enough without us invading his privacy?"

Declan ignored my objection and continued fastidiously accessing Jasper's private locker. I sighed and glanced at my EDC (everyday carry) compact pouch which was spread out on the bench beside him, grateful that at least my pen, notepad, zipties, and a black, stainless steel folding tactical knife had been left undisturbed.

A moment later Declan crowed triumphantly before snapping the lock off of the door and swinging it open on its creaky hinges. There was a thud as a heavy bag dropped out of the locker and landed at Declan's feet. He unzipped it before I could protest, and whatever I was going to say completely slipped my mind the moment I saw an abundance of pink and brown fifty and hundred-dollar bills spill out of the canvas gym bag.

I stared at the numerous portraits of Prime Ministers William Lyon Mackenzie King and Robert Borden before locking eyes with my cousin.

"Janey Mack," he muttered quietly.

NINE
"MONEY HORSE"

"How much is that?"

"Not sure."

"Ballpark it."

"Jaysus, I dunno," replied Declan, his hands rifling through the overflowing canvas bag. "Hundred grand or so? Some big stacks on the bottom."

"Damn it," I exclaimed, before punching a locker so hard it left a dent.

"Ya all right there, Fella?"

I took a moment to compose myself, then tucked my toiletry kit into my duffel bag and zipped it shut. "Yes. Come on, let's go home."

"Home? I don' mean to be a buzzkill, but what are ya wantin' to do with these scads o'cash?"

"Just leave them where you found them."

"Are ya off yer nut? Think o'the renos we could do at the Shillelagh with this!"

"It's not ours. Put it back."

I started to walk away, but halted when I heard a locker door slam shut. I turned around to see my cousin staring at me with his striated orange, green, and black tattooed arms crossed in defiance, the bag of cash still lying at his feet.

"What?" I protested.

"The bloody state o'ya!" snapped Declan. "Forget keepin' the money. Ya know this had somethin' to do with Jasper gettin' killed!"

"What am I supposed to do, D? Jasper wasn't a client. The cops can handle it."

"Them cow-tippin' Barneys who patrol the sons o'the soil out here ain't up for the task an' ya know it."

"The Mounties is the official law enforcement agency for all of Surrey, not a private police force. They are more than qualified."

"They're at least three steps behind!"

"I'll call in an anonymous tip on the ride home."

"Bollocks. I ain't goin'."

"How ya going to fight crime when you're half-cut and too busy fooling around with grandmas, Bub?"

"At least I ain't afraid o'usin' me balls," snarled Declan.

I was used to taking a ribbing from him, but that one hit a nerve. "What did you say?"

"Ya heard me."

I got in Declan's face and snorted so angrily it rivaled the bull that had chased me around the arena not long before. We glared at each other for what felt like an eternity, neither of us backing down. Eventually, Declan spoke.

"I know it's been tough for ya since all that shite went down with those MMA blokes an' ya got dumped by yer roller skatin' She-Hulk sexpot. Not to mention yer Detective honey blackballin' yer arse. But ya gotta be better than this."

I took a deep breath and pushed my damp hair back out of my face, and spoke at last of what had driven me from work as a

PI, and haunted me for the better part of a year. "How can you be so glib after what we did?"

"Ain't nothin' glib about takin' a life," said Declan, solemnly. "An' it don' ever get easier. But we've had no choice but to knock off some baddies in our crime fightin' time together. I'm sorry to say it, Boyo, but each one o'them had to go."

I gritted my teeth, knowing he was correct, but there was one death that still felt different from the others. They were committed in self-defence.

"Even Cassian Cullen?" I replied, uttering the moniker of the mixed martial artist whose homicidal warpath was responsible for the staged suicide of a good man and former client Elijah Lennox. Cullen was without question the most lethal and deadly foe I had ever encountered, whose cruel cunning and viciousness had left an incalcuable body count in its wake, dating back to his time in the Canadian military's special forces and as a prisoner of war in Afghanistan.

I realized in that moment I hadn't spoken the brute's name aloud since I defeated him in life-or-death combat, despite arranging for Declan to take him out with a sniper shot, whether or not I survived that final encounter.

"There's a difference between committin' cold-blooded murder an' assassinatin' fer the greater good, Jed. Remember what that ol' ape ya call a Pa said to ya back when *he* took out that biker boss on the Lion's Gate?"

"Kendricks," I said, referring to the man who had ordered a hit on my friend and former tag-team partner, had Declan shot and hospitalized, burned our family pub to the ground, and kidnapped my father. Suddenly the thought of taking out such monsters didn't seem like such an egregious transgression. I shook off the haunting memories and replied.

"He said that with guys like that, it was him or us. That some men are so dangerous and deadly they don't ever stop coming for you or your loved ones, regardless of whether they're behind bars."

"Aye. Which means ya gotta ask yerself, if ya ain't movin' forward an' helpin' folks—savin' people like only yer arse can—than what the hell has all o'this been for?"

Although I still hung my head, for a moment the heaviness that had been weighing down my soul began to feel a little bit lighter.

"'Tis high time to scuttle the pity party an' get back to doin' what ya do best."

"Beers, bodyslams, and breaking two-by-fours over my head?"

"Bustin' cases wide open," he said assuredly.

I tried to remain tough and hold my cousin's gaze, but it was pointless. His words cut through me faster than it would take him to pound a pint of Guinness. I didn't share his clarity or the ease with which he had reconciled the past, but for the first time I felt some kind of spark within, as if the man I used to be had been prodded, ever-so-slightly, from a dormant state. A few quiet moments went by until I felt coarse yet tender fingertips pat the side of my bearded face. I looked up and locked eyes with him.

"Stop beatin' yerself up, *Dearthair Fola*," which was Irish for *blood brother*. "Ya know if it could be done over, we'd still do it the same."

I nodded slowly as I took his words to heart. Declan reached down into the bag, grabbed a handful of hundred-dollar bills, folded them, then tucked the cash in my shorts pocket.

"What the hell are you doing?" I asked.

"You're a PI, yeah?"

"So?"

"So, PIs get paid. That right there is your retainer."

"D, I'm not taking—"

"Ya bloody well are," snapped Declan, cutting me off. "Jasper trusted ya. He would o'wanted this."

My cousin's mind was made up and I knew better than to try and push back. Instead, I grabbed the canvas bag of cash, zipped it up, opened my locker, and stuffed it inside. "This is as good a place as any to stash this cash for now," I said, grabbing my EDC multitool sheath, looping my belt through it, and cinching up my cargo shorts by fastening the black canvas strap around my waist.

"Deadly!" exclaimed Declan.

"What?"

"What do ya mean, what? I feel like I just watched Batman put on his utility belt."

I patted the leather pouch on my hip. "I guess we've got some work to do."

"We're suckin' diesel now!" Declan exclaimed, clapping his hands together and rubbing them excitedly. "All right, what's next?"

"We review the facts," I replied, surprised at how self-assured and filled with vigour I was. Perhaps my cousin was onto something after all.

"An' those are?"

"Someone flung—or more likely swung—an axe into Jasper's skull."

"An' it could o'been a two-man job cuz o'that jagger wire mark 'round his neck."

"That's possible. And let's not forget the washer on the broken neck chain at the bottom of the log boom pool."

"What the hell is that about?"

"You mean the hardware as jewelry?"

"Aye. Did the tree-fellin' fecker also wear an anchor bolt as a brooch?"

"Let's table that for now."

"Ha!"

"We know he had a bad breakup with his rodeo clown boyfriend Kelly Lewis."

"He's the one who roughed you up?" asked Declan, reading between the lines.

I nodded. "And as soon as I mentioned I was a PI he assumed Jasper hired me and had me choked out."

"Except the bastard right buggered that."

"I don't think he wanted me dead. He just seemed caught off guard and is definitely hiding something, which is probably why he panicked and called in his Hulkster-armed accomplice to make me see stars."

"Which is how ya wound up here lookin' like a polluted Pennywise who pissed himself."

"Pretty much," I said, both acknowledging and ignoring the less-than-flattering description. We stood there silently in the locker room, while I kept mentally replaying the handful of encounters we had with Jasper, trying to remember something ... anything. Of course, it didn't help that during most of the times I was trying to recollect I had been despondent and drunk at a saloon. After a moment, a memory sprung to mind.

"You recall when Jasper mentioned his family?" I asked. "His grandfather, in particular?"

"His Chop-Chop Pop Pop?"

"Yes. Jasper said something about how making real bank from loggersports would be the best way he could honour his memory."

"Aye."

"I don't know. I guess it was the way he said it. He had a little cocksure grin, like he knew something we didn't."

Declan scratched his close-cropped hair, trying to recall the moment. He had been even more intoxicated than I was, not to mention preoccupied with cowgirl cleavage on the nearby dance floor, so I wasn't expecting an epiphany.

"Ya think the bloke was somehow makin' cabbage from jugglin' chainsaws an' the like?"

I shrugged. "All I know is there's now a big bag full of his cash in my locker."

Declan nodded in agreement. "What now then?"

"We follow the money."

3:56 P.M.

TEN
"THE PIT BOSS"

A giant fireball roared as it erupted into the air like hot lava spit out of a volcano, igniting a heat wave so sizzling it refracted the light and distorted my vision. The sudden and extreme temperature, combined with the peppery plume of hickory smoke that whooshed over us, caused my eyes to water.

"*Hadouken!*" cried Declan, with such vigour that Ryu from *Street Fighter* would have been impressed.

I held my breath for a moment until we had walked through the smoldering grey cloud. Once we had made it to the other side, we both spotted what we were looking for, although the objects of our interest couldn't have been more different.

One of the perennial attractions at the *Colossal Cloverdale Rodeo* is their Cowboy Rib Fest, a literal hotspot destination set up along a patchy grass field at the far end of the Country Fairgrounds, a brisk ten-minute walk from the Stetson Bowl. The stretch of land was narrow and butted up against a chunk of real estate regularly used by production companies for the seemingly endless amount of television and film series filmed in the quaint and charming pocket within Surrey, British Columbia. I could see in the distance, behind the procession of pop-up grills and food trucks, numerous paved roads, storefront facades, and other special indoor and outdoor buildings which were used as sets, although they all had been co-opted by the Greater Vancouver city for the weekend in order to allow for more carnival games and attractions. It was only when I noticed a large banner advertising caramel candy apples for sale covering the blue-and-white sign for *The Smallville Gazette* that I realized I was just a kryptonite stone's throw away from Superman's adopted hometown.

It had been a bit of a hike for us to make our way from the locker room to this pitmaster's paradise, but given our renewed determination to hunt down Jasper's killer, we made the trek without complaint.

A long row of grills ran along a side-by-side spread of searing stations. Each featured six-by-ten, industrial sized, propane-powered, cooking grills crackling loudly, and spewing orange embers into the air as they roasted racks of ribs, beef steaks, pork chops, chickens, every kind of animal flesh that could be doused in flame, sauce, and seasoning. Industrial-sized smokers and portable charcoal BBQs were sprinkled in among the heavy-duty bars of stainless steel sitting atop the multiple burners. The master meat chefs at the separate stands worked below large, overhead placards depicting images of mouth-watering, charbroiled grub.

I spotted the specific pit I had been looking for, but when I turned to inform Declan, I found myself alone. I stood still, looking around for him, in-between a line up for Fraser Valley Chilliwack sweet corn on the cob and a gaggle of tykes with puffy red-and-blue cones of cotton candy, who loitered around an oversized, inflatable slide that anchored the adjacent "Kids Zone" play area.

After a few moments I gave up and shook my head at my cousin's all-too-familiar disappearing act. However, as I made my way toward my destination, I spotted an oasis in a desert. Smack dab ahead of me was a refrigerated cart-on-wheels, and it was all

I could do not to burst into a sprint. The stripey-capped attendant looked at me curiously as I skidded to a stop in front of him.

"Please tell me you have milkshakes!"

Stripy Cap shook his head. "Just popsicles and sno-cones."

"Banana flavoured?" I asked.

A wave of relief washed over me when he nodded. I fished cash out of my pocket as Stripey Cap scooped ice into a paper cone and began to douse it in sweet yellow liquid.

"Extra syrup, please."

My instruction was obeyed and a moment later I was biting into chilled relief from the hot sun, blazing grills, and long day. It was almost as good as a DQ shake.

Almost.

A calm came over me as my frozen treat scratched an itch that had been growing since I knocked back my preferred, post-match beverage before finding Jasper Adams's body. Then an unmistakable Irish brogue cut through the noise of the crowd like a razor-sharp blade through basted beef.

"Hold up, Jed!" Declan hollered. He had a twenty-ounce plastic cup filled to the brim with blonde ale in one hand, while the other held some delicacy that looked like a slinky flayed out of a spud deep fried on a stick.

He held up his carnival food and nodded. "Bone Apple Tit, Mate."

I ignored his continued butchery of the language of love and stayed focused. "What the hell is that?" I asked, eyeballing his starchy monstrosity.

"A tornado potato."

"A what?"

Declan took a chomp of his native land's dietary staple. The swirling tater bounced up and down from his chin like the bellows of an accordion until he used his tongue to corral it all up into his mouth.

"Tornado. Potato."

"You have those back home?"

Declan glared at me as if I had questioned Bono's ability to croon like a legend.

"I'll bloody well pretend I didn't hear that," he replied, before licking some lingering salt off of his lips. "What about you?" he said, nodding toward my sno-cone. "That banana?"

I barely managed a nod as I took another bite of my icy treat.

"I'm surprised ya ain't dancin' a bloody jig."

I ignored his comment and gestured toward his portable cooler backpack. "What's the point of lugging that thing around if you're just going to buy a beer everywhere we go?"

He stared at me incredulously. "This is a Bohemian Pilsner, Jed," he snapped, proudly holding up his brew as if taking offence. "Should I have paired me salty tornado potato with a Bud Light?"

"You really like saying 'tornado potato' out loud, don't you?"

"Aye," replied Declan, without missing a beat.

I sighed, and like so many things with my cousin, let it go. "Come on," I said. "I found him."

We munched on our respective snacks as we approached the last stop in the long line of cookout camps, one that shared the same moniker as the food truck parked on the grass beside it.

DDT BBQ featured several twenty-something bodybuilders working the pop-up grill, and their sweaty and hairless torsos all glistened from the blistering heat broiling an assortment of meat.

An extra shiny kid in a skimpy undershirt struggled with a pair of tongs as he tried to turn over a rack of ribs. When he leaned in close a burst of flame shot up off the grill and singed his arm. He yelped before dropping the tongs and rubbing his forearm.

"Goddamn it, Zander!" bellowed a familiar voice. "Tell me you're lathered up in baby oil and not essential oil!"

"Flynn used the last of it," he said, defensively, rubbing his stinging appendage.

"That shit is flammable you moron!" snapped my part-time boss Bert Grasby. "Get the hell out of here and have Braxton check you out with the first aid kit."

Zander nodded obediently and scurried off behind the DDT BBQ base. Seeing me, Grasby threw his arms up in frustration. "It's impossible to find good help these days."

His rotund face was even redder than usual from the all-encompassing heat. Instead of his usual embroidered track suit, he wore a creamy-white, sleeveless, hoodie with matching shorts, made of the same velour material that was his signature style and preference. It was a bad call, especially since his outfit was splattered with blotches of brown barbeque sauce, and he must have been sweltering. But Grasby didn't seem to care. He picked up the tongs from the grass, snatched the overcooked ribs from the grill, and tossed them in a garbage bin.

"I don't suppose either of you wants to make a few bucks working the gridiron?"

"Not unless you're talking about a football field," I replied.

Grasby nodded, seeming to have expected such a response. Declan took a big swing of his pilsner, and nodded toward the muscular young men in Grasby's employ.

"Jaysus Christ, Fella. How many o'these tubesteak Tarzans ya got workin' fer ya?"

"Hey, fuck you, Declan! They're not all queer."

"Just gay for pay then," piped my cousin.

"Enough, the both of you!" I snapped, having had my fill already and knowing if I didn't interject, I would witness a descent down a rabbit hole of snarky barbs and insults. "I need your help, Grasby."

"With what?"

I recapped Jasper Adams's murder in the loggersports area and the discovery of his body after the rushed finish to my match with "Cowboy Cobb" Calhoun.

"Fuck!" barked Grasby. "How come I'm just hearing about this now?"

"Cuz his body is still bloody warm, ya gutternsipe."

"That's not all," I said, and continued by telling him about my encounter with Kelly Lewis and how I was choked out and left unconscious. I left out the part about the cash in Jasper's locker, however. I was going to play that one close to the chest for the time being.

"What can I do to help?" asked Grasby.

He may have been an acquired taste to many, but ever since our interests aligned while I was working my first case the potbellied promoter had become a staunch and reliable ally.

"You're running a BBQ pit and XCCW is putting on shows at this country fair. Surely you can grease some wheels and introduce me to the top brass around here."

"I suppose. But why?"

"Because I have some questions for them."

"Ah, c'mon, Ounstead. I thought you were done with that Sherlock Holmes shit."

"Not just yet."

Grasby sighed and slumped his shoulders. His volleyball-sized tummy protruded further than usual when he put his hands on his hips.

"Do you know if the cops are shutting things down?"

"No idea."

"Wind yer necks in," said Declan. "Last I saw it was just the lumberjack pit they had cordoned off."

"So, we're still slated for tonight's show then," said Grasby, hopefully.

"That's your business. I only signed on to work this afternoon."

"Tit for tat, Ounstead. Main event this evening and I'll give you what you want."

"Not interested."

"Even if I put the strap on you?"

That surprised me. For over a year since my return to the ring I had danced around the XCCW Championship, but until recently I never really considered becoming the top dog within the promotion because I had only ever agreed to wrestle part-time. Although he initially wanted me to take the belt from the former champ El Guapo, Grasby had grown impatient and christened the steely old warhorse "Cousin Pappy" Vinny McKinney as his main man.

Although it was a far cry from the gold I held while wrestling in the WWE, I'd be lying if I said that for a moment I wasn't tempted. There really was nothing quite like making an entrance to the ring with the biggest bling, no matter how big or small the audience may be.

I pushed aside the nostalgia and stood firm. "I couldn't do that to Vinny," I said earnestly. "Not when he finally snagged the top prize in the twilight of his career."

"And if I told you it was his idea?"

"What?"

"His rotator cuff is toast. Needs surgery. His doc gave him the green light for one more match to hand-off the title, but that's it. No comeback. He's done."

I slurped the last of my banana sno-cone and considered the *quid pro quo*.

"You'd be doing him a favour, Ounstead. Letting him go out with some dignity by dropping the belt to a high-profile star like you before being put out to pasture."

"Not a bad bargain there, Boyo," said Declan, nudging me with his elbow.

"All right, Grasby," I said reluctantly. "It's a deal."

The portly, faux-velvet-garbed man clapped his hands together so victoriously you might have thought he had just negotiated an end to the rivalry between the Vancouver Canucks and the Calgary Flames.

"What now?" I asked.

"Now you meet the Seven Heads of the Rodeo."

A.J. DEVLIN :: 63

ELEVEN
"HOOT-AND-ANNIE"

The portable was nearly a kilometer away from the fair-grounds. Located in the back corner of an oversized strip mall parking lot, it still had an abundance of white lines and empty parking spots surrounding the transportable building, despite the bustle of Saturday afternoon shoppers making their way in and out of the Home Depot store with renos on the brain, carts full of paint cans, or pallets stacked with plywood.

I had driven Grasby and Declan in my Ford F-150 pickup truck, but despite the extended cab and relatively roomy backseat, my cousin was still miffed that I had allowed Grasby to ride shotgun. Declan pounded back an entire Harp Lager tallboy on the minutes-long drive and had popped the top on a second one as we entered the headquarters for the *Colossal Cloverdale Rodeo and Country Fair*. Although he seemed wary of the speed at which the former IRA operative crushed cans of beer, Grasby kept his head down and his mouth shut until we entered the building and he introduced us to the four people who awaited us.

They were seated around several folding tables pushed together to create the centerpiece of a makeshift boardroom, save for one small Latino man, who texted on a smartphone while pacing back and forth. His spiky dark hair with platinum-blonde frosted tips and short-sleeved shirt covered in flames were matched by his tawdry, orange-tinted, translucent glasses. Upon seeing us, he clicked his phone off, stormed over, and glared upwards.

"Since when do you call a meeting?" he demanded of Grasby, giving him the stink-eye.

"Special circumstances, Quentin."

"You can't just do that! And on *the* big Saturday afternoon? That grub hub can fall apart in a heartbeat if I'm not there. Do you even know how much business you could be costing me?"

"You won't lose a dime and we both know it," Grasby replied, pointing at the barbeque stains on his sleeveless velour top and shorts. "Besides, this will only take a minute."

"I still don't like it. Ribfest is MY turf and call." Quentin shifted his attention to Declan and me, as if noticing us both for the first time. "What's with the roid monkey entourage?"

"Pull yer wire, ya poxy wee bollocks," growled my cousin.

Quentin's eyes widened momentarily in fear before he correctly intereptreted the context clues present in Declan's Irish slang and quietly took a seat at the table.

Grasby proceeded to introduce us to the remaining three people.

"Thank you all for coming on such short notice. Everyone, this is Jed Ounstead, former WWE superstar, current XCCW main event talent, and esteemed private investigator."

My cantankerous kin cleared his throat before taking another swill of his beer. Grasby continued, clearly irked. "And this is his cousin. He's, uh ... Irish."

"That'll do, Pig, that'll do."

If Grasby recognized the heartfelt quote from the ending of the movie *Babe* he certainly didn't show it. Then again, since it was Declan, he may have figured being referred to as swine was simply a case of getting off easy.

"Over here are Fred and Tammy Milligan," he said, waving a hand at the middle-aged couple. "They own Milligan's Traveling Carnival and Amusement Park and this is their first year at the Rodeo."

The modest husband and wife nodded their heads and said hello. They were dressed in casual clothes and had the look of folks who had been putting in long hours for even longer days.

My part-time employer continued. "Which leaves us with—"

"Someone who's wondering if you're trying new gimmicks *outside* of the ring, Grasby," said a sultry voice. A striking woman in her mid-twenties wearing a hot-pink, short-sleeved, button-down put her calloused yet feminine hands flat on the table and stood up slowly. Her shirt was tucked tightly into her form-fitting, classic blue jeans, and she sported matching dusty brown cowboy boots and a Stetson hat. "Are you trying to renegotiate for a bigger slice of the pie with the Seven Heads last minute cuz your baby oil brigade has been packing more asses into the seats than expected? Because we have a flat rate deal."

She locked eyes with me and strode over to us, moving with a lithe athleticism and a level of self-assuredness that almost took my breath away. She smelled of sweet sandalwood and smiled, extending a hand toward me. I was lost for words so I just shook it repeatedly as I looked into her sparkling green eyes, only then noticing her strawberry blonde hair and freckles around her high cheekbones.

After a few moments Declan coughed into his fist and muttered *"Dúisigh"*—Irish for "wake up."

I snapped out of my smitten state and managed to blurt out a greeting.

"Hello," I said, lamely.

"'Hammerhead' Jed," she said, smirking. "Ain't you a tall glass of sweet tea. I used to have a poster of you in my room."

"Really?"

She shrugged. "They were sold out of all the Hemsworth brothers' posters at Walmart."

I chuckled heartily. She flashed a genuine smile and I felt a flutter in my chest, before I realized I was still shaking her hand.

"And you are?"

"Georgiana June Tibbs. But everyone just calls me Annie."

"Nickname, eh?"

"Yup."

"I know a little something about that."

"I'll bet you do," she said, flashing a demure yet darling smile. "My father Gus and I run the rodeo events at this country fair."

"And where is Gus?"

"He's got his hands full at the moment with some dinks."

Declan nearly choked on his beer. *"DINKS!"* he crowed, before doubling over, clutching a hand to his temple, and feigning head pain.

"Are you okay?" asked Annie, genuinely concerned.

"Too ... much ... piss ... to take!"

"Grow up, Jackass," snapped Annie. "A 'dink' is rodeo slang for a bronc with no buck in it that's gotten loose in the arena."

Declan inhaled sharply as if to go for the jugular with a response, but noticed my uncomfortable expression. Although it might not seem that way to most, he could read me like a book and could tell I was already a bit sweet on Annie. He slowed his hearty laughter, acquiesced, and headed toward the exit.

"Where are you going?" I asked.

Declan shooed me away with a wave of his hand. "Fag," he grumbled, before begrudgingly sauntering out of the portable. I watched him leave, only to turn back around and find the faces of Annie, the Milligans, Quentin, and Grasby staring at me in shock.

"Irish for cigarette," I said, by way of explanation.

"*That* guy is your cousin?" asked Annie.

"Yeah. And sometime sidekick."

Annie huffed. "I think I liked you better when you tag-teamed with 'Mad Max' Conkin." The mere mention of my former partner only brought to mind memories of his broken neck and how his accidental paralysis not only changed his life permanently, but mine as well. Annie must have seen some kind of melancholy on my face because a moment later she wrapped her hand around my forearm and gave it a squeeze.

"You okay, Big Guy?"

I pulled it together and cleared my throat. "I'm fine."

Annie smiled softly as her hand slipped away slowly, and I only then realized her touch had triggered a tickle of goosebumps on the back of my neck.

"Grasby, you said I was going to meet the 'Seven Heads of the Rodeo.' You speak for wrestling and this chuck wagon chump here does the Ribfest," I said, motioning toward Quentin as he threw his hands up in the air in protest while aggressively working a toothpick around his mouth with only his tongue. "That means if Annie and her Dad handle the cowpoke contests—and the Milligans rep the carnival—then I only count four honchos on hand."

"That's cuz we're still missing a few," he replied. "Randy Pippen isn't here, but he runs the loggersports, so he's likely on site dealing with the cops and the fallout from your lumberjack buddy's murder. Then there's Jim Kootnekof. He coordinates the Marketplace located in the row of red barns beside the casino and behind their amusement park," said Grasby, nodding to Fred and Tammy.

"And the last person?"

"I don't know him. Some dude acting as the proxy for the proprietor of the Agri-Zone, who's back in Calgary."

"Agri-Zone?"

Annie interjected. "Yeah, it's like a whole super-sized animal area. There's multiple petting zoos, pony rides, a reptile habitat, and even more critter attractions. I actually just met the guy earlier today. Kind of a cagey fella. And a little weird."

"Weird how?" I asked.

"I don't know. I mean, I went over there because we just found out we have a pregnant mare and wanted to ask if he'd consider stabling her for a couple of days as a professional courtesy. He was nice and all, but only agreed to speak with me if I accompanied him 'for a balmy stroll'."

Annie used her fingers to do air quotes for the last part or her sentence. "He actually said 'balmy stroll' instead of 'walk?' I asked.

"Yup."

"So, he likes some exercise," said Grasby. "What's strange about that?"

"Nothing, I guess. It's just ... he's kind of a fancy fella. Was dressed all prim and proper, you know? I mean there are literally animals galore all over that place, which means he's knee deep in hay, dirt, and manure, but the guy's walking around in a crisp three-piece white suit without even a speck of dust on him. And then when we went on our walk, he brought two pets, each on its own leash. A wiener dog and a goat."

"That is weird," concurred Grasby. "What's that guy's name again? Simmons? Sparks?"

"Sykes," I replied, with certainty.

Annie clapped her hands together and stomped her boot on the floor like she was doing a line dance. "That's it!"

TWELVE
"CATCHING A WEASEL ASLEEP"

Grasby elected to stay behind to discuss business with Quentin and the Milligans. They began bickering back-and-forth about how a rowdy bunch from Ribfest had snuck their brews out of the beer garden and into the carnival, which had led to some drunken incidents for which Fred and Tammy had been woefully unprepared and understaffed. As a result, the married duo was demanding that Ribfest send over some of their security guards to help wrangle the troublemaking, intoxicated goons before they caused any more havoc. It was only when I left the squabbling entrepreneurs behind me and made my way down the metal steps into the parking lot that I realized Annie had followed me out of the building.

"Hold up, Sugar."

I did as she requested.

"You know, you move deceptively fast," she continued. "Must be the long strides you take with those tree trunks you walk around on."

I turned to face Annie, who looked even more attractive under the natural light. "That's my secret."

"What is?"

"Never skip leg day."

She giggled. "I don't care how much iron you can squat, ain't nothing going to get your tushy tighter than squeezing your gams to stay in the saddle."

To add emphasis to her point Annie playfully slapped her own backside.

"See? I can bounce a quarter off of this thing."

I couldn't help but smile. "I don't doubt that for a minute."

Declan, who was about ten feet away alternating between puffs of his cigarette and using the empty Harp Lager can he had crushed and fashioned into an aluminum sphere as a Hacky Sack, swiveled his head in our direction.

"Did she just say somethin' 'bout her arse?" he asked excitedly, as he stopped kicking upwards and the metal ball fell and clattered against the asphalt.

"Watch it, D," I cautioned, pointing a finger directly at him.

Declan took a long drag of his smoke and sauntered over to us. "What's our next move then, Boyo?"

"Looks like the Agri-Zone."

"Mind if I tag along?" asked Annie.

"Sorry Love, but me an' me cuz work alone."

"Not this time," I found myself blurting out instinctively.

"Are ya feckin' kiddin'?"

"Annie, how big is this ... what did you call it? A super-sized petting zoo?"

"That's putting it lightly. We're talking nearly forty-thousand square feet of hens, hogs, and horses, in addition to pretty much any other farm animal you can think of."

"They don' have any goddamn peacocks over there, do they?" asked my cousin, intently.

"A whole bunch, actually."

Declan shivered like a cold chill just ran down his spine. "I bloody hate peacocks," he said quietly.

"Why?" asked Annie.

"Those creepy tail feathers for starters," he spat. "'Tis like a hundred eyes o'Anubis glarin' all at once, waitin' for ya to join the choir eternal an' get mummified."

I sighed at having to hear Declan launch into the backstory of his own personal kryptonite for the umpteenth time. I looked at Annie and was about to try and change the subject when I first saw it.

"I think you've seen one too many old monster movies," said Annie.

"Sod off, Calamity Jane!"

"Seriously, how can you hate peacocks? They're so cute. Shoot, I fed a handful of sweet corn to one this morning."

Declan jumped backwards from Annie like he just found out she was carrying a contagion. I ignored him, as my eyes were still locked on the item hanging around her neck.

"Sweet Jaysus, tell me ya at least sanitized yer paws, ya skitter," sniped Declan while cringing.

"Yes, of course. They have hand washing stations you have to go through at the entrance and exit. Seriously, what's the deal with the peacocks?"

Declan took another drag of his cigarette before somberly launching into a monologue like a long-suffering prisoner of war recounting time spent locked up and tortured.

"I suppose it all started when I was just a wee wain," he said, before sucking back so hard on his smoke it crackled before there was nothing left but the filter. He flicked the butt away, crossed his arms, and exhaled a stream of smoke so smoothly Humphrey Bogart himself would have been impressed. "Ya see, me an' me fam, we used to spend our summers at a cottage just outside o'Cork an'—"

"What the hell is that?" I demanded, pointing at the makeshift necklace around Annie's neck and cutting short my cousin's troubled recollection of the turquoise peafowl that had haunted him since his youth.

"Bloody hell, Jed! I was just gettin' to the part where …"

Declan trailed off when he recognized the same thing I had. We both stared at the small, shiny washer that was attached to a silver chain—exactly like the one I saw on the bottom of the log boom pool underneath the deceased and floating body of Jasper Adams.

"What?" asked Annie, pulling the circular hardware off of her neck and raking the flat metal ring along the gleaming ball beads of her necklace. "You mean this?"

THIRTEEN
"THE DIRTY DUKE"

"Yes," I said, pointing at the washer. "What is that?"

"It's a necklace."

Declan and I exchanged a curious glance.

"We can see that, Annie. But it's a bit odd as jewelry goes, don't you think?"

"Aye, an' don' be givin' us any more o'that bounce a coin off o'yer arse sweet talk. What's the scoop, Lassie?"

If Annie was nonplussed she didn't show it. Instead, she just pulled the chain over her head and handed it to me. "Just a common household washer on a simple chain, Boys."

"What are ya, some kind o'cowgirl Miss Fixit or somethin'?"

I held the necklace in my hand. Definitely nothing special as far as I could tell. I passed it to Declan for him to take a closer look, but kept my trap shut in hopes that Annie would explain further. She did.

"It was a gift."

"From?"

"Kooty."

"An African antelope?" asked my cousin, scratching his head.

"That's a Kudu," I replied.

"*Koot-ee*," said Annie again, phonetically. "As in Jim Kootnekoff."

I recognized the name. "You mean one of the Seven Heads of the Rodeo gave that to you? The Marketplace guy?"

"Yes."

"Why?"

"He's a Doukhobor."

"A bloody what, now?"

"A Doukhobor," I said, familiar with the relatively obscure religious sect. "They're radical pacifist Protestants from Russia who settled in Western Canada, commune-style, over a hundred years ago."

"Like a bunch o'tranquil Charlie Mansons?"

"Except with less brainwashing and butchery and more spiritual Christianity."

"An' what are these necklaces then, like their own personal Helter Skelter bollocks?"

"Not quite," said Annie. "Doukhobors are above all else people of peace. And while most of the Russian-born pretty much died off by the seventies, some, like Jim carry on their traditions."

"And these washer necklaces are one of those?" I asked.

"Kind of. Although this is more of a Kooty thing. Think Tony Robbins if he were eastern European and looked like a grey-haired scarecrow instead of the Missing Link. Jim uses these 'pendulums' as part of his motivational speaker presentation."

"Listen here, Love. If ya want to see me flap me arms and cluck like a chicken before havin' yer way with me all ya need to do is ask. No need to lull me into a trance."

Annie laughed. "You're funny. Now I get why Jed keeps you around as his sidekick."

"*Sidekick?!?* exclaimed Declan, before punching me in the shoulder, utterly aghast. "I'm the bloody big gun he brings in to get his beefy arse out o'trouble time and time again!"

I sighed and tried to keep things on track. "We can define the parameters of our dynamic duo later. I want to hear how this necklace is motivational."

Declan lit another cigarette. "Sidekick," he bemoaned. "If ya think I'm gonna start wearin' a yellow cape with green ginch then yer thicker than them two-by-fours ya crack over yer noggin."

"Can you zip it and let the lady talk?"

Declan huffed before yielding.

"The pendulum?" I said, to Annie.

She began to swing the washer on the chain back and forth. A moment later her hand was still and the metal ring was doing all of the work through momentum alone.

"Look," she replied, motioning with her other hand toward the oscillating disc. "Let's say you want it to move higher to the left. So, you try and fight the pendulum."

Annie used her thumb and forefinger to give the chain some zip. It responded by swinging back harder in the other direction.

"You see? Maybe for a short moment you can lift it higher, but sooner or later it's going to go back to the side you like less—harder and bumpier—with the extra power you've given it."

Annie's pendulum swung back and forth aggressively with the added force just like she had described.

"Now, if instead you are willing to let the pendulum swing, you don't lock your energy into one side. It doesn't jerk back and forth. It's smooth. When the washer is high, you *focus* on it, which allows you to gain greater perspective and control."

"Okay, but inevitably it's going to go back to the side you don't like."

"Right. But notice how fluid it is now when it swings that way. You see, with my focus being on this side, it's almost like time moves slower over here. And when it goes the other way, I don't fight it, so it's over quicker and back to where I want it to be."

I nodded, starting to understand the logic, despite the fact I felt like I was being fed a bit of metaphysical mumbo jumbo. "Like a salmon swimming with the current instead of against it."

A delightful smile broke out across Annie's face. "Exactly. It's like life, you see? You can't stop the ups and downs. You're going to swing both ways no matter what. But if you focus on one side—and let go of the other—you'll be rewarded with more command of the highs which will feel much longer than the inevitable lows."

"It's about detachment," I said, understanding her point.

"Not bad, Ounstead. Maybe you should ditch the 'Hammerhead' nickname for something that gives off a more open-minded vibe."

I felt a little surge of energy crackle between us while Annie and I both stood there smiling at each other.

"What a load o'shite," snapped Declan, taking a swig from another can of Harp Lager I hadn't even noticed him open. He then stifled a belch since we were in the company of a lady.

"There's truth to what she's saying, D," I said, surprising myself with both my conviction and the fact I was so quickly jumping to Annie's defence. "My freestyle wrestling team in university used to have a sports psychologist who talked about attaining harmony both on and off the mat to maximize performance."

"Aye, well, that's all well an' good, yeah? But ever since ya mentioned salmon I realized I'm bloody famished, so I'll see ya back at the rodeo after I get meself some fish an' chips."

"Hold up," I said, as he turned to leave. "How are you getting back?

"Ya know me better than that," replied my cousin with a wink.

"I need to talk to Sykes, which means I'm heading to the Agri-Zone."

"I'll join you," said Annie. I quickly nodded my approval.

"Do you think you can head over to the Marketplace and try and track down this Kooty character?" I asked Declan. "Because I'm going to want to talk to him next."

My cousin took another swing of his beer and nodded. "I'll sniff out yer Duke o'Whores for ya, Boyo. An' I'll ping ya on yer utility belt when I do," he said, nodding toward the iPhone pouch on my EDC multi-tool sheath.

With that Declan was in the wind, making a beeline toward a curly-haired, curvy woman exiting the Home Depot. She was struggling to carry several floral hanging baskets toward her car. My cousin drained the last of his beer, crushed the can flat in his hands and flung it across the asphalt like he was on the ninth hole during a game of frolf, then began chatting up the latest object of his affection.

"I guess that just leaves you and me," said Annie, blushing slightly.

I opened my mouth to respond, but quickly closed it when I felt my cheeks turning rosey red as well.

FOURTEEN
"ROPING THE BRISKET"

There was silence in my Ford F-150 as I drove Annie back toward the fairgrounds, but it was far from awkward.

If anything, it was comfortable. It hadn't occurred to me to ask the young cowgirl riding shotgun in my truck how she had gotten to the off-site portable headquarters for the impromptu summit of the Seven Heads of the Rodeo or if she even needed a ride. She just hopped right into the passenger seat, rolled down her window, and looked contently out at the suburban side streets as we cruised, the wind in her hair causing her strawberry-blonde locks to flap gently over her shoulders.

A honk from the car behind nudged me out of unconscious ogling. I threw up a submissive hand in front of my rear-view mirror and waved, keeping my eyes on the road as I resumed driving back toward the parking lot reserved for performers and athletes, for which I still had a green parking pass on the dashboard. By the time I had rolled to a stop in an empty stall and turned off the ignition I had figured out something to say.

"So, uh, you and your dad work together, eh?"

"We do, but he often does the lion's share depending on my competition schedule."

"Sounds familiar."

"How so?"

"Well, I may be a wrestler-detective and partner in our private investigation firm, but my pop is a retired thirty-year VPD legend who keeps our business afloat. Especially lately."

"Lots of squared circle action in the springtime?"

"Something like that," I said, declining to mention the melancholy that had haunted me since my last case and the morally conflicting events before my PI sabbatical.

"I suppose it is the beginning of Speedo season."

My heartrate spiked as I felt flushed with embarrassment. "You saw me in the ring earlier?"

"Maybe," said Annie, with a hint of a smirk on her face.

"I usually wear pants."

"Uh-huh."

We got out of my truck and started making our way to the private performers and competitors' entrance to the fairgrounds.

"What events do you compete in?" I asked, desperate to change the topic before the possibility of Annie having witnessed me executing a cringe-worthy bronco buster on the ugly mug of "Cowboy Cobb" Calhoun became a point of conversation.

"More like what events *don't* I compete in."

"Really, I'd like to know."

Annie sighed and began listing her horseback specialties. "Barrel racing, pole bending, saddle and bareback riding—if it's done on a bronc, I've got it covered. But I'd have to say my specialty is roping the brisket."

"I'm not bad at that last one myself, as long as I have a side of horseradish and can chase it with a banana milkshake."

"What about a banana cream pie? Cuz I make a sweet one."

"Will you marry me, Annie?"

She blushed and chuckled, then swatted my arm. "It's not nice to tease," she said coyly. "And just so we're clear, 'roping the brisket' is a particular steer roping technique. Give me a lasso and a moving target, I can pretty much take down anything."

"Never thought I'd find myself jealous of cattle."

"They're all castrated."

"Did I say 'jealous of cattle?' I meant come at me with rope and I'll be ready for battle."

"Nice save."

"Hey, I am half-Irish, after all. The malarkey makes me prone to a little hyper-*bull*-e."

Annie groaned. "Are all pro wrestlers such dorks?"

"Just the ones who regularly use two-by-fours for celebratory self-inflicted head trauma."

"How do you break those planks of wood over your head every night and still manage to form sentences, anyway?"

"Trick of the trade, my dear. Trick of the trade."

"Well bless your heart and your bumpy ol' noggin then."

The gate attendant recognized either Annie or me, as he let us walk on by and into the country fair with a curt nod. I kept my head down and dared not look at my new cowgirl compatriot, but if the vibe I was feeling between us was any indication, she was doing her best to keep herself from grinning a little bit too.

We kept the ensuing chitchat amicable, but to a minimum as Annie picked up the pace and entered the Ribfest area I had recently visited. Due to the horde of hungry carnivores, we were forced to switch our march to single file. As a result, I fell in step behind Annie and followed her toward the Agri-Zone through the maze of flaming grills, long lines, and satisfied, finger-licking customers hunched over weather-beaten wooden patio tables. Soon a converted ice arena and adjacent outdoor field, peppered with people and pens containing a collection of critters and beasties on hand for the super-sized mammal menagerie, appeared in the distance. It was then that Annie's words took a more pointed turn.

"So, you've got history with this Sykes hombre, I reckon?"

"I do indeed."

"Good or bad?"

"Our relationship definitely began as a *quid pro quo* one, although we've certainly become chummier of late. I dare say we might even be considered friends."

"What's the deal with the wiener dog and the little horn-head on a leash?"

"You're speaking of Napoleon and Brutus, two prized purebreds that anchor a couple of Sykes's animal-themed businesses. And it's probably best to refer to them as a dachshund and a goat. He may have his fingers in some murky transactions, but Sykes takes pride in conducting himself like a proper gentleman."

Annie gave me a bemused look as I pulled out my performer's pass and flashed it to the Agri-Zone attendant, who swung open a metal gate and waved a hand for us to enter. "You know some weird people," she said, matter-of-factly.

I did my best to smother a laugh. "Wait until you meet Pocket and Tubbs," I said, referring to the loquacious three-foot dwarf and his four-hundred-pound BFF who were both stalwart friends and my occasional tag-team partners in the XCCW.

If Annie mustered a response, I didn't hear it as my focus was suddenly hijacked when I recognized a familiar face on the other side of a large enclosure housing a sounder of swine that had their snorting snouts caked in mud as they trotted about in all directions within their sty.

I stood there staring until it was as if the target of my gaze felt my eyes upon him, lifted his head, and looked directly back at me. Time stood still as I locked eyes with Kelly Lewis, who had changed out of his gear and into a simple white T-shirt, a pair of dark blue jeans, and yellow hiking boots.

Annie elbowed me. "What is it, Jed?"

"Oh, nothing," I said, as Jasper Adams's former lover's eyes widened in surprise. "I just spotted the rodeo clown who tried to have me killed less than an hour ago is all."

FIFTEEN
"DUCKS OFF"

Kelly Lewis wasted no time making a hasty retreat.

He spun on a dime, broke into a dash, and before I even knew what I was doing I found myself in hot pursuit. I had no time to try and explain things any further to Annie as after a few quick steps forward I was at a sudden and literal impasse.

On my left, dozens of children clustered around a circular, above-ground, man-made pond serving as a temporary home and cool aquatic respite for dozens of ducks and geese. The children giggled and milled about as they crushed crackers and tore up pieces of bread to feed the waterfowl, blissfully unaware that they were serving as a barrier to my efforts to confront the man responsible for my loss of consciousness and lingering ache in my trachea.

I pivoted and took off to the right, around a pigsty until I slammed right into a line of leash-bound alpacas being led out of the petting zoo by yellow-shirted attendants. They gasped in horror as my full weight crashed down upon a large and particularly fluffy-fleeced creature, knocking it to the ground. The alpaca let out a wail and toppled over faster than a frost-bitten Tauntaun taken down by the cold on planet Hoth. Shrieks and screams from both adults and children rang out across the family-friendly venue. I pushed myself up with my hands, only to find myself face-to-face with the buck-toothed beast. The llama-like mammal looked at me innocently with its big black eyes. Overwhelmed with guilt, I petted its long furry neck.

"Sorry about that, Bub," I said soothingly, as I scratched behind its ears. For a moment the alpaca and I shared an intimate gaze and I thought my accidental tackle was forgiven—until the long-necked bugger spat directly in my face. Still, I could hardly blame the woolly critter given the sudden and forceful way I had bowled it over. If I had any chance of catching Lewis, I couldn't exactly linger, so I bounced back up on my feet, wiped the spittle from my face, and, with no other choice, leapt over the fence and into the hog pen.

Pigs squealed and scurried in all directions as I weaved in-between and hurdled my way over the pack of them. My Converse sneakers chewed up chunks of mud behind me as I cut through the large sty and closed the gap between Lewis and me. He stopped briefly to watch the commotion, but seeing that I was gaining on him, continued his escape. But the tide turned in my favour as I had cleared the far side of the wooden enclosure with a leap so perfect that gold-medal hurdler Edwin Moses himself would have been impressed.

Once clear of the obstacles, the crowd thinned out, leaving only an alarmed Lewis and me sprinting across what was left of the field. I started gaining ground fast. My confidence growing with each stride, I stayed on Lewis and narrowed the gap between us. Sensing me nipping at his heels, he hung a hard right. Within moments I realized where he was headed—directly toward the long line of people patiently waiting at the pony ride station.

"Get out of the way!" screamed Lewis, and his high-pitched heads-up caused such alarm children and parents alike scrambled in all directions.

But it was too late. The chaotic scene was all the opportunity I needed, except this time I *intended* to make a flying tackle. Throwing myself forward into a dive, I wrapped my arms around Lewis from behind and pulled him tight as we tumbled to the ground. We rolled over a few times before I lost my grip, but the chase was over, and whatever opportunity he might have had to get away was gone. Although I had halted his escape, I only succeeded in escalating the conflict, for by the time I climbed to my feet Kelly Lewis crouched before me, vibrating with anticipation, waiting to take me on.

I held up my hands in defense. "I only want to talk."

"Fuck you, Private Dick."

"Jasper was a new pal and seemed like a good man. I just want to know what happened."

Kelly's eyes began to water and his fierce demeanor was replaced with a trembling lip. "You mean you don't think I killed him?" he asked, his voice rife with emotion, oblivious to the parents and children who slowly formed a circle around us.

I wasn't surprised Lewis had heard the news about Jasper's death by now, but for the life of me I couldn't figure out why, if he was mourning, he would be creeping around the Agri-Zone. It seemed like an odd play if his grief was as genuine as it appeared to be.

"No, Kelly, I don't."

"Then why are you after me?"

"Like I said, I'm only looking for answers. Starting with why you had your barrel-armed buddy try to choke me out with a flank strap."

"I panicked, okay? And you leave Buffalo out of this."

"You mean the animals?"

"No, I mean the man. *Buffalo*. He's harmless and only put you to sleep because I asked him to."

So, "Buffalo" was the big-armed brute who had me seeing stars in record time. Not to mention another nickname for me to remember. I put my hands on my hips, growing frustrated with the mounting miscommunication. "Look, Kelly, I think we want the same thing here. I'm trying to find Jasper's killer. And so far, all I can think of is maybe it has something to do with the money in his locker."

The whites of Lewis's eyes widened until they were the size of saucer plates. I silently cursed to myself as I realized I may have overplayed my hand.

"Take it easy," I said, softly. "I only just found that cash after you—"

"You shut your fucking mouth!" he screamed, startling the circle of onlookers who had now fully surrounded us.

Any further attempt on my part to defuse Lewis's agitation was cut short the moment he snaked a hand behind his back and unsheathed a Bowie knife so shiny when the sun glinted off the blade it nearly blinded me.

"Back the fuck off, Ounstead!" he warned.

"I can't do that, Kelly. Not until I get some answers."

That was it for Lewis. He let loose a primal roar and charged at me with the weapon. I still didn't know much about Jasper Adams's former beau, but realized pretty quickly the man knew how to handle a knife. And since the Bowie was infamous for being able to cut like a razor, chop like a cleaver, and stab like a sword, my life was suddenly on the line.

Fortunately, I have a former IRA operative for a cousin, and he liked to unwind and pass the time practicing self-defence techniques together. One of Declan's preferred styles is KMTKF — Krav Maga Tactical Knife Fighting—a brutally efficient Israeli style of combat.

Lewis came at me strong by snaking out his Bowie toward my upper right chest. I blocked him at the wrist with a hardened palm. He retracted the knife and struck again, this time low and away. I swept downwards with my other hand, executing a "Sand The Floor" defensive half-circle motion with such precision that

Mr. Miyagi would have been impressed. I could tell the blade-wielding bull-wrangler was growing frustrated. Lewis tossed the knife upwards, caught it in his left hand with an overhand grip, then took his most dangerous swipe yet with a jab toward the side of my neck. At this point my KMFKF training had taken over and I reacted instinctively as if on autopilot. Except instead of sparring with plastic blades with Declan, I was fending off lethal strikes from a bloodthirsty rodeo clown.

Lewis continued with a flurry of increasingly aggressive attacks, including stabs toward my sternum, ribs, and abdomen, all of which I swatted away. I moved fast, efficiently, and I dare say even gracefully, so for a moment I felt as if I were kung fu training with a Wing Chun dummy.

Festering with rage, Lewis kept swinging his Bowie harder with each successive strike. He let out another bellow, this one more anguished, and in his vexation opened himself up by arcing his knife in a wider stabbing movement. Recognizing this mistake, I was able to deliver an open-handed blow to his biceps. While his blade hand was still rotating backwards from my fierce chop, I managed to connect with an uppercut to his Adam's apple where the top of his throat met his jawline. He gasped, hacked, and clutched his throat as he stumbled backwards, and I took the moment to pull my hands in close to my chest, steady my footing, and centre myself before another round of attacks.

It was only then I realized that the Agri-Zone had grown silent save for some clucking chickens, oinking pigs, and one cow off in the distance lowing, while nearly everyone present had formed a very wide circle around Kelly Lewis and me as we engaged in battle.

Lewis snapped his head from side-to-side, cracking his neck, and sugar-footed his way around me with an impressive Muhammad Ali shuffle, all while getting his bearings and priming himself for another attack. In a flash, he lunged forward and I was caught off guard by how much ground he covered so quickly.

I was trying to dodge left as he raised his blade up above his head when I heard a whooshing sound.

A split second later a thin noose of white rope looped around Lewis's wrist and suddenly cinched so tight the Bowie knife went flying out of his hand. I was certain I heard a pop or a snap of either ligament or bone breaking before my attacker howled in pain. By the time I realized what had happened, Annie Tibbs had not only lassoed Kelly Lewis, but had him face down on the ground, her knee in his back, as she hog-tied his hands behind him in what I'm sure would have been a record had she been in an arena and with a four-legged animal instead.

Lewis yelped in pain. "Ow!" he screamed. "What the fuck—what are you doing?!?"

Annie responded by elbowing him at the base of his skull, knocking him out instantly. A few moments of total silence ticked by before the crowd broke into thunderous applause and hooted and hollered for my cowgirl saviour. Annie stood up, took off her hat and tipped it to her fans, and basked in the adulation like the seasoned pro she was.

"How's that for a finishing move?" she asked, cheerily.

I tried to respond, but was still in such a state of shock my mouth was unable to form any words. Instead, I just stood there dumbly, doing my best not to spoil Annie's heroic moment in the spotlight.

"Shouldn't you be breaking a two-by-four piece of wood over your head in celebration right about now, Big Guy?" she asked, before giving me a sly wink.

I couldn't help but smile.

SIXTEEN
"TWO-JUMP CHUMP"

The crowd milled about, buzzing with excitement over the knife fight and lasso action, and I overheard folks debating whether or not what they had just witnessed was some kind of pro-wrestling shoot the Agri-Zone staged as part of the country fair's entertainment. I walked over to get a better look at Kelly Lewis, still unconscious. Nonetheless, I kicked his Bowie knife aside and out of reach. I also noticed his hands were tied so tightly behind him his fingers had turned as red as tomatoes. I unsheathed my stainless steel tactical knife from the carry-pouch on my right hip.

"Hold your horses there," said Annie, as she wrapped the remaining slack of the thin white rope around her elbow. "You're telling me you had that sucker on you the entire time?"

"I did."

"During a knife fight?"

"That's right."

"Why didn't you pull your blade?"

"Annie, if I pulled this" I said, holding up the weapon, "then things would have ended very differently."

I spun the blade's metal loop around my index finger, knelt next to Lewis, pulled up his bound hands, and sliced them free from the tightly-tied cord Annie had used to subdue him.

"What the hell are you doing?" she asked, as I folded my knife shut and slid it back into the leather pouch looped through my belt.

"Trust me."

"I know this hombre, Jed. He's slicker than pig snot on a radiator."

I reached down, opened a flap from my sheath, pulled out a zip-tie, and held it up for her to see.

"Hot damn," she said. "You're just a regular beefcake boy scout, ain't ya?"

"You should try my game bird campfire chili," I replied, before fastening Lewis's hands securely behind him with the sleeker plastic band.

"Wouldn't mind that one bit," she said, her voice so heavy with flirtatious innuendo I half expected her to jump in my arms after she finished coiling the rope she had used around her arm.

I did my best not to blush and checked Lewis's neck for a pulse. It seemed a bit faint, but it was there, and he was breathing normally.

"You really did a number on him," I said, climbing to my feet. "Those were some pretty impressive moves."

Annie scoffed. "Kelly ain't nothing but a two-jump chump compared to the big-ass bullocks I take down."

"Where'd you get the rope?"

"Compliments of that poor herd of alpacas you steamrolled," she said.

"You were on me the whole time?" I asked, realizing that not once in my pursuit of Kelly Lewis had I looked back over my shoulder or even wondered what Annie was up to after I left her in the lurch.

"You got some brawn and agility, Hoss, I'll give you that. But do you really think you can match the strength and speed of the steer I'm used to?"

"I'm your huckleberry," I replied.

That elicited a genuine chortle from Annie, who still came off as cute despite snorting a bit at the end. "So, what now?" she asked.

"We wait for security, I guess. Unless the Mounties show up first. And something tells me they won't be far off now that Jasper's murder is common knowledge."

Annie looked at me quizzically and I informed her of the exchange Lewis and I had mid-combat, during which he almost broke down in tears when I revealed that I didn't believe he was the killer.

"You know he was playing you, right?"

"He seemed pretty sincere to me. And I trust my instincts."

"Did your instincts clue you in to the fact that Kelly has a long history as a pill-head with unhinged behavior?"

"Are you serious?"

"Oh yeah. He's bipolar, Jed. And it's not uncommon for him to go on-and-off his meds."

"Is this just hearsay or are there records of this?"

"Kelly's been reprimanded and suspended plenty of times. Hell, we almost kicked him off the tour completely once. The rest of the Seven Heads will back Gus and me up on that. They've—we've—also gone out of our way to cover for his ass more times than I can count."

"Why bother if he's so much trouble?"

"Family's been with the rodeo since the beginning. His grandpappy and folks are long gone, but they were beloved and the fact is Kelly is a third-generation broncobuster."

I chuckled despite myself.

"What's so funny?"

"Nothing. It's just now I know where that term actually comes from."

"Broncobuster?"

"Yeah."

"Isn't that the name of one of your wrestling moves?"

"Today it was."

"So, it's like some kind of cowboy body slam or something?"

"A story for another time," I said. "Maybe over that campfire chili."

Annie seemed to enjoy my sliding that callback into our conversation. She stepped toward me and slipped in close, placing a hand on my chest which caused me to instantly flex my pecs. "Geez," she said, impressed. "Maybe time in the saddle isn't the best way to build tight muscle after all."

We gazed in each other's eyes for a moment. I took a breath and inhaled the honeyed smell of sandalwood that enveloped her, then gently brushed away a few stray strawberry-blonde hairs that had escaped from underneath her hat.

"You're pretty adorable," I let slip softly, before I could stop myself.

Annie smiled. "*Hammerhead* Jed," she cooed, before touching the tip of my nose with a brightly coloured pink fingernail that I only then realized matched the colour of her shirt. "Sweeter than a banana cream pie."

I began to dip my head and lean in just a little when we were interrupted.

"Holy shit! You're him! The 'Hammerhead!' We just watched you wrestle a couple of hours ago!"

A dumbfounded dude with a dad bod stood so close to us that I realized if I continued in my efforts to lay a kiss upon Annie he would have been locking lips with us as well.

"Hi," I said, awkwardly, as Annie and I each backed away from the man and one other.

Dad Bod chugged back some of the twenty-ounce beer in his plastic cup with one hand while fumbling with his phone with the other. "Can I get a pic?"

"Sure," I said, remembering the promise I made to myself as a child when I was at a WWF house show at the Pacific Coliseum and was rudely shooed away by "Ravishing" Rick Rude for making a similar request. Although he was an unabashed heel and was likely just staying in character, being so unceremoniously rebuffed left an emotional scar and was why in that moment I made myself a promise that if I were ever to make it as a pro-wrestling superstar any fan who ever asked for a photo would always go home satisfied.

"Marcus! He said yes!" crowed Dad Bod, triumphantly, and a moment later a plump teenage version of my beer-swilling supporter shambled over to us.

"How about one with us all showing off our guns?" asked Marcus.

I nodded politely. Dad Bod struggled awkwardly with his phone, as given my size, one of his stubby arms was far too short to take a selfie.

"Annie?" I said, in a pleading voice.

The cowgirl grinned and took the phone, freeing up Marcus, Dad Bod, and me to all focus on taking the snap. We started with us all flexing our biceps, then moved on to a few other variations before taking a final shot of us where I had my arms wrapped around their shoulders.

When we were finished Dad Bod patted my biceps and triceps repeatedly. "Jesus, those cannons are even bigger than they look on TV, aren't they?"

Even Marcus got in on the action and prodded away at my arms as if I were a lab specimen.

"That was fun, Guys," I said, and they took the hint once Annie handed back the phone. Father and son thanked me profusely before both hunching over the electronic device and scrolling through their sure-to-be future social media posts as they walked away.

Annie and I reunited outside the pony ride station, where the miniature horses had resumed their walking circuit. A crowd lingered despite a defeated and unconscious Kelly Lewis on the ground, so we stepped to the side for a bit of privacy. I desperately looked for any chance to recapture the magic that had been between us, but the moment was gone.

"I don't suppose you have any smelling salts on you?"

Annie patted her empty back pockets on her jeans before turning her hands palms up. "Only ones I know of are back at the Stetson Bowl."

Before I could respond, I heard a loud—and familiar—bark. I turned to see a reddish-brown dachshund running toward me, weaving in and out around ankles as if it were racing around plastic poles at a Superdogs show. Although the hound was on its own, it dragged behind it a leather leash attached to its collar.

I broke into a smile as I bent forward and the little animal leapt into my arms. "Napoleon! You little devil, how are you?" I asked as the dog yipped excitedly and licked my face. I nuzzled him right back and scratched the base of his neck, which caused the peppy pup to settle down and moan in pleasure.

"You two need a moment?" asked Annie.

"Sorry, this guy and I just have a bit of history."

Napoleon squirmed in my arms and rolled over, turning his belly up, which I began to scratch.

"Isn't this Sykes's pet?" she asked.

"It is."

"He sure likes you."

"I happen to know a few of his sweet spots from the doggy spa."

"Doggy spa?"

"Like I said, we have history."

After an extended tummy rub, Napoleon jumped out of my arms and trotted off a few steps, before stopping and looking back. He barked impatiently.

"I, uh—have to go," I said to Annie.

"With the wiener dog?"

"Dachshund," I said, correcting her. "Sorry, it's just that, well, he's a purebred, you see? He comes from a long line of championship canines who specialize in flushing out burrow-dwelling animals and—"

I stopped, amazed at how quickly I found myself sounding like my fastidious bookmaker associate, despite the fact we hadn't seen each other in quite some time. Annie just stared at me blankly.

"Napoleon will take me to Sykes," I said, before picking up the end of the dog's leash.

"What do you mean he'll take you to him? It's a dog, Jed, not an Uber driver."

"Trust me, Annie. I got this. You mind keeping an eye on him until the cavalry arrives?" I asked, nodding toward a still conked-out Kelly Lewis in the dirt.

"I reckon I can manage that."

I reached a hand into my EDC pouch and withdrew an *Ounstead & Son Investigations* business card. It was tattered and worn around the edges, but still had my mobile number on it.

"Give me a shout when security or the Mounties arrive. And especially if Lewis wakes up beforehand, because I'd love to have first crack at questioning him."

Annie nodded and tucked the card away into the front pocket of her pink, button-down shirt. With that I headed off across the Agri-Zone, letting a dachshund lead the way to an old friend whom I was hoping would be able to provide me with something I had been sorely lacking up until now.

Answers.

SEVENTEEN
"A BOVINE GAME OF MANURE CHANCE"

The term "cow-pie" was a bit of a misnomer.

You'd think when it came to cattle-dung things would be pretty straight forward, but as I quickly found out, that wasn't exactly the case. Your standard deposit of cow-crap has the consistency, texture, and certainly the smell you would expect. However, the flattened multiple dollops that Napoleon was leading me toward looked less to me like plump, Norman Rockwell-esque, windowsill-cooling pastries made of excrement, and more like flattened shit-frisbees. My furry escort scampered toward the neglected baseball diamond behind the indoor arena which housed the section of the Agri-Zone I hadn't yet visited. The infield had been converted into a lush green mini-field, with an obvious layer of instant lawn that had been laid atop of the added topsoil and patchy green and yellowish grass underneath. The entire area had also been cordoned off with a combination of silver metal poles equidistantly spaced apart every six feet, connected by orange plastic snow fencing that created a large, rectangular pen. The instant lawn had been laid flat among the landscaped turf and the rolls of grass were separated by crisscrossing straight lines into at least thirty squares, each with its own random number. The cordoned off area was pristine, save for the collection of manure patties and a single, young-looking, Holstein cow that stood in the middle of the pen chewing cud.

Napoleon yipped excitedly and stared up at me with big brown eyes. I took the hint, bent over, and unclipped his leash from his collar. I watched as his pint-sized paws hit the baseball field with the signature speed that had led the dachshund to win the Weiner Dog Racing Championships at the Hastings Racecourse and Casino, an event that I had attended as a special guest of the prized pooch's master.

Napoleon made a straight dash to the enigmatic gentleman who had become a trusted ally and friend, and while we had stayed in touch over the previous months, we had not seen much of each other, save for a single time he had called on me for a favour. Sykes had a reputation in Vancouver as the city's most esteemed and honourable bookmaker. He had requested my assistance in collecting an outstanding debt from a hard-partying rookie sensation from the Canadian Football League's BC Lions. As usual, Sykes seemed less concerned about the retrieval of the money and more about the overall optics of the assignment. I was able to parlay my celebrity into gaining access to an exclusive fundraiser at the posh Vancouver Club, where I discreetly collected the money owed, although it required me to defeat the intoxicated quarterback in an arm-wrestling match in the venue's kitchen before the gridiron superstar took a break from snorting lines of nose candy, and meekly forked over his outstanding balance. Sykes had been very pleased with the non-violent resolution.

I followed Napoleon's tiny paw prints as they made their way to the man himself. Dressed impeccably in a light-yellow shirt and the crisp white linen suit Annie had described earlier, still without a speck of dirt on it, Sykes stood adjacent to the grass area inside the orange fence that housed the cow, paying neither much attention.

Instead, my bookie buddy was preoccupied with a white goat that, when not climbing up and down a miniature see-saw, was hopping on and off of a tiny trampoline. The animal would also routinely trot over toward the object in his master's hand and chew on it, which appeared to be a bright green spiked rubber cactus. Had I not already been familiar with Sykes's surprisingly popular goat yoga business venture, I may have found the plethora of visual and tactile stimuli for his horned animal perplexing.

"I thought goats ate tin cans," I said to Sykes, lobbing a verbal jab at him from fifteen feet away. He provided his effortless answer in his usual commanding yet cool voice, which somehow mysteriously remained audible despite the loud squeaks coming from the cactus as the goat munched on the emerald rubber.

"And on what do you base such an assumption?"

I shrugged. "Saturday morning cartoons, mostly."

Sykes let out a familiar sigh before responding. "Unfortunately, I am afraid the insipid daybreak children's television programming that surely framed your pop culture perspective as a youth was rife with factual inaccuracies."

"Then why the rep for munching metal?"

"That falsehood is derived from the fact these glorious ruminant mammals have on occasion been witnessed eating the label and glue attached, not the can itself."

By the time I reached my enigmatic sometime-associate, Napoleon had joined the goat, one that I barely recognized as Brutus given how much he had grown since I had last seen him. Napoleon barked excitedly and Brutus bleated in response, before the two of them began to frolic and dance around one another like a couple of cross-species BFFs. Sykes placed the cactus chew toy into a duffel bag by his feet and replaced it with a bag of Bocce's Brushy Sticks Dental Bars then tossed the brown chicken-flavoured plaque busters in-between dachshund and goat. Napoleon and Brutus both scampered forward and grabbed their chewy snacks. Moments later they lay down on the grass beside each other and chomped on them enthusiastically.

Although his gold Versace sunglasses hid his eyes, there was no mistaking that the man was happy to see me. "Mr. Ounstead," he said with more zest in his voice than I was used to hearing. He extended a well-manicured hand. "A pleasure as always."

"For me as well, Sykes," I said, before we both matched our shake with a smile.

"I see you have upgraded your wardrobe," he said slyly, nodding toward my prototype *DO NOT GO GENTLE* two-by-four struck-by-lightning pro-wrestling tee.

"Something like that."

"Wild men who caught and sang the sun in flight, and learn, too late, they grieved on its way, do not go gentle into that good night."

"You know your poetry."

Sykes shrugged ever so slightly. "That is my favourite passage by Dylan Thomas, although I must confess, I am more of an Oscar Wilde aficionado myself."

Sykes nodded toward Brutus the goat, before clasping his hands behind his back like a dignified aristocrat.

"As you can see, young Brutus is maturing very quickly," he said, emphasizing the hard "T" in the word "maturing," before motioning to the kid.

"It's okay for goats to have dog treats?"

"Considering these are top-of-the line, grain-free, mint-flavoured delicacies that optimize oral health while freshening the breath of both Napoleon and Brutus, then yes, in this case, it is."

"I guess hay and halitosis make for a bad combo in the goat yoga business."

A breeze passed by, causing Sykes to pat down a single, out of place, jet-black hair on his head as he responded.

"Would you say the chance of finding spiritual and physical alignment is more or less probable if the animal nearby has a prominent tongue coated with sulphur-producing bacteria?"

"With all the beer breath I've been smelling around here, I don't think it really matters."

"Touché," said Sykes. "I concur that pristine oral hygiene is likely not a priority for most of the attendees at these ... *rural* festivities."

I smirked. "Speaking of which, how'd you land this plum gig? And why are we talking next to a penned-in cow with yellow spray-painted squares covered in several dung piles?"

I had to give it to Sykes—he continued to surprise me with the venues at which we would meet in order to conduct our business.

"Fair questions. However, before we begin, I must first apologize."

"For what?"

"As you know I care little for your other profession, hence why I was not in attendance at your matinee performance today."

"It was just a ten minute outdoor wrestling match at a suburban rodeo, Sykes. I'm not starring as Curly in *Oklahoma!*"

"Nevertheless, I was aware of your presence here and had an emissary en route to deliver a small congratulatory gift, something which unfortunately did not come to pass given the murder of your loggersports companion Jasper Adams."

I had long ago given up trying to deduce how Sykes came by his information and was always in the know. Yet I trusted him completely and knew whatever information about me he obtained was in safe hands.

"Is that why you sent Napoleon to get me?"

"Partially. I also assumed you would want to discuss the events that just transpired in my Agri-Zone."

"*Your* Agri-Zone? I thought the proprietor was from Alberta."

"You of all people know I have connections in Calgary after the charity wrestling exhibition I helped organize between you and your childhood hero Bret "The Hitman" Hart. Take me at my word when I say that I have a vested interest in acting as an effective proxy for my Calgary associate regarding his faunal menagerie. A knife fight occurring in broad daylight amidst the general public—including children no less—is the antithesis of the image I am working so diligently to create and cultivate."

"Yeah, sorry about that. I didn't exactly see it coming, and if I knew what I know now, I would have played things differently."

"You are referring to Mr. Lewis and his history of mental illness?"

"For starters."

"I see." Sykes walked over to a small, black, Igloo Playmate cooler beside the mini trampoline. He opened it and withdrew a stainless steel cocktail shaker and an empty glass, strained a light green beverage into the tumbler, and garnished it with a lime wedge. He tasted the drink and sighed satisfactorily. "Forgive me," he said, a moment later. "Where are my manners?"

Sykes returned the cocktail shaker to the cooler and retrieved something that made my heart skip a beat—a large, chilled Dairy Queen milkshake with such a perfect amount of condensation on the paper cup that it might just have been used in a TV commercial.

"*I can resist everything except temptation*," I said, quoting Sykes's favourite poet back to him as I licked my lips.

"Marvelous, Mr. Ounstead," replied Sykes, chuckling heartily and handing me the dairy delight. "Banana, but of course."

"Thank you," I said, before pointing at the odd sight of a cow in a pen full of numbered grass squares in front of me. "Do I even want to know what's going on here?"

"This would be my latest enterprise, albeit with a certain degree of bucolic panache."

"Actually, I think I've heard of this before."

"Is that so?"

"This isn't my first rodeo. Well, first time wrestling at a rodeo I mean."

"Indubitably."

"This is *cow-pie bingo*, isn't it?" I asked, motioning toward the steam rising off of the fresh pile of poop that landed on four, a number I knew from a brief stint in New Japan Pro Wrestling years earlier was considered unlucky in the land of the rising sun due to tetraphobia.

"*Cow-pie bingo* is such rudimentary terminology."

"How else do you describe placing bets on where a cow is going to crap?"

"By referring to such a surprisingly lucrative country fair activity far more eloquently."

"Road apple roulette?"

"*A Bovine Game of Manure Chance.*"

"You should trademark that," I said, dryly.

"Speaking of happenstance," replied Sykes, ignoring my dig, "is that what you think led Mr. Lewis to attack you with a blade?"

"No, I think I inadvertently brought that on myself."

I told Sykes about my investigation so far, which included the conversation Kelly Lewis and I had over s'mores, how he had me choked out by some beast of a man named "Buffalo," and that the mere mention of the bag full of cash in Jasper's locker sent my recent knife-wielding attacker into a blind and near-lethal rage.

"So, it seems likely that Lewis is the murderer," I said, summarily.

Sykes nursed his cocktail, his well-groomed features betraying nothing. "I acknowledge your method of deduction, Mr. Ounstead, but I believe you are more out-of-practice than you realize when it comes to your investigative skills."

"And why's that?"

"Perhaps I should let Bartholomew explain."

"Bartholomew?"

Sykes nodded and took another sip of his drink. "Yes," he said, before rolling his tongue, eliciting a high-pitched whistle and waving a hand toward himself. It was hard to tell at first because of the designer shades that hid his eyes, but I realized he was instead flagging down someone behind me. I turned around and saw a six-foot-six, three-hundred-plus-pound man, in a pair of gargantuan, denim overalls, nearly as wide as he was tall, lumbering toward us while carrying two hay bales over his massive shoulders. Both bales were wrapped in thick strips of tape which had the word *"ORGANIC"* written in large font.

"Allow me to introduce my employee for this weekend."

Sykes nodded and Bartholomew dropped the hay with the ease a normal-sized person would handheld bean bags. He waved at me from less than a foot away, while his hairy and tree-trunk-sized arms glistened with sweat. This monster of a man had close-cropped blonde hair that was more yellow than the dried grass he had been carrying. A jubilant and innocent smile spread across his big doe-eyed face.

"I knows you," he said, in a booming deep voice.

I stared at the slabs of beef the giant man had as upper limbs and instinctively rubbed my still tender neck. "Yeah. And I think I may know you, too."

"Oh boy. I'm suh-suh … sorry about making you go 'night-night.' Mister Sykes says is okay now. I just did what cousin asked."

"Cousin?"

"Uh-huh. Cousin Kelly."

I glanced at Sykes, whose face was as impassive as ever.

"Your cousin is Kelly Lewis?"

Bartholomew nodded excitedly and offered a gorilla mitt. I shook it politely, and the titan squeezed my hand so hard I thought he might crush a few metacarpals.

"Yup. And you're famous. You're the 'Hammerhead.'"

"Jed is fine, Bartholomew."

The giant shook his head vigorously and I thanked the stars when he let go of his vice-like grip. I tried not to wince as I wiggled my fingers in an effort to stave off numbness, but the big man didn't seem to notice the movement.

"No, no, no. Only Mister Sykes calls me Bartholomew. I like nicknames. I call you yours and you can call me mine."

"Okay then, *'Buffalo,'*" I said.

His pumpkin-sized, cherubic mug lit up with a high-wattage smile. "Ha ha, 'Hammerhead!' How did you know?"

EIGHTEEN
"THROW A FAKE"

Buffalo and I looked at one another for a long moment. While he stared at me blankly, still grinning ear-to-ear, I found myself instinctively tightening my core and tensing my body as I stood before the man who had choked me out in record time. His swole arms hung limply by his side like a couple of shoulder strapped meat cannons and it was clear he wasn't going to say anything until I did.

"Sykes? Do you think you and I could have a word in private?"

"As you wish, Mr. Ounstead. Bartholomew, could you please feed that *"Moo-Moo"* a handful of the yummy hay before working with it on the exercise we were practicing earlier?"

Buffalo nodded obediently, ripped strips of straw off of one of the organic hay bales he had carried, and lumbered over toward the animal in the grass bingo pen. He hand-fed the heifer some hay and petted it on its head.

"Good Moo-Moo," said Buffalo.

Sykes topped up his cocktail then returned to my side.

"What's its name?"

"I beg your pardon?"

"It's a girl cow, right?"

"That is correct."

"What's its name then? Cleopatra? Athena? I know you like the names of your animals to have historical significance," I said, motioning to Napoleon and Brutus, who were both still lying side-by-side on the grass and quietly chewing away on their dental sticks.

"Benefits of a classical education," retorted Sykes.

"You're getting sloppy. That's a Hans Gruber quote."

Sykes chuckled and flashed his luminous white teeth again. "Very good, Mr. Ounstead. Very good. Perhaps my assessment of your abilities being rusty was a tad premature."

"So, what is it?"

"I beg your pardon?"

"The cow's name."

"It is a simple bovine, Mr. Ounstead. It has no name."

I almost choked on my banana milkshake upon hearing his words, wondering what it was exactly that made a wiener dog and a goat worthy of classical monikers while a cow was not. I decided to let it go and push forward in my efforts to elicit answers from Sykes.

"I need your help, Sykes."

"Indeed. And there are several factors at play. The first being that it is quite possible Kelly Lewis was not responsible for the murder of Jasper Adams."

"And the fact Lewis and Jasper were disgruntled ex-lovers and the goliath who works for you and nearly strangled me to death on his cousin's orders doesn't make you think otherwise?"

"Not necessarily."

Sykes proceeded to explain how Bartholomew "Buffalo" Lewis was essentially a jacked-up Lennie from *Of Mice and Men*. Kind, harmless, and endlessly devoted to his older cousin Kelly. Both had toured with the rodeo for years and, according to

Sykes, the childlike colossus was an additional reason for the Seven Heads of the Rodeo's reticence to cut ties with Lewis completely. Doing so would leave Buffalo without a job, or more importantly a purpose, and according to Sykes the giant with a gentle soul would be devastated, distraught, and utterly lost without his cousin and caretaker. Upon taking over the Agri-Zone on behalf of his Calgary-based business partner, my calculating companion had taken a shine to the simple behemoth as he lumbered about the country fair and hired him for some odd jobs, which I knew from experience was par for the course for Sykes, who seemed endlessly drawn to the abnormal. He was like a one-man magnet for all things misfit and maverick.

"I hear you, Sykes, but I'm still not seeing how that disqualifies Lewis from being a suspect."

"I never said he should be. There just remain certain facts you seem to be overlooking."

"Such as?"

"Mr. Lewis called upon Bartholomew to render you unconscious after you revealed your credentials as a professional investigator, correct?"

"Yes."

"And we can both agree he was clearly grief-stricken by the news of the death of Mr. Adams and that he did not begin his attempted assault on you with a knife until the mention of the duffel bag of money you found in the locker of the deceased?"

"Uh, yeah ..." I said, starting to connect the dots Sykes was laying out before me.

"This is all in addition to Mr. Lewis's established history with mental illness. As you know, bipolar condition in particular is often associated with instantaneous mood swings and erratic behaviour."

"You're saying he was triggered both times he came at me."

"I am saying it might be a pattern worthy of consideration."

"But what about the sack of cash? Surely that has to be a possible motive."

"I concur. Just not in the way you think."

Before I could respond, a thunderous and ear-piercing hybrid sound of gargling and screaming sliced through the open air and startled me so badly I nearly jumped out of the pair of yellow Chucks that were tied snugly around my feet.

"AAAAARRRGGGGGLLLLLLEEEEEEGGGGG!"

Ever the cool cucumber, I followed Sykes's gaze as he looked straight ahead. Leaning over the top of the orange mesh fence with a torso thicker than a beer keg was Buffalo, his mammoth meathooks cupped around his mouth. I wasn't the only one jolted by the blaring cry as a moment later the cow emitted a high-pitched wailing moo before crapping out a wad of manure that plopped onto the grass like a super-sized Olympic discus.

Buffalo threw his arms up in the air so quickly I was pretty sure I felt a gust of wind whoosh past me before he began jumping up and down. Even Sykes, despite his penchant for being utterly unflappable, gave into his emotion and raised his tumbler in a victory toast.

"Outstanding, Bartholomew!" he proudly declared.

"I can't wait to show Cousin!" bellowed Buffalo with unbridled enthusiasm.

"He doesn't know about what just went down?" I asked.

Still excited, Sykes turned his head to look at me, and in doing so, his upscale eyewear slid slightly down the bridge of his nose, revealing his eyes. I always forgot how icy blue his irises were, and despite their frosty appearance, they were crackling with electricity.

"He does not. And it is best for us all, Bartholomew especially, if that remains the case for now."

I nodded, my racing heartbeat slowly returning to normal after the jarring sound. "Are you going to explain whatever the hell that was? Because I almost joined the cow in leaving a startled deposit on this field myself."

"Mr. Ounstead, you are aware that the crux of my business model is and has always revolved around the taking and placing of wagers, are you not?"

"I am."

"So, in a Bovine Game of Manure Chance, would it not be advantageous if one were able to encourage said creature to defecate at a certain time and place?"

"Are you telling me that's why Buffalo just bellowed like a Chewbacca pissing out a kidney stone? Because you're rigging this backcountry bingo by potty-training a cow to crap on demand?"

"I am a man of honour, Mr. Ounstead, and, as such, do not care for the term *'rigging.'* Not to mention that encouraging such an animal to evacuate its bowels with precision is far from an exact science. This is more of an … experiment, if you will, based upon the latest research in the fecal patterns of cattle. And let me assure you that being on the cutting edge of bovine behavioural cognitive processes requires a significant financial investment. That being said, if a random sound were to happen to induce a painstakingly-trained mammal such as this to defecate, it would hardly be seen as pre-meditated and strategic, and in turn could potentially make the outcome of the wagers I am taking this weekend *very* lucrative indeed."

I sighed and shook my head, frustrated that I was discussing dung in such detail when I was still wrapping my head around the possibility that Kelly Lewis didn't kill Jasper. Sykes adjusted his glasses while I sucked back the remainder of my banana milkshake, and as always, the dairy delight brought me clear-headedness and calm.

Buffalo went back to petting the cow and feeding it hay, while I tried to get my conversation with Sykes back on track.

"You said something about the bag of money still being motive."

Sykes nodded. "Are you familiar with the particular importance of the loggersports events this weekend at this very country fair?"

"More than the usual wood-chopping, tree-climbing, and axe-throwing you mean?"

Sykes nodded as he took an unusually big swig of his lime cocktail. Since I had only ever seen him nurse drinks before, I figured he still must have been in a celebratory mood.

"I suppose I'm not," I said.

"These lumberjack festivities are being sponsored by STIHL, the German manufacturer of chainsaws and other such handheld power equipment used in our logging games. Although not public knowledge, those behind the scenes are—for lack of a better word—*abuzz* about the fact that representatives from the company headquarters in Stuttgart are here in town for a very specific reason."

"Which is?"

"To award the winning competitor of the all-around events category an opportunity to serve as an official spokesperson to represent their Timbersports brand in the Pacific Northwest. Rumour has it that in addition to a hefty cash prize, the ongoing, multi-year contract would be quite lucrative. It was my understanding that your friend Mr. Adams was considered a frontrunner to win both the prize money and contract."

I lowered my head for a moment as I snapped back in time to the moment Jasper and I were getting drunk together at the bar. The memory was foggy—but it was there. I played it over in my mind again and again, in addition to the conversation Declan and I had in the locker room when I was changing out of my stolen clown costume, where we had zeroed in on something similar Jasper had said to me while he smiled smugly to himself.

"That's not to say that making a living exclusively from loggersports wouldn't be nice."

What was it that Jasper knew? Had he just been letting his mind wander with a "what if?" scenario? Or did the self-satisfied way in which he said such a thing have a deeper meaning—as if he knew he was in the hunt for and on the cusp of potentially snagging a STIHL sponsorship, and being able to kiss his day jobs goodbye in order to make a living exclusively from being a professional, paid, competitive lumberjack?

Despite the limited time we had spent together, after hearing firsthand the way he had spoken about his grandfather, it was hard not to think that securing such an honour and plum gig would have made his "Chop-Chop Pop Pop," as Declan so affectionately referred to him, very proud indeed.

I cut my thoughts short and turned my attention back to Sykes. "You said Jasper was a frontrunner. Which means there were other loggers in contention."

"Correct."

"You think one of them may have used that as a reason to take Jasper out?"

Sykes sipped his cocktail and smiled ever-so-slightly. "It is your profession which requires such speculation and investigation, Mr. Ounstead, not mine. I am simply sharing some potentially relevant chatter with an old friend."

A while back having Sykes refer to me as a friend would have thrown me for a loop. But our relationship had evolved over the time we had known each other, and I'll be damned if I hadn't grown to consider the animal-loving, wager-taking, enigma of a man a pal.

"Any particular rival woodcutters spring to mind whom you think may have had the motive or the means to eliminate Jasper?"

"I understand that the STIHL sponsorship had been essentially shortlisted to two men—Mr. Adams, and a gentleman known as Harland McGraw."

"Never heard of him."

"No, I imagine you would not have, nor will you have much luck trying to find him by his given name. He is much better known by his competitive nickname, 'Hot Saw' McGraw."

"Where can I find this 'Hot Saw?'" I asked.

"Unfortunately, at the moment, I do not believe you can. Both Mr. McGraw and Mr. Pippen have already been taken to the local Royal Canadian Mounted Police detachment for questioning."

"You mean Randy Pippen. The loggersports head honcho and one of the Seven Heads of the Rodeo."

"The one and the same," said Sykes.

"Did Pippen have a favourite between Jasper and McGraw?'"

"Most certainly. Mr. Pippen much prefers the more polished and blue-blood Harland McGraw and has been known to favour him. He was apparently less than inclined toward your friend and his more salt of the earth, man of the people, growing-up-on-the-green-chain image, despite the popularity of your late companion among the dedicated fans of these logging tests of strength and skill."

I nodded, taking it all in. I slipped my phone out of my pocket and checked the screen. I had one text message from an unknown number. I opened the message.

Kelly in custody at the security station inside the arena. Still out cold. RCMP on their way. Is that chili of yours hot? Cuz in case you haven't noticed I like things spicy, Big Boy.
Annie

I did my best not to blush. If Sykes noticed my momentary infatuation he chose to ignore it, instead shifting his gaze between Napoleon and Brutus, still chewing their dental sticks side-by-side like the best of friends, while Buffalo continued to smile innocently and pet the cow as he fed it handfuls of organic hay.

With Lewis still unconscious and the Mounties on their way there was no sense in heading over to the security facility to meet with Annie just yet. And although the STIHL sponsorship opened up an entirely new avenue of investigation—one that could be the break I had been looking for in terms of making headway into the who and why of Jasper's murder—there wasn't much I could do with both Pippen and "Hot Saw" McGraw off site.

Which left me with Declan, who last I knew was tracking down the Doukhabor motivational speaker Jim Kootnekoff,

AKA "Kooty," the big cheese who oversaw the Marketplace at the *Colossal Cloverdale Rodeo and Country Fair*.

"A penny for your thoughts, Mr. Ounstead," said Sykes.

"What do you know about the Marketplace and Jim Kootnekoff?"

"Alas, with my Agri-Zone responsibilities, I am afraid I only know of him by name."

"What about his motivational speaking?"

Sykes simply shook his head.

"Ever heard of the necklaces he's known for peddling?"

Sykes's left eyebrow shot up so high on his forehead it looked like it was on an invisible fishhook. I told him about the washer on the chain I had found at the bottom of the log boom pool and how given the fact Jasper was known not to buy into Kootnekoff's unique brand of self-improvement, it was more than likely the rudimentary jewelry had belonged to the killer.

"Most curious," conceded Sykes. "It appears as if your next avenue of investigation awaits."

"How far away is this hayseed bazaar, anyway?" I asked.

"On foot, and making your way through the fairgrounds crowds on this Saturday afternoon, I am afraid such a footslog could take up to twenty minutes."

I cursed silently to myself. "I don't have that kind of time, Sykes. Not with Lewis in custody with security while the Mounties are on the way. I need to get to the Marketplace fast to question this Kooty character and get back so I'm present the moment Lewis comes to."

"A solid strategy," agreed Sykes, before draining the last drops of his lime beverage.

"You don't happen to know of a quicker way for me to get over there, do you?"

A satisfied smile slowly crept across Sykes's face.

"Oh, Mr. Ounstead. Despite all of our dealings with one another it seems you still underestimate me."

NINETEEN
"BURN THE BREEZE"

The ostrich ran like the wind.

I desperately hung onto the base of its long neck and did my damnedest not to squeeze it too hard. The fast-footed fowl's massive two-toed feet danced across the dirt pathway, leaving a trail of dust behind us that I dared not look back at over my shoulder, despite feeling tiny specks of dirt nipping at the back of my ears before whooshing away as if blasted by a leaf blower.

All I could think of as I clung to the flightless bird was that Annie wasn't kidding when she said that riding horses kept her thighs taut, as my quads were on fire as they struggled to stay wrapped around the creature's black-feathered torso. My hair flapped backwards and I had to blink repeatedly as the air dried out my eyes when we reached a speed that must have been close to fifty kilometers per hour.

I initially expressed great hesitation at the thought of hitching a ride on the back of an ostrich as a potential solution for getting to the Cloverdale Rodeo's Marketplace as soon as possible, but Sykes wasn't having any of it.

"Are you crazy?" I exclaimed. "Look, I know you're into quirky stuff with animals, and hey, no judgement," I said, raising my hands. "I get it, it's your thing. But you've got to admit, even for you this is pushing it."

"Have you ever travelled via ostrich before, Mr. Ounstead?"

"No, Sykes, I haven't. I've also never gone waterskiing with a beaver."

"Despite some controversial and inaccurate opinions, ostrich riding is much more common than most realize. In fact, the practice is actually a rather widespread activity in North America and remains a very popular tourist attraction in South Africa."

"Look, I appreciate that you're chock-full of fun facts like this, and maybe when Jasper's killer is behind bars you can tell me all about the mating habits of the penguins at the Cape of Good Hope over another banana milkshake or something. But for now, I think I'll just try and push my way through the crowds and find this Kooty character myself."

"What a shame. I could expedite your arrival in a fraction of the time."

I gritted my teeth and hung my head. Sykes may have been a lot to take at times, but with the exception of Declan, my father, and Rya, there probably wasn't a person I trusted more.

"Even if I hopped on one of your big bird's backs, I'm almost six-foot-four, have leaned out, and added some mass since we've last met. I tip the scales at a meaty two-forty and change now, Sykes. Don't these things have a weight limit or something?"

"In point of fact, they do, with the general rule of thumb being that just under ninety kilograms is considered the maximum weight an ostrich can safely support on its back while running."

"Well, there you go then. I'm nearly fifty pounds over that."

"I said *general* rule of thumb, Mr. Ounstead. I believe Odysseus would be an exception in your case."

"Sweet mother of God," I said, as I face-palmed myself, not even bothering to inquire as to why the damn ostrich had earned a distinguished designation while the poor potty-training cow had not.

Seven minutes later, Odysseus the ostrich had carried me so far that I could see the adjacent row of long red barns—which served as the country fair's shopping area—on the horizon. Unlike the ten-year trek his namesake had traversed, once my rapid-transit land fowl had gotten onto the beaten path—which was essentially a straight shot through a greenbelt of evergreen trees that connected the Agri-Zone and Elements Casino and its horse race track with the outbuildings that served as the Marketplace—the trip went very quickly.

Odysseus and I had been accompanied on our backtrail jaunt by Sykes's ostrich wrangler Garth, a stout and stoic, fifty-year-old petting zoo veteran who seemed quite comfortable taking instruction from my bookie buddy and being mounted on a flightless bird of his own, all the while ensuring my avian Uber shuttled my oversized ass swiftly and safely to my destination.

Garth made some clicking sounds out of the side of his mouth as we neared the end of the dirt trail, which was in walking distance from the supersized swap meet. Both Odysseus and Garth's ostrich obediently slowed to trots and eventually full stops. I hopped off of my new feathered friend and gave him a few gracious pats on one of his shaggy wings.

"Definitely faster than a pony ride," I conceded.

Garth just nodded, then dug a handful of figs out of the pocket of his jeans and fed both Odysseus and his broad-beaked brethren. Having worked up an appetite, Odysseus snaked out his neck like a coiled cobra striking and furiously pecked at the treats in Garth's open palm, causing a few of the small pear-shaped fruits to fall onto the ground. Garth bent over and scooped them up, but when he stood back up, I noticed a necklace had sprung free from underneath his starched white undershirt. Except it wasn't just any kind of necklace. It was a stainless steel washer with a silver ball chain looped through it.

"Interesting piece of jewelry," I said, motioning toward the metallic disc around his neck.

Garth hocked a loogie, spat, and the wad of phlegm arced through the air like a marble-sized saliva shotput.

"Uh-huh," he said, nonchalantly, before resuming feeding figs to the ostriches.

"You get that from Kooty?"

"Yup."

"You're one of his followers then?"

Garth didn't like that one bit. "I ain't no lemming," he snapped. "But I believe in the man and his teachings."

"Believe what, exactly?"

"Wish it. Will it. Wield it."

"That like a catchphrase or something?"

"More like a mantra."

"I see," I said, pretending to understand, despite becoming more perplexed at how a rodeo rhetorician could inspire such devotion to self-help seminars that as far as I could tell were built around nothing more than a ninety-nine cent trinket that could be quickly cobbled together from the bottom of any household toolbox.

"So, how exactly does it work?"

"How does what work?"

"I mean, do you *'wish'* for an ostrich, *'will'* it to be fast, then *'wield'* the opportunity to turn a profit by charging for rides or something?"

Garth stared at me long and hard for what felt like an eternity. Finally, he spoke. "Are you fucking with me?"

"Wouldn't dream of it. Does Sykes know about your, uh, affiliation with Kooty?"

Garth snorted again in another attempt at clearing his sinuses. Although it was grating on the ears, I was appreciative that this time the obnoxious sound was not followed by more projectile mucous.

"Sykes don't know squat. And he don't need to either, ya hear?" growled Garth. "Lord knows that bastard is nosey enough as it is."

"He definitely doesn't miss much," I said, by way of agreement.

"Well, he's gonna goddamn stay in the dark, if you know what's good for you," he said gruffly, patting the washer still dangling around his neck. "Cuz this here's my business."

"You got it, Bub. As long as you tell me where exactly I can find this guru of yours."

Garth hocked and spat again, which caused me to wince and look away. "Just walk into any of them red barns ahead and ask around. Kooty'll be kickin' about somewhere."

I thanked Garth for both his ostrich and navigational assistance, then headed off toward the Marketplace in an effort to find an inspiring Doukhobor on a dais in mid-diatribe.

Imagine my surprise when I encountered something even more unconventional.

6:03 P.M.

TWENTY
"SHIRK AND SHAVER"

"Well, stick a banana up my butt and call me Betty!"

"What the hell did you just say?"

"You're that 'Hammerhead' pro-wrestler guy with the big match tonight, ain't you?"

I gritted my teeth. I was so caught up in trying to track down Jasper's killer I had completely forgotten the Faustian bargain I had made with Grasby in order to get an audience with the Seven Heads of the Rodeo.

"Jesus, you're huge. Whaddya, eat the cobs with your corn too in-between all them gravy smothered steaks?"

"Speak that way about a banana again and the only smothering will be my hand over your big mouth."

"Easy, Hoss," the man said while putting his hands up in the air submissively. "Just trying to break the ice. Kind of goes with the gig."

The average-sized man in black western boots and Levi's wore a white T-shirt with a hypersexualized green female frog on it, in which the amphibian's bulbous butt was elevated, right underneath text that read *"FROGGY STYLE."* The lewd tee was tucked tightly into the ill-mannered individual's waistline, and I half expected him to tip over from the sheer weight of his shiny silver longhorn bull belt buckle that had nearly the same circumference as a frisbee. He stood in the middle of the first red barn I had entered, in front of a kiosk adorned with more novelty Tees and sexual innuendo-themed attire than you'd find on the wall in the back corner of a Hot Topic store.

"Forgive me," he continued. "We just don't see fellers like you around these parts much. Not with all the city slickers who roll in here playin' cowboy for the weekend and tryin' to get a taste of the rustic life."

I gave him a slow nod, before turning my back on the banana blasphemer and taking another look around the rest of the barn-turned-Marketplace. The venue was absolutely bustling with people, many jammed shoulder-to-shoulder as they shuffled their way up and down aisles full of the finest gadgets, health products, impulse buys, and collection of *As Seen On TV* crap as far as the eye could see. Directly across from me and Froggy Style a squad of young Korean women in matching purple medical scrubs scurried about their booth trying to showcase their inventory and make some sales. Customers stepped on-and-off of acupressure foot pads, received neck rubs while seated forward-facing in upright massage chairs, and tried out kneading and vibrating Shiatsu seats. Froggy Style either didn't care, or had simply seen it all before, as he continued with his pitch.

"I gotta say, I'm loving your T-shirt," he said, pointing at the **DO NOT GO GENTLE** credo across my chest above the graphic of a two-by-four with a lightning bolt through it.

"Thanks."

"What's that on the back there?" he asked, inquisitively.

"It's nothing," I said, trying to wave away his interest with a hand. "This is only a prototype."

"C'mon, Hoss, don't be shy! Lemme see."

I sighed and turned my back, allowing Froggy Style to read the additional text.

"Rage, rage, against the dying of the MIGHT?" he asked, confused. "What's that?"

It finally occurred to me that the play on words of the famous Dylan Thomas verse I thought was so clever may have been asking a bit much from the casual sports entertainment fan.

"I'm a pro-wrestler and it's, uh, from a poem—"

"I'm not an idiot," he snapped. "But isn't it supposed to say *'rage against the dying of the light?'*"

"That's why there are weights underneath," I replied, referring to the garment's other image of an Olympic sized barbell curving downwards due to an abundance of cast iron plates.

"Ha!" exclaimed, Froggy Style, slapping me on the back as I turned back around. "I love it! That's genius. And I'm not just blowing smoke up your ass either, I do this for a living. How much?"

"Like I said, it's just a work-up. Not for sale."

"What about a trade?" he continued, ignoring me. "What are you, like a double XL? I think I gotta Rewind Beer Co. shirt that size around here somewhere."

"I'm good, Bub."

"Are you sure? It's pretty sweet. Has a *Magnum, P.I.* retro theme and comes with their beer logo over top of the brown, orange, and yellow colours from TC's chopper."

How the uppity bugger had known to scratch my Tom Selleck nostalgia sweet spot was beyond me, but I'll be damned if his pitch didn't momentarily have me considering making the swap. Seeing that I was nibbling at the baited hook, he tried to sweeten the deal.

"C'mon, Big Fella. I'll even throw in an ALF Chia Pet."

Being the sentimental snob that I was, I lost interest as soon as Froggy Style tried pushing the burnt sienna, cat-eating alien from planet Melmac on me.

"Is it this way to the Jim Kootnekoff motivational speaking?" I asked, pointing toward the rear of the Marketplace barn.

"Kooty? Nah, not this year. They moved him next door. He's at the Yuk Yuk's theatre in the casino now. Takes the stage every two hours too so you can still make the next show."

I started to head off when Froggy Style yelped. "Wait!" he pleaded, before scrambling behind his kiosk and rummaging around the shelves beneath the cubicle. He popped back up like a submerged buoy a moment later and handed me a plastic bag.

"I tell you what, this is on the house. But if you wanted to repay me for my generosity, maybe you could consider me as a potential business partner to mass produce those babies?" he asked, patting the exclusive T-shirt on my torso.

A business card appeared between his fingertips. I reluctantly accepted both the bag and fluorescent neon wallet-sized credentials which loudly touted *"Dicky Diamond's Duds'n'Stuff."*

"I'll think about it," I said, and that was all it took for Dicky's face to light up brighter than the pyrotechnics that would go off back when I walked toward a WWE ring. I slipped the card in my cargo shorts pocket, and only then noticed the additional item to my eighties ale top, which came in a less than discreet box.

"Is this what I think it is?" I asked.

"That's just the basic model. Come back and I'll cut you a deal for the bionic one."

I looked again at the penis pump on top of my T-shirt in my shopping bag, but when I went to speak, I simply couldn't find the words. Dicky gave me a supportive pat on the shoulder.

"Gotta offset all those steroids, am I right, Gigantor?"

Five minutes later, I was inside the Elements Casino when music began to pulse from behind the doors to Yuk Yuk's comedy club. I slipped into the theatre past a distracted usher assisting a confused elderly couple with directions to their seats. I hung back for a few moments as my eyes adjusted to the dim lighting. Kooty's motivational speech had begun, and the iconic bass for Survivor's "Eye of the Tiger" was rocking so hard I made a mental note to add the vintage tune to my weightlifting playlist. I slipped into an aisle seat in the rear of the theatre, in which almost all of the one hundred auditorium chairs were filled with folks anxiously awaiting inspiration.

About a minute later, the anticipation had reached a fever pitch, however before David Bickler's iconic vocals hit, there was a record scratch followed by the ringing of reverberating sound similar to that of an amp being unplugged.

This was followed by utter silence, save for the hushed crowd looking around confused and whispering back and forth with one another as they tried to figure out what was happening. And while I may have been completely unfamiliar with Kooty's presentation style, even I could tell something had gone awry.

Suddenly, a different pounding bass blasted out from the speakers and the moment I recognized the beat I cursed to myself, because I knew what was coming next. The poor crowd, on the other hand, had absolutely no idea the shitshow they were about to witness.

A dynamic figure in amber-tinted sunglasses and a tan Stetson cowboy hat emerged from behind the red curtain like an adrenaline-charged Arsenio Hall, fist-pumping and taking puffs of a cigarette, all the while doing a jig to the instrumental beat of "Shamrocks and Shenanigans" by House of Pain.

The only problem—it wasn't Kooty, a Doukhobor, or even a legitimate motivational speaker. It was my cousin.

TWENTY-ONE
"THE IRISH COWBOY"

HARNESS *HAPPINESS!*

That's what the giant sign hanging over the stage read. Three large silver discs—clearly not metal, but covered instead in cheap aluminum foil—hanging from the rafters, swaying slightly, and resembling both Annie's necklace and the chain and washer I had found underneath Jasper's floating body in the log boom pool.

A shimmering bright font on a large projector screen sparkled and danced across the display with the now-familiar words—WISH IT! WILL IT! WIELD IT!

Declan sashayed back and forth on the dais waving his hands up in the air as he tried to rile up the audience. He grinned ear-to-ear as he kept his groove going, crowing enthusiastically into the headset microphone hovering near the corner of his lips.

"*Boom sha lock lock boom*, ya wally glunterpecks!"

I hung my head in embarrassment, but given my cousin's borderline inhuman tolerance for alcohol, I couldn't tell if he was three sheets to the wind or simply just extra buzzed from the thrill of having a large crowd hungry for some life advice in the palm of his hands.

"Golly, his arms are covered in so many tattoos," I overheard a frumpy, fifty-something woman mention to her milquetoast husband, while gawking at the full-sleeved orange, green, and black tats adorning Declan's striated biceps, triceps, and forearms.

"He sure doesn't look Russian, does he?" chimed in the meek man.

Declan glanced backstage over his shoulder and made a slicing motion with his index finger across his neck. The classic tune by the Irish-themed, hip-hop trio faded. He flicked away the butt of his smoke, then clapped his hands together repeatedly.

There was some mild applause as a portion of the perplexed crowd joined in, still unsure of what exactly was going on, but apparently willing to go along with it for the time being.

"All right, ladies and lads! Keep smackin' yer mitts together an' let's hear that boola bus!"

The uncertain clapping grew a bit louder.

"Now, who's ready to grab life by the barse and take charge o'their futures *tits sweet?*"

The influx of Emerald Isle slang combined with Declan's own distinctive terminology, including his beloved bastardization of the French expression *tout de suite* for "right away," was too much for some people.

"You're not Jim!" shouted a surly-looking silver fox in a polo shirt.

"Where's Kooty?" demanded another audience member.

"Who the hell are you?" screeched a woman.

"Keep yer Alans on, Mates. Me name is Declan St. James. An' ol' Koots asked me to fill in for him."

"Is he sick?" asked Silver Fox.

"Let's just say he's in no condition to take the stage this afternoon."

"I want my money back!" bellowed a ripped skinny fat dude in a tank top, whose muscular arms contrasted with his prominent pot belly and chicken legs. He jumped to his feet and let loose a few obscenities to drive home his request before the rest of the equally distressed crowd turned restless and began getting out of their chairs.

Declan furrowed his brow as the tide turned against him. A moment later he spotted me in the back of the audience and his frown turned upside down.

"Quit yer ragebaggin', folks! We got us a celebrity here among us! Give it up for professional wrasslin' superstar 'Hammerhead' Jed Ounstead, who owes all o' his fame an' fortune to the three Ws program!"

My cousin pointed in my direction and a hundred heads turned to stare at me. Realizing I couldn't leave Declan in the lurch, I begrudgingly walked forward while the crowd politely clapped until I climbed up onto the stage and took my place at his side.

"What took ya so bloody long," he snapped, covering the microphone with a closed fist. "I sent yer arse like ten texts."

I realized I hadn't checked my phone since I received Annie's message and mounted Odysseus. I silently cursed the carry-pouch looped around the belt of my cargo shorts. The leather sheath may have come in handy during investigations, but the thing negated the vibration of a mobile phone. I reached into my EDC case and flipped on my iPhone's ringer, when Declan noticed what was in my other hand.

"Jaysus, ya stopped to go shoppin'?" he asked incredulously, before using a couple fingertips to open and peer inside the bag. Seeing the male enhancement item I had been given by Dicky Diamond, Declan grinned devilishly. "Good on ya, Jed."

"The Doukobor, D," I growled.

"In the back," he said, nodding behind the stage. "He's waitin' for ya."

I knew there was a catch, but between the undercover rodeo clown action, petting zoo knife fight, and ostrich ride, I had experienced enough tomfoolery for one afternoon and decided to take him at his word. But before I could head toward the back, Ripped Skinny Fat Dude stomped up the aisle on his gaunt gams and stabbed an accusatory finger at me.

"Liar! He's been famous for years. The three Ws program had nothing to do with it!"

I froze in my tracks. Ever the consummate sweet talker and brimming with malarkey, Declan seemed confident he could handle the cantankerous crowd.

"Go on, now," he said to me in a hushed tone. "I'll keep these eejits busy an' buy ya some time to question that Russki bastard."

He unwrapped his fist from around the headset microphone, spread his arms wide, and stepped forward into the spotlight. "Easy, Boyo! Ya gotta crawl before ya can walk, am I right?"

"What the hell does that mean?" snapped Ripped Skinny Fat Dude.

Declan rubbed his hands together, turned away from the crowd for a moment, then spun back around and produced a small red and silver can of Hell's Gate Premium Lager as if it had magically appeared out of thin air. The crowd oohed and aahed at the optical illusion.

"Wish it!" he crowed.

He popped the top of the beer.

"Will it!"

Declan threw back his head, chugged the entire three hundred and fifty-five milliliter brew, smacked his lips, belched, then crushed the empty can on his forehead.

"Wield it!"

Declan flung the flattened metal disc out into the audience and threw his fists in the air victoriously. The crowd suddenly seemed awfully motivated by my cousin's demonstration, because I could still hear their chuckles and applause by the time I made my way backstage to the room where I finally found the enigmatic spiritual leader whose cheap branded jewelry was somehow inextricably linked to the death of my lumberjack buddy.

TWENTY-TWO
"ACKNOWLEDGE THE CORN"

New-age music filled the small green room, its darkened walls draped in mauve-coloured velvet. A dozen scented candles were strategically placed around the jerry-built sanctuary, furnished with a couple of beanbag chairs and a craft service table bearing a meatless platter of pungent artisanal breads, nuts, deviled eggs, spices, and cabbage. These combined with the overpowering aroma of green tea and jasmine made the room smell less like a staging area for a show and more like a hipster coffee shop near Vancouver harbour's iconic bright yellow Sulphur piles.

In the centre of the space, lying prone atop an island of cushions, was none other than Jim Kootnekoff himself. Annie wasn't far off when she referred to him as a grey-haired scarecrow, as the gangly man's stringy mane was spread out like the head of a wet mop. The motionless motivational speaker was face down, his hands tied behind his back with what looked like a severed extension cord. I tossed aside my shopping bag from *Dicky Diamond's Duds'n'Stuff* and knelt beside the man better known as "Kooty." I jabbed him a few times in his bony ribs until he moaned loudly. I helped the disorientated Doukhobor sit up, and his elongated legs immediately crisscrossed as he settled into a Sukhasana position, better known as an Easy Yoga Pose. He kept his head lowered and took a deep breath, then, despite being barefoot in jeans with his wrists still bound, began sliding himself over to the wall.

I was caught off guard by whatever the hell Kooty was doing but decided to let it play out. The persuasive preacher reached the edge of the room—and with his back still on the floor—butted his ass right up to the wall. He then began to kick his legs out up and out against the wall, as if he were a disorientated upside down Radio City Rockette. However, after a few attempts, Kooty managed to "kick" his heels into a full lotus position, then roll off the wall and over his shoulders, before popping back up in front of me with his legs perfectly criss-crossed and ankles resting atop the inside of his knees.

He inhaled and exhaled deeply before opening his eyes. "That's better," he said, pleasantly.

I again found myself in Sykes's debt, because I recognized the sixty-something's style of seating and its degree of difficulty thanks to a complimentary goat yoga class courtesy of my bookie benefactor. Despite a genuine effort on my part, I did not find the inner peace I was looking for following my ferocious encounter with Cassian Cullen, the psychopath I bested in combat and whose execution I orchestrated months earlier before I walked away from my life as a private eye. Of course, it's also possible that tranquility and harmony eluded me because a goat pooped on my back while I was in the plank position.

Kooty tossed his gunmetal-gray locks behind him with a practiced snap of his head, then looked right at me. The gaze from his hazel eyes was so sudden, piercing, and penetrating, it felt like staring at the back of a DVD shimmering in sunlight. I recoiled instinctively, finding myself taken aback as if by some mind-probe. Jim's angular features only accentuated his inscrutable aura, and after closing his eyes again for some more deep breathing, he reopened them and smiled slightly.

"Thank you, Friend," he said, with a suave and silky voice.

I stood up and cleared my throat before blundering out a response. "For what?"

"Helping me."

"Do you remember what happened?"

Kooty realized his hands were restrained, but unlike most other people, he made no effort to struggle against his bindings.

"There was an Irish fellow," he said calmly. "He entered my quarters, confirmed my identity, then began to sing a song."

"It wasn't David Bowie, was it?" I asked, knowing all too well my cousin's affinity for the rocker's omnisexual alien alter ego Ziggy Stardust.

"On the contrary, it was a beautiful little folk song. What were the lyrics?" he asked himself, before closing his eyes yet again in an effort to recall the moment. "*Too-Ra-Loo* something. But after that my memory is blank."

I rubbed my tired face. *Too-Ra-Loo-Ra-Loo-Ral*, I thought to myself. The famous Irish lullaby. As in a tune one sings before bed. Or, in Declan's case, before he puts someone to sleep, like the poor, plump rodeo clown who had been choked out in his trailer only to have his costume stolen. I made a mental note to try and make things up to the jester if I ever had a moment when I wasn't bouncing around a damn country fair like a small metal sphere in a Cowboy-themed pinball machine.

I grabbed a chair by the craft service table, spun it around, and took a seat, resting my elbows on the top of the backrest. It felt good to finally sit down. I followed Kooty's lead and took a few deep breaths myself. My heart rate slowed while the adrenaline tapered off, and only then did I realize how sore my lower back and legs were from both my match and the ensuing hijinks.

"You're Jim Kootnekoff. One of the Seven Heads of the Rodeo, motivational mentor, and the big kahuna in charge of this Marketplace here."

"Call me Kooty," he replied. "And yes."

"Your necklaces are quite popular," I said, nodding toward the washer and chain combo I had been seeing all afternoon hanging around his neck. It wasn't any bigger or fancier than the others, just the same piece of humble hardware jewelry.

"This isn't a necklace."

"Sure seems like it."

"It's a totem."

"A totem?"

"Yes. A special one, in fact. You see, life is all about momentum. And this simple saucer here," he said, pointing downwards with his chin, "think of it as a pendulum—"

"Spare me the hippie spiritual spin, Bub. I get it. Emphasize the highs, mitigate the lows and all that."

"Don't be so trite. I can sense your inner conflict. And also ..."

Kooty's voice faded away but he had piqued my curiosity.

"Also, what?"

"The ones you miss."

My heart skipped a beat. Could the grizzled guru be telling the truth? Did he have some kind of psychic power allowing him to see the permanent hole in my heart left by losing my beloved mom as a teenager, or the new emotional crater that had opened up since Rya stopped speaking to me? Or perhaps I was just so wrapped up in my own self-loathing that pensiveness was plain as day on my face and more obvious than my love for banana milkshakes. *Damn it,* I thought, licking my lips as the melancholy suddenly had familiar company. I know they say the average man thinks about sex once every few minutes, but my fondness for my favourite frozen treat had to have been just as frequent.

"Yessss," cooed Kooty. "Don't run from it. Take on the turmoil. Focus your power."

"Then what?" I snapped. "Your little swinging metal disc is just going to make everything okay?"

"It can. In time."

"Bullshit."

"You haven't even tried."

"That's because some things can't be undone," I blurted out, only then realizing—and wondering why—I was sharing so much so fast.

"Whatever may have occurred, you can get past it. I feel your energy, Friend. It's powerful. And immense."

"I can't just—"

"But most of all, your aura is kind," he said, smiling softly.

I nearly choked up. I barely even knew this strange man but, in some ways, felt more understood in that moment than the last time Rya had kissed me on my cheek and confessed her love for me. And although she claimed that it was platonic, I was pretty sure it was more than that for her, just as it was for me.

"Welcome the pain," continued Kooty. "Embrace it and you can harness—"

"What?" I snapped, interrupting him. "Happiness?"

Kooty paused before responding.

"Forgiveness," he said.

I jumped to my feet and turned my back on the man, storming off toward the green room door as I tried to pump the brakes on the epic brain busting he was doing. I calmed myself and returned to the chair, except this time I turned it around and sat down facing him proper. Kooty avoided my gaze and stretched his long neck, waiting for me to speak.

"Look, I appreciate what you're trying to do, okay? You've got some mental mastery, I'll give you that. I see now why there are a hundred people out there all eating up your schtick."

"My truth."

"Fair enough," I said, figuring it was the least I could concede.

Suddenly, the crowd outside the lounge laughed collectively before breaking into a round of applause. Whatever Declan was doing out there, it sure sounded like he was killing it. Kooty winced a bit. I thought it was over the sound of his seminar proceeding without him, but instead he appeared to be suffering from physical pain as he shifted his shoulders uncomfortably, his arms still secured behind his back. As he ignored the noise of the elated audience, I opened my EDC pouch and retrieved my tactical knife. I flipped it open as I walked behind Kooty and cut loose his hands from the electrical cord. He made no motion aside from a sigh and soft moaning as he rubbed his reddened wrists. I put my blade away and returned to my chair.

"Did you know that one of the lumberjacks in the logger-sports pit was murdered a couple hours ago?"

Kooty's eyes widened in surprise. "I did not."

"It's my understanding that you're familiar with some of them."

"Several."

"Jasper Adams is dead."

"Oh, no. I am deeply saddened to hear that."

"Did you know him?"

"A little. I reached out with an offer to assist him in bettering himself after I received word he was in contention for a corporate sponsorship, but he was uninterested."

"You have quite the following here at this country fair. Like Annie Tibbs."

"Annie," he said, smiling. "She is a delight."

"I'll say. But it seems like most folks come to you. Why make an effort with Jasper?"

"It wasn't just him. My offer was to all of his fellow lumberjack competitors as well."

"Who were these other colleagues?"

Kooty closed his eyes again as he recalled the names. "Buck Lockhart, Thomas Gayford, Harland McGraw. A few more whose names I can't recall."

"What can you tell me about McGraw?"

"First and foremost? I don't particularly like the man."

"Why?"

"I find him to be selfish, impatient, and petulant. Especially after it became clear he and Jasper would be competing for such a high stakes and desirable position."

I nodded slightly. That certainly sounded like it could be a potential motive to me, and "Hot Saw" McGraw had officially made my list of people I wanted to talk to.

More hoots, hollers, and clapping from my cousin and his congregation. Kooty didn't even flinch.

"Why reach out to McGraw if you didn't care for him?" I asked.

Kooty unfolded his long legs and stretched them out in front of him. He slid his hands down his worn-in light blue jeans, and did some more deep breathing until his lengthy fingers reached and cupped the balls of his feet, with his nose touching his knees in an impressive display of flexibility. He slowly sat back up and crossed his legs together, this time with his bony feet underneath his thighs, before answering my question.

"Because I believe that during times of change, we are all at our most malleable. I hoped that perhaps Harland's good fortune might lead him to choose another path."

"Did he?"

"At first."

"How so?"

"He came to some of my seminars, bought several necklaces, and even began wearing one proudly. This isn't uncommon among my students, as often surrounding themselves with multiple totems in addition to wearing one around their neck keeps them inspired. What was unusual, however, was the way Harland indulged his ego and began to boast about the edge my mindset was giving him."

"The edge?"

"Yes. Harland wants the corporate contract very badly. I was trying to teach him how to use the three Ws to manifest his own destiny."

"So, he became one of your, uh, disciples or whatever?"

"I prefer the term *pupil of positivity*."

"Look, Bub, I don't care if he was more jacked up than Tom Cruise with a new girlfriend on Oprah's couch. Did the guy drink your Kool-Aid or not?"

"He did—until apparently he didn't see results fast enough and was still lagging behind Jasper in several events. He grew restless and told me he was done."

"But he kept wearing the necklace, didn't he?"

"I don't know."

I leaned back in the chair as I absorbed the information. At this point I had no reason to doubt Kooty, and I'll be damned if he hadn't started to grow on me with his thoughtful and earnest answers. Not to mention that he had barely brought up the fact Declan had rendered him unconscious, tied him up, and hijacked his spiritual summit.

"I wrestle for one of your fellow rodeo bigwigs. Bert Grasby."

"I see," said Kooty, still showing no sign of recognizing me.

"I'm also a licensed private investigator and was mid-match when Jasper's body was found floating in the boom run pool. We may have been new pals, but we had a connection of sorts and I think I can find his killer, perhaps even quicker than the cops can."

"On that ... we agree," said Kooty assuredly.

Again, the mystifying man seemed to have some kind of faith in me, despite us just meeting. In fact, I almost felt he had more confidence in my abilities than I currently did. The only thing I knew for sure was that the more I looked into matters, the harder it was getting for me to walk away from Jasper's homicide.

"I just found out about this STIHL sponsorship from a trusted source," I said. "But none of the other Seven Heads of the Rodeo even mentioned it."

"Most likely because they aren't aware."

"How did you come across this information?"

"It was told to me with a request for confidentiality."

"Shouldn't that discretion go out the window after what happened to Jasper?"

Kooty nodded. "You make a solid point."

"So, who was it then? McGraw?"

"Randy Pippen."

Pippen. The only country fair kingpin I hadn't met aside from Annie's father Gus, for whom I at least had a frame of reference, thanks to my charming, redheaded, young lady friend. I felt my pulse quicken at just the thought of the lovely and lively cowgirl, and nearly blushed over the embarrassment I felt over the romantic musings taking place in my head. I waited for Kooty to continue but he had clammed up.

"Why keep a lid on it?" I asked. "I mean, especially if you don't care for McGraw?"

"Why does a therapist not share what is told to them by a client in a session?"

I nodded, respecting the fact that, whether I believed in Kooty's new-age ideology or not, the man had a code.

"May I stand?" asked Kooty.

"Go ahead. You're not a prisoner. And I'm sorry about the roughing up earlier."

Kooty slowly climbed to his feet, stretching his elongated limbs in all directions like a lithe Rip Van Winkle after a long slumber. He began to rotate his hips, arms akimbo, and aside from a few pops and cracks in his joints his movements were impressively smooth and fluid.

"I take it you know the man who incapacitated me?"

"My cousin. He helps me with my investigations."

"When not helping himself to some ale, it would seem."

"He tends to fluctuate between inebriated and enthusiastic."

"And that's him on stage riling up my audience?" asked Kooty, acknowledging for the first time the sporadic applause and laughter coming from the stage.

"Look, if you want to press charges, I understand. But do you think you could hold off for a little while? At least until I have a chance to see this thing through? The guy may be a shit-disturbing pisstank, but he's saved my ass more times than I can count, so if I'm going to have a shot at finding justice for Jasper, I need him by my side."

Kooty waved away my request with spindly fingers. "No harm, no foul, Friend."

"The name's Jed. Jed Ounstead."

I offered a hand to Kooty. He gazed at me again with his penetrating hazel eyes, then shook it and smiled. My meaty mitt was enveloped in his tentacle-like grip, and when we broke the shake I stared at the item that had suddenly appeared in my palm.

A small washer on a silver ball chain.

I looked up at Kooty and he smiled. "Focus your power, Jed. You'll be amazed at what you can accomplish."

"Yeah, maybe," I replied, before tucking the necklace away in my cargo shorts pocket and not my EDC pouch. "Thanks," I said, earnestly. "And not just for the info, but also for the, uh … talk."

Kooty gave me a pat on the shoulder. "Help me reclaim my place on stage and we'll call it even."

I chuckled. "You got it. Although, I must say, my cousin seemed quite taken with your three W's system. And it was well received by the audience."

"Well received?" exclaimed Kooty, as we headed toward the exit of the small velvety and vegan green room together. "How does he even know how to present it?"

"He may have used beer as a prop."

Kooty scoffed despite himself. "Inebriated and enthusiastic indeed."

The audience roared as the Doukhobor and I took to the dais together. After giving Declan a reassuring thumbs up, my cousin took off his Stetson hat, bowed for the crowd, and wrapped up his charade. He introduced Jim Kootnekoff with a boisterous and heroic preamble, then handed the authentic motivational speaker the microphone and its battery pack. Kooty clipped it to his beltless jeans before sliding the headset over his silver mane and nodding politely at Declan and selling our seemingly planned transition.

Kooty slipped into his presentation without missing a beat and with all eyes on the self-help sage, my cousin and I moved off to the side of the stage. Declan scooped up his beer backpack and popped his cowboy hat back on his head as we descended the steps to the main floor before he smacked me aggressively on the arm.

"Stop the ball!" he exclaimed.

"What?"

"Where's yer flute chute?"

"I left it with the T-shirt in Kooty's quarters. And I didn't buy it. Dicky Diamond gave it to me."

"Ya got it for free from Dicky D?"

"Yes."

"I hate you."

"Excuse me?"

"Ya got a bloody horseshoe up yer arse, ya know that?"

"Are you kidding me? I don't want pervy swag."

"I could give a bollocks, Mate! Did it ever occur to ya I might?"

"I figured you already had one."

"Aye, but it's the top o'the line electric one. What the shite am I supposed to do if it runs out o'juice an' I don' happen to have any batteries on hand? Jaysus, Jed, use yer goddamn head, that's valuable shite yer just tossin' away!"

With that my cousin bolted back up the stairs and into the backstage area to retrieve the bag I had left behind. Before I could even begin to chastise him, the haunting chimes from the melody for "Carillon" by Ennio Morricone echoed from my EDC pouch.

I saw the name on the call display and answered immediately.

"Mr. Ounstead," said Sykes. "I assume Odysseus was able to get you to the Marketplace posthaste?"

"If he ran any faster he may have become the first ostrich ever to take flight."

"Excellent."

"What's up, Sykes?"

"It has come to my attention that the loggersports pit has been re-opened. While Mr. Adams's body has been taken away by the coroner, and the boom run section remains sealed off, it is business as usual with regards to the rest of the area."

I switched the call to speaker and checked to see if there had been any additional text messages from Annie. There were none.

"I'll head over there, then."

"My suggestion exactly. Especially given the fact that Mr. Pippen and Mr. McGraw have both returned to the previously scheduled competitions after their time with the RCMP."

"Already?" I asked, somewhat surprised.

"It seems they have been cleared of any involvement for the time being."

I hesitated before responding.

"Not by me."

TWENTY-THREE
"BIG CHIPS ARE FLYING"

Two-inch chunks of white pine showered down from above like New Year's Eve confetti as the deafening roar of the high-powered, modified STIHL chainsaw drowned out the rabid fans in the bleachers surrounding the popular logging event.

Moments before, an abnormally bottom-heavy man wearing safety glasses, noise-reducing earmuffs, and very snug protective orange overalls stood fast while brandishing his mechanical tool. He held the saw above his head, showcasing a spinning chain that had a set of teeth chunkier than a junkyard dog's and were moving so fast they were only visible to the human eye when he slowed down the device to entice and excite the audience.

After a healthy round of applause, a starter horn blasted and Orange Overalls lowered his chainsaw again into the propped up large section of a log. Pine chips started flying so fast and far that I wondered if the front row of the crowd was too close to the action and perhaps in some kind of lumberjack equivalent to Sea World's "Splash Zone."

The organizers must have known what they were doing, however, as the bits of wood landed no more than a couple feet away from the spectators, who remained collectively enthralled by the impressive display of woodcutting action.

Declan and I stood side-by-side next to the seating area, and I glanced at him to see if he had any reaction to what was going on in front of us. After being refused admittance into the fire-hazard zone until he extinguished his cigarette, Declan moved onto another one of his preferred vices and was sipping yet another can of Hell's Gate Lager. His day-drinking supply must have been running perilously low. While downing one three-hundred-and-fifty-five milliliter Hell's Gate brew that magically appeared in his hands as part of his misdirection during his hijacking of Kooty's *Harness Happiness* forum could have been a one-off, the fact he was drinking another meant he was likely out of Harp Lager tallboys altogether.

Declan nudged me with his beer hand and pointed at Orange Overalls while yelling, but given the ear-splitting sound of the chainsaw, he may as well have been silenced by a mute button. Despite his sleeveless, striated, and Celtic tatted arms, with his amber-tinted aviators and cowboy hat my cousin looked less like an ex-IRA operative and more akin to an off-duty sheriff working security at a St. Patrick's Day parade.

I shook my head, making it clear I couldn't understand. Declan rolled his eyes and tried once more to talk over the roar of the chainsaw. Again, I heard nothing, until Orange Overalls switched off his tool as the thin wooden disc he had been cutting popped off the log and landed on the dirt, rotating a few times like a slowing spinning coin before flopping flat onto the ground. With my ears still ringing, I was just able to hear the latter half of my cousin's sentence.

Unfortunately, so was the crowd.

"— do himself a bloody favour and carve off a piece o' his Kardashian-sized rump cuz he feckin' looks like he's smugglin' a couple o'pumpkins up his arse!"

Declan took a big swig of his lager and didn't seem to notice that everyone present in the pit had heard the latter part of his commentary—including the big-bootied competitor himself. Or, more likely the case, while almost everyone else was either shocked or aghast by the public body-shaming of the poor pulp cutter, my cousin just didn't seem to care. Even the announcer had apparently overheard, as his voice stumbled over the loud speakers.

"That's uh, Denny, uh … Swan. Denny Swan everyone! With a time of thirteen point seven seconds, which puts him in third place. Let's hear it for him, Folks!"

A smattering of nervous applause was offset by chatter and snickers over Declan's all-too-audible comment, which seemed to hang in the air longer than the tiny bits of sawdust that hovered above Orange Overalls. The big-butted bastard blinked repeatedly as he stood next to the log he had just cut in a respectable time, looking like a lost kid at a shopping mall with nothing but a blank look on his face.

"We're gonna take a little break!" crowed the announcer, and you could all but hear the relief in his voice. "But be sure to return in thirty minutes for the semifinals of the hot saw competition!"

Feedback from the microphone screeched through the speakers before cutting to silence, but I was already stepping over and around piles of woodchips and small split logs that could easily cause one to roll an ankle as I made my way toward the sign-in and prep station. Declan hustled to keep up with me.

"Where ya barrellin' off to?"

"That's gotta be Pippen," I said, motioning across the woodcutting zone toward a burly bald and goateed man in a tight black T-shirt and jeans. He stood under a large banner that read **EVENT STAFF AND COMPETITORS ONLY** and was giving an earful to a woman with a clipboard who stood next to him. The poor lady took copious notes while Pippen kept pointing back and forth between the hot saw log and a stack of replacement trunks of wood. I wasn't sure if it was protocol for the timber to be replaced in-between competitors or not, but Pippen seemed preoccupied enough that I figured now was as good a time as any to try and gain an audience with the man.

"How do ya know what he looks like?" asked Declan. "He wasn't at the portable party with them other rodeo dopes."

"He fits Sykes' description. And he wasn't there because he and 'Hot Saw' were being grilled by the cops."

"What would the garda want with his turkey Kermit?"

"Turkey Kermit?"

"Ya know, his meat puppet."

"Are you talking about penises again?"

"An' yer not?"

"Damn it, D, I can't tell if it's all the beer or if your mental health is genuinely suffering from a debilitating fixation."

"Ya said his '*hot saw*,' didn't ya?"

"I said Pippen *and* 'Hot Saw.' As in 'Hot Saw' McGraw, Jasper's loggersports rival."

I filled Declan in on the information I had obtained from Sykes and how our late lumberjack pal had been in direct contention with McGraw for a highly desirable STIHL sponsorship. Declan simply nodded as he took in this latest scoop, but didn't seem particularly interested. Instead, in yet another flagrant act of disobeying the multiple no open flame or smoking signs posted on poles around the chainsaw competition area, he flipped a cigarette in-between his lips and lit the tip with his Zippo.

"I don't give a shite what ya say, there ain't no way some o'these loggin' ludders 'round here ain't callin' their willies 'hot saws.'"

"Just can it and have my back," I snapped.

"Aye, don' I always?" said Declan, falling into step with me as we approached the last remaining member of the Seven Heads of the Rodeo whom I hadn't met, with the exception being Annie's father Gus.

Declan and I began our jaunt into the loggersports pit, which was surrounded by the amusement park, but also nestled behind the small outdoor XCCW pro-wrestling ring and bleachers, where I had been grappling before I first heard the scream that kicked off a most unpleasant afternoon.

Pippen had finished barking at the poor girl with the clipboard and sent her on her way by the time we approached. The bleachers had emptied and most of the crowd had cleared out after a thirty-minute competition break had been announced, which left us alone with the elusive top-dog of the Timbersports.

He paid us no mind as we approached, and was lifting several custom chainsaws by their elongated handles two or three at a time from a stockpile on the ground onto a large wooden table, which appeared to have been carved by one of the very tools it was housing. Although he looked strong for his size, Pippen was grunting repeatedly, with beads of sweat forming on his brow, as his bald head and face turned pink from the exertion of lifting the saws.

"Ya want a hand with those, Boyo? Cuz if ya hoist anymore I think ya might shite yer Wranglers."

Pippen gave us a curious look, then stood up and put his palms on his lower back and thrusted his hips forward, causing a few loud cracks from his spine.

"Jaysus! Ya just snapped, crackled, an' popped!"

I nudged Declan, concerned we were headed down a similar path as when he lipped off the security guards outside of the rodeo arena.

"What? Ya heard the bloke's back. Sounded like a bloody Rice Krispies commercial."

Unlike the big beefy bodybuilding rodeo security guys, Pippen seemed to have a sense of humour. He smirked then relaxed his body. "Actually, I might take you up on that offer," he said.

I nodded to Declan who slid off his beer backpack and went to work. Pippen seemed impressed that, despite his wirier stature, my cousin seemed able to lift and load the chainsaws onto the staging table with relative ease.

"What about you?" he asked. "Guy your size, we'd have this finished in a jiff."

"He needs to work off the beers he's been knocking back," I replied. "Besides, I'd much rather talk to you about Jasper Adams's murder."

I retrieved my private investigator's license and flashed it for Pippen. He pulled a pair of eyeglasses out of his pocket, slid them on, then leaned forward and squinted a bit as he examined my credentials.

"PI, eh?"

"Not to mention a new pal of the deceased and an associate of Sykes."

That combo caught his attention. Pippen gave me a careful once over before responding. "I see," he said, slipping off his glasses and tucking them back in his pants.

"It's my understanding you were just questioned by the RCMP?"

"That's right."

"What did you tell them?"

"Just the truth about Adams."

"Which is?"

"That I know who killed him and why."

TWENTY-FOUR
"COOKIE CUTTER"

"You know who butchered Jasper?"

"Yep."

"Care to enlighten me?"

"Sure, as long as you pick up some cookies for me."

I glanced around the now empty hot saw section of the loggersports pit. There was no concession or craft service table, just stacks of logs, split timber, and a whole lot of wood chips and shavings covering the dirt ground. Even the bleachers were bare due to the abundance of NO FOOD OR BEVERAGE notices displayed around the area beside the NO SMOKING posters.

I glanced at Declan, who was still hard at work lifting the chainsaws onto the smooth surface of the long, wooden table while flagrantly disobeying the abundance of signage forbidding the lit cigarette dangling between his lips. I turned my attention back to Randy Pippen, who used the round neckline of his crew-neck T-shirt to dab the perspiration that lingered on his forehead from loading the power tools before Declan kindly took over the task.

"Uh, all right, I guess. What are we talking about here though? Oatmeal Raisin? Macadamia Nut? Because there's a food truck with desserts just outside of the entrance that sells some," I said, jabbing a thumb over my shoulder.

Pippen chuckled. "Not those kinds of cookies, Sherlock."

"Are you sure? It would just take me a minute, plus it's right by a sno-cone cart," I blurted out, doing my best not to lick my lips. Although it was no DQ milkshake, given all the hustling I had been doing in the heat, an ice-cold banana-flavoured treat would have hit the spot.

Pippen pointed at the collection of circular wooden discs that had collected around the base of the chainsaw cutting area. "I'm talking about these kinds of cookies. Help me clear them out of the way for the semifinals and I'll tell you what I know."

"Roger that," I said. Without another word I began stacking the wooden cookies on top of one another, until I had at least a dozen in a pile as if I were cleaning up a stack of barbell plates at the gym.

"Jesus Christ, you're a strong son of a bitch," said Pippen. "You ever thought about getting into competitive woodcutting? I bet you could split a poplar right in half in the Standing Block Chop."

"The only splitting I'm interested in was the kind that was done to the back of my friend's skull," I replied, hefting the stack of wooden cookies up and off of the ground.

Pippen mumbled an apology then led me behind the sign-in station and around the corner toward a refuse pile consisting of more cookies, random chunks of wood, a couple broken metal mounts for logs, and a few giant tires.

"Dump 'em anywhere around here," he said.

I leaned forward and gave the cookies an underhanded heave as they fell forward and splashed across the logging debris like giant coins being tossed into a waterless fountain. I was wiping the sawdust off of my hands on my cargo shorts when I saw them.

Coiled and uncoiled silver wires, spread out across the pile of debris. I pointed at the shiny filaments. "Those are jagger wires."

"So?"

"Before Jasper took an axe to the back of the head, he was choked out by one. Cut his neck deep."

"I know."

"Who has access to this pile?"

"Everyone. But it's not like this is the only place you'll find wire."

"What do you mean?"

"This is a loggersports pit, Man. There's wire every which way you turn."

I tried not to frown as the momentary jolt of excitement that I had made some headway quickly faded.

"Who killed him, Pippen?" I asked, finally.

"Kelly Lewis. He's a rodeo clown and he and Adams were—"

"I know all about Lewis," I replied, hearing the disappointment in my own voice. "And I don't think he did it."

"He's a whack job."

"He's bipolar. Which doesn't automatically make him a killer. I also saw the anguish on his face firsthand not too long ago. He was absolutely devastated by Jasper's death."

"Sounds like guilt to me," said Pippen. "Especially after their fight."

That nugget caught my ear. "What fight?"

"The one he and Jasper had by the boom run pool not long before the body was found."

"You saw this fight?"

"Just the tail end of it. Lewis was screaming to high heaven about Jasper not loving him anymore and giving up on their dream or something. Said this was their big chance to make it happen and that Jasper was throwing it all away."

I nodded slowly, processing this news. I knew Lewis was unstable, but the timing of this spat bothered me because it was the last known sighting of Jasper alive and established both him and his emotionally volatile ex-lover at the scene of the crime. Also, what did Lewis mean by them giving up on *their* dream? I hadn't a clue, but I might if I could get back to the security station and question a conscious Lewis before the RCMP took him into custody.

"You told all this to the Mounties?"

"Yes. They didn't say one way or the other, but I sure got the feeling they figured Adams's death was a crime of passion."

"More like a gong show."

"Hey man, I'm not a detective. All I know is it makes sense to me, but I'm still down one great lumberjack. I ain't happy about any of this shit."

"What about McGraw?"

"He was off-site from this pit when Adams was murdered."

"Do you know where?"

"No."

"But I thought he was your boy."

"Excuse me?"

"Isn't it true that you would have preferred it if McGraw landed the STIHL sponsorship over Jasper?"

"That's only because I think he's a better fit to represent my loggersports competitions. McGraw will schmooze and promote. He'll get out there and boost the brand."

"Why couldn't Jasper do all that? Especially if he was better?"

"The guy was a maverick. He was good—damn good—but he always did things his way. Not really a team player. Plus, McGraw was a lot more competitive with Jasper when it came to the STIHL Six."

"The STIHL Six?"

"Yeah, STIHL's select half a dozen disciplines that makeup their prestigious Timbersports brand. Springboard, Stock Saw, Underhand Chop, Single Buck, Standing Block Chop, and Hot Saw.

I nodded slowly as if I fully understood, despite the fact that I was only familiar with a few of the events he mentioned from my recent conversations with Jasper and because the timer on my PVR recorded past the end time of episodes of RAW or SMACKDOWN and occasionally caught the opening of STIHL wood chopping competitions. Pippen seemed genuine, however, and from the time I spent with my deceased lumberjack pal, I could definitely see Jasper preferring to do the lone wolf thing.

"Then your preference for McGraw had nothing to do with him being part of a blueblood family?"

Pippen shrugged. "I mean, he comes from money, so it didn't hurt he'd often cover a lot of his own expenses without trying to get me to reimburse him. And I guess being one of the McGraws means he has to stay on the straight and narrow."

"How'd his family make their fortune?"

"Cedar siding. His father owns the biggest business in the Pacific Northwest, with some of the finest western red you'll ever see. Rumour has it George Lucas bought a shitload when he wanted the best of the best for renovations at Skywalker Ranch."

"Impressive. And probably a lot tougher to break over your head than the standard two-by-fours available at Lowe's."

"Why on earth would you break a two-by-four over your head?"

"I ask myself the same thing all the time," I said, smirking to myself. "I want to talk to McGraw. Is he here?"

"Yeah, he's warming up for one of his next events."

"Where?"

"Hold on, now," snapped Pippen. "You said you'd help me with the cookies."

"I already did."

"I got like two more piles back there for you to carry," he said, again stretching out his lower back, but this time without any snap, crackles, or pops. "A deal's a deal, right? I held up my end."

"Tell my cousin I said for him to do it and point me towards McGraw."

Pippen sighed but didn't push back. "He's in the alley."

"What alley?"

"The axe-throwing one."

"Axe-throwing? Are you kidding me? Jasper was found dead from a hatchet to the head."

"Hey man, don't push your theories on me. I'm just doing my job. I'm lucky the cops even let me re-open for our big Saturday night of semi-finals after this nightmare today."

"How do I get to this axe-throwing alley?"

"Down that way fifty meters or so then turn left," he said, pointing toward a well-worn foot path in the dirt. "You can't miss it."

I started off toward the area where I could find "Hot Saw" McGraw. I had taken about ten steps when I turned back around and asked Pippen one more question.

"Who was better at the axe-throwing? Jasper or McGraw?"

Pippen didn't hesitate when responding. "'Hot Saw.' Aside from the event that gave him his nickname, he dominates when it comes to axe-throwing. It's not even close."

I turned back around and resumed my trek, and despite Pippen's and the police's apparent certainty that Lewis was the culprit, I was finding it very hard to believe that Harland "Hot Saw" McGraw—who just happened to be an expert blade flinger who recently started wearing a motivational washer on a chain necklace exactly like the one I found underneath Jasper Adams's corpse—was above suspicion.

TWENTY-FIVE
"BULLSEYE"

THWACK!

The blade of the axe sank into the soft wood. The tool hit its mark dead centre—perfectly placed in the middle of the bullseye. The surrounding rings of red and white, on the giant-sized, sanded, and smoothed wooden cookie served as the axe-throwing target. There were more dents, splits, and cuts than I could count where axe blades had pierced and pummeled the pine.

I stood behind and to the left of Harland "Hot Saw" McGraw, in his blind spot. He was a good fifteen feet away from his target. I watched as he pulled one axe after another from the stump in which over a dozen hatchets, cleavers, and tomahawks stuck out at an angle.

With each new tool he yanked free, he flipped it in the air, caught it by the handle, and began his wind-up routine. He was shorter, but bigger than Jasper, and around five-foot-ten. I made him for at least a burly two-hundred and twenty pounds, with a meaty build and arms and legs of a girth similar to the many logs lying everywhere in the competitive woodcutting pit. A shock of bright, flat-top, platinum-blonde hair sat atop his head and his chiseled jawline and posh, sleeveless, grey-and-white camouflage track suit, made him look like an upscale, urban militia survivalist.

"McGraw," I said, as I approached him in-between his practice throws.

The man better known as "Hot Saw" turned to face me with an axe in hand. The steel blade glinted so brightly in the sunlight it made me squint for a couple of seconds.

"How'd you get back here?" he asked.

"I need a word," I said, as I approached him.

"Hey, I ain't got no loggersports hookups, okay? You're a big boy though, show up at the next try-outs and I'm sure you'll do fine."

"That's not why I'm here."

McGraw sighed, then turned and flung the axe at the target. *Bullseye again.*

In fact, he hit the target so perfectly the blade of the axe clanged against the one that was already in the centre red circle, which caused a spark from metal on metal, before the two hatchets rested side-by-side in the worn-in wood.

He placed a big black boot upon a stump and unzipped a front pocket on his camo pants, then retrieved a small notepad and a pen. He flipped through the pages until he found a blank one.

"Who do I make it out to?"

"Excuse me?"

"The autograph."

I tried not to let slip a chuckle. I had given more than my fair share of autographs over the years, but not once was I ever so audacious that I assumed someone would want it without asking first. I decided to play along.

"Jed Ounstead," I said.

"Ounstead. Is that with a 'w' or a 'u?'"

"It's with a PI."

McGraw stopped writing and looked up at me, confused. "PI?"

"Yeah, you know. Short for private investigator."

"What? Why are—who the hell are you?"

"Just a guy working a case. This one being the murder of Jasper Adams."

McGraw didn't like that one bit.

"Fuck off," he said, putting his notepad and pen back into his pocket.

"I know you were just cleared by the Mounties. But since you and Jasper were both up for the STIHL sponsorship, that makes you a person of interest."

"I said fuck off!" yelled McGraw. "I don't have to talk to you, and even if I did, do you think I'm stupid enough to do it without my lawyer present? Hit the bricks, Shithead."

McGraw stormed over to the throwing target and angrily ripped his hatchets out of the bullseye. He shot me a dirty look as he marched back to his throwing perch and plunked the axes back into the stump housing the others. He selected a particularly large axe and pulled it free, then began practicing his swing like a golfer before a drive. I watched in silence as he threw the bigger blade with two hands, its forward rotation slicing through the air, before landing dead centre in the red circle yet again.

McGraw continued throwing axes and paying me no mind. I hesitated before leaving, instead reviewing the facts and what I knew to be true to this point.

Jasper was murdered by an axe to the back of the head.

Pippen confirmed McGraw was not in the loggersports pit at the time of the killing, a point on which the RCMP likely concurred since they released him from custody so quickly.

McGraw came from a wealthy family.

Kooty made it clear that McGraw wanted the STIHL sponsorship.

But unlike Jasper, McGraw couldn't have desired it for the money. Which meant his motivation must have been the prestige associated with the title and honour of repping STIHL. If he didn't need the dough, and if McGraw's family already had a lot of it, was it just a coincidence Declan and I had found a bag full of bills stuffed inside Jasper's locker that up until now only we knew about, save for Sykes whom I had told and, apparently, Kelly Lewis? How many people did Jasper know, let alone those who worked at, or were associated with, a country fair, who would be able to get their hands on that kind of cash?

Dots connected quickly in my head, and while it was certainly a gambit, it wasn't a thought without merit. I didn't see a downside to my spur-of-the-moment theory since McGraw had shut me down and clearly wasn't going to talk to me anymore. So, I figured what the hell.

"Okay, 'Hot Saw,'" I said. "You win. But if you're not going to talk to me, then I guess I have no choice but to go to the RCMP and tell them about the big bag of cash you used to pay off Jasper so he would withdraw from competing for the STIHL sponsorship."

My words landed harder than any axe McGraw had flung. He jerked upward so quickly mid-throw that his two-handed axe flew wildly, flipped blade-over-handle at twice the speed I had witnessed earlier, before soaring ten feet over the red-and-white mark and beyond.

His cheeks flushed crimson, and when he looked at me, I could see the fear appear on his face faster than it took one of the axes he had been hurling to hit its target. We stood in silence staring at one another, and while his mouth was agape, I did my best to keep mine from curling into a satisfied smile.

"*Bullseye*," I said out loud.

TWENTY-SIX
"OVER-ROTATION"

I closed the gap between us while McGraw continued to gawk at me, wide-eyed and in a state of shock. I moved swiftly and with purpose, like a panther closing in on its prey. I had him caught off guard and had no idea how long it would last. He was rattled, so the time for me to pounce and try and get him to talk was now, before he pulled it together, composed himself, and kept his word about not needing to speak with me.

When I was five feet away, I saw panic flash in McGraw's eyes. After glancing around, and realizing it was just us alone in the axe-throwing alley, McGraw yanked a small hatchet free from the stump and braced himself in position—not for attacking, but poised to repel one. By the time I was only a couple of steps away he had the weapon cocked behind his ear.

I thought of backing off, but decided against it. Maybe I sensed that McGraw was on the ropes, or perhaps it was the fact I had just gone toe-to-toe with Kelly Lewis in a knife fight and felt good about my self-defence skills. It didn't matter—I wasn't going to stop unless he swung his hatchet at me.

"I'd re-think that move, Bub. You might have gotten away with one murder this afternoon, but they'll nail you for two."

"I didn't kill him!" McGraw yelled, before jumping back defensively and weakly slicing his hatchet through the air. It was far from a killing blow, one I would even call pathetic.

I slowed my pace, as if to encourage him to engage in more nervous chatter. "He died from an axe to the head, McGraw. Look at where we are and what you can do."

"I swear! You have to believe me! I didn't—I would never kill Jasper!"

"You resented him because unlike you he came from a genuine lumberjack lineage. He was your top rival. And you *really* want that STIHL sponsorship."

"Which is exactly why I tried to pay him off!" he exclaimed.

Boom Sha Lock Lock Boom.

Declan's impromptu motivational speaker's entrance theme echoed in my head. I had him now. "So, it *was* your money."

"Yes," he conceded, still holding the hatchet, but lowering it slightly. "I thought that he would just take it and bow out. I mean, that's what he said he'd do."

"Jasper wouldn't promise that."

"No, not Jasper. His boyfriend. Kelly Lewis."

Now things were starting to make sense. Lewis being triggered by the mere mention of the money before he pulled his Bowie knife, and the fight Pippen overheard between him and Jasper in which the former yelled about *"giving up on their dream"* and *"throwing it all away."* Whatever that was exactly and how it involved at least a hundred-grand didn't really matter, just that Lewis had seen an opportunity for a payday and clearly Jasper couldn't bring himself to take it, which tracked after what he had shared with me about his grandfather and loggersports. Their fight occurred after Jasper and I had commiserated over our complicated relationships with our lost loves, which meant that when Lewis went at him by the boom run pool not long before the murder, it must have been some kind of last ditch effort by the rodeo clown to sway his ex.

Did Jasper even know that a payoff had occurred? If he did, he certainly didn't take off with it like Lewis seemed to want him to, but instead chose to continue competing in the day's woodcutting events. And if he didn't know, and Lewis had somehow stashed the money in his former lover's locker without his knowledge, it was still pretty clear that Jasper wouldn't take a bribe. Could that rejection have caused Lewis to snap and murder the man he loved? He was bipolar and I had experienced firsthand how his intense mood swings could result in violence—the guy had tried to stab me to death. But something just didn't sit right with me about that. Despite how unhinged he could be, I still wasn't sure Lewis would or could actually kill Jasper.

Maybe I was overthinking it. What the hell did I know, anyway? Truth was, I was far from well acquainted with either man, and had been out of the investigation game for the better part of a year. Even Sykes, who was one of my biggest supporters, had commented on my sleuthing skills being rusty.

Or perhaps, given all my pining over Rya, my brief encounter with my better-than-ever ex-girlfriend Stormy, or the sudden fluttering of my heart when I thought of Annie Tibbs and her freckles and strawberry blonde hair, I was just a hapless and hopeless romantic not wanting to see the truth that was staring me in the face.

In the end, all of my pointless pondering did me no favours, because it kept me from seeing Harland "Hot Saw" McGraw swing an axe at me until it was far too late.

TWENTY-SEVEN
"SCOOP HIT"

I felt weightless, as though I were swinging in the world's most uncomfortable hammock, before noticing a less-than-pleasant pulling sensation on my armpits and ankles as I regained consciousness.

"Jesus Christ, how much does this fucking guy weigh? I feel like I'm lifting a bag full of anvils here."

"Aye, he's a big ol' slab o'beef, I'll give ya that. Plus, now that he's wrasslin' full time the eejit's doubled down on his workouts an' nutrition."

"You mean he's still trying to get bigger?"

"Let's just say when he's not pumpin' up his pipes or chesticles in the gym the mad bastard's suckin' back on so much protein powder an' banana milkshakes there's entire species o'monkeys in Madagascar that are endangered now cuz o'his big arse."

I open my eyes to see Declan's staring straight down at me, and although his face was still mostly hidden by the brim of his Stetson and his amber-tinted aviator sunglasses, I could still detect a certain amount of concern.

"There's me boy!" he crowed, before dropping me in dirty sawdust like a foil-wrapped hot potato right off the grill.

My shoulders hit the ground with a thud. I looked up and saw Randy Pippen, who had been holding my ankles, follow suit and let go of my legs. I tried to sit up but immediately felt woozy, only then experiencing the throbbing sensation from the top of my head where Harland "Hot Saw" McGraw had hit me with an axe. But considering there was no gash or blood, and just a small goose egg that I could feel on the crown of my noggin, I realized he must have hit me with the flat side of the tool's blade.

"Took a wee bit o'a beauty sleep there, didn't ya, Princess?"

I groaned as I pressed both of my palms against my temples, which felt with each pounding of my pulse as if they were a heartbeat away from exploding.

"McGraw?" I croaked, as I fought off a wave of nausea and continued to massage my aching skull.

"He took off out of here like a shot," griped Pippen. "What the hell did you say to him?"

"Excuse me?"

"I just want to know why the semifinals for my highly popular hot saw competition are about to start and I'm missing my marquee attraction. For Christ's sake, Ounstead, the guy's named after the event."

"Keep yer Alans on there, Mister Poopin'," cautioned Declan, before lighting a cigarette and taking a long drag. "Give me *Col Gaolta* a goddamn minute."

"It's Pippen!" he exclaimed. "How many times do I have to tell you that?"

I dragged myself to my feet and braced myself against a stack of rubber tires, only then realizing we were near the pile of debris that Pippen had me haul a stack of wooden cookies to earlier. The hot saw section of the wood chopping pit was abuzz with chatter while the song "Green Grass and High Tides" by The Outlaws played over the loudspeakers. I took a couple of shaky steps forward and peered around the plastic tent we were behind to see an excited crowd taking their seats in the bleachers, waiting for the chainsaw action to commence.

"So, what? The Deadeye Douche just bolted, then?" asked Declan.

"Yeah. And now he's on the lam because I busted him for a bribe."

"What the hell are you talking about?" asked Pippen.

I filled in Pippen and Declan about my conversation with McGraw and how he had confessed to paying off Kelly Lewis—under the assumption Jasper would be game to take the cash and drop out as a contender for the STIHL Timbersports sponsorship.

"Son of a bitch," muttered Pippen. "Harland killed him after all. I guess he must have snuck back into the pit when I wasn't looking."

"McGraw swears he didn't murder Jasper, but I honestly don't know. I mean, with his desperation to become the STIHL rep for the Pacific Northwest and his axe-throwing prowess, there's no denying he had a clear motive and the means."

"Aye, but let's not forget about the Bowie-bladed bastard with the mental disorder," chimed in Declan. "Take it from me, ya never want to count out crazy."

Lewis, I thought to myself. Killer or not, the guy had been instrumental in setting up a payout with McGraw, whether my detective instincts were rusty or not. Anyway you cut it, of one thing I was certain—the attempted bribe to get Jasper to drop out of the STIHL sponsorship had played a critical role in the homicide.

I flipped open my EDC pouch to retrieve my phone, only to see I had three missed calls from Annie. I tried to ring her back, but it went straight to voice mail.

"Howdy! This here's Annie, and I reckon I must be off ropin' a steer or somethin' cuz unfortunately I ain't able to pick up the phone right now—"

I almost felt sad having to end her recorded message early, as hearing her perky voice provided me with the first bit of welcome relief I had received since taking the blunt force of an axe to the head.

A buzzer blared followed by the announcer's voice booming over the speakers. "Take your seats, Folks! The semi-finals for the hot saw competition will begin in five minutes!"

"Sorry, Boys," said Pippen. "Duty calls."

"I appreciate the help, Pippen," I said, and the loggersports honcho nodded politely before trotting off around the tent to oversee the impending event.

"We have to get to Lewis in the security station," I declared. "And if the Mounties haven't taken him away yet, then I need to call him out on the attempted payoff. I think that might get him to talk."

"Let's crack on with a run then!" Declan replied enthusiastically, as he slung the straps of his beer backpack over his shoulders and tightened them.

I wobbled on my feet a little just at the thought of breaking into a run. I held a hand to my still pulsing head. "Can't do it, D. Not yet."

"Shite, yer right," he conceded, snaking out a strong hand and helping to steady me.

"Damn it," I snapped in frustration.

"What is it, Mate?"

"There's not enough time to get ostriches here either."

"Jaysus, Jed, how hard did that chancer hit ya?"

"Never mind," I said, waving away his confusion. "We just need to find another way to get across this country fair—"

"Tits sweet?" interjected Declan excitedly.

"Yes, D," I said, in a rare moment of acceptance of his dirty dialect. *"Tits sweet."*

"Deadly," he said, as a grin spread across his face. "Lucky for yer arse, I got us a solution."

TWENTY-EIGHT
"RASCALLY RIDERS"

"Let's go, Flo! Kick this bloody geezer-mobile into top gear already!"

Declan stood behind the seat of his geriatric gal pal on the black floorboards of the three-wheeled, ZooMe classic, Radio Flyer red power scooter, pointing ahead with a hand that held a can of Hell's Gate Lager like a beer-swilling navigator, while his other palm was clasped firmly atop one of Flo's shoulders. I had to give it to the older lady, because she had certainly picked us up well prepared for a fast ride. Flo had swapped out her eyeglasses for a pair of vintage brown leather goggles that were strapped around her head, and her blue-tinted white bouffant fluttered about in the wind as she followed Declan's orders and increased their speed by cranking back on the motorized machine's hand-throttle.

I did the same on the second ZooMe, loaned to me by one of Declan's past-her-prime playmate's friends. Flo herself had traded with another member of her roaming rodeo scooter gang, leaving behind the slower four-wheeled, metallic blue Rascal I had first seen her operating when she and Declan showed up while I was dressed like a cruddy clown desperate to get into the change room—the very place where we found the bag of cash in Jasper's locker, and the likely catalyst for his killing.

Simpler times, I thought to myself, as I realized I needed to increase the tempo of my *"geezer-mobile"* to keep up with my inebriated cousin and his speeding senior sweetheart.

My head snapped back as my ZooMe lurched forward, and by the time I was pulling even with Flo and Declan, we must have been going close to fifteen kilometers per hour. With its oversized front tire and tread, and deluxe, electronic keypad controller mounted between the handlebars, the humming of the 350-watt engine made for quite the souped-up tricycle.

We were moving at a good clip and the crowds were scrambling out of our way as we left the loggersports pit behind us, rolling through the surrounding funfair rides toward the security station by the Agri-Zone where, to the best of my knowledge, Kelly Lewis was still being held. By the time we began to cut through the heart of Milligan's Traveling Carnival and Amusement Park, our scooters had slowed to a crawl. Throngs of pedestrians, families, and folks were puttering about this way and that, not to mention the overflow of people spilling out of the long lines surrounding the bumper cars, giant sky swing, and roller coaster.

Declan wasn't pleased one bit by the delay and expressed his frustration with his signature restraint and charm.

"Bloody hell, move yer arses ya flabby cotton candy gobblin' gobshites! Jaysus, if I see one more tayto tummy floppin' about I swear I'm gonna catch Type II diabetes through me eyes!"

Declan glanced back over his shoulder and shot me an apologetic look.

"Sorry, Boyo. Looks like we may be stuck in this traffic jam for donkey's years."

"Just keep pushing through," I said, pulling my ZooMe scooter behind his and Flo's so we were at least travelling more efficiently in single file.

I dug out my iPhone from the EDC sheath on my hip and tried calling Annie again. Straight to voice mail, except this time I hung up before her recording played, not wanting to be distracted by the soothing sound of her voice. I exhaled and massaged the still aching bump on my head, frustrated by our current predicament, and feeling the pressure to keep my investigation moving for fear of losing momentum.

I was pretty sure I was ahead of the Mounties so far as well, with uncovering the attempted bribe, multiple motives, means, and a direct connection between Kelly Lewis, Harland McGraw, Kooty's necklaces, and axes.

The cops, I thought to myself. More specifically, the RCMP. I was stressing so much because the moment they got their hands on Kelly Lewis he would be out of reach for the immediate future, and I would have no way to question him about recent revelations. And, like it or not, we certainly had an established rapport. Sure, it may have been one primarily based upon bull wrangling, strangulation, and a near death knife fight—but I'll be damned if I didn't think he was more likely to crack and start talking to me rather than the police.

Until now, I had still been thinking of myself as a civilian. But that just wasn't the case. Sabbatical or not, I wasn't just a licensed private investigator—I was also an Ounstead, and the only child of a retired Vancouver Police Department living legend who had more connections to law enforcement than Declan did to Guinness and cigarettes.

Frank answered on the second ring. "I hope you're not calling in the middle of one of your little half-naked stunt shows."

My old man was never one to shy away from his lack of enthusiasm for my other profession, which had been a sore spot for him ever since I chose to *not* become a third generation VPD member, in order to pursue my dreams of a life in the squared circle instead. Although we had grown closer since I had become a PI and joined Ounstead Investigations—recently rechristened by him as *Ounstead & Son*—my father wasn't keen on the extended hiatus I had taken from the family business. Nevertheless, and to his credit, just like Declan, he had given me the time and space I clearly needed while I grappled with the outcome of my last case and the enduring regret it had left in its wake.

"It was a professional wrestling matinee match, Pop. And let me tell you, it was a doozy."

I summarized the events that had occurred since I had called an in-ring audible, prematurely rolled-up "Cowboy Cobb" Calhoun, and come across Jasper Adams's floating corpse. I heard my old man perk up immediately.

"Jesus jumped up Christ, Boy! That's a hell of an afternoon."

"And then some."

"So, you're liking this axe-throwing, cheap-shot artist then? Or the rodeo clown headcase? Hell, maybe they were in cahoots?"

"I honestly don't know. I'm grinding it out and doing the work, Pop. But I'm feeling pretty rusty."

"Been a while since you've caught a case. That's normal."

"Is it? I mean, maybe things are just different now? You know, after …"

"After what? You single-handedly put a stop to a murderous psychopath who was above the law? Not to mention provided justice for the dead and saved countless lives by doing so?"

"Yeah," I said, knowing better than to try and play Devil's advocate with my father when he was so sure of himself. My old man let out a long sigh and I heard the clatter of the bows of his half-rimmed reading glasses hitting the desktop in our company's office on the second floor above The Emerald Shillelagh, our family pub. I reminded myself how unusual it was for Declan to have booked off an entire weekend when he was the main reason the downtown tavern not only stayed in business, but remained very profitable. That financial security also allowed both my father and me to occupy ourselves with work better suited to us and that we greatly preferred. Perhaps I had been too hard on Declan when all the guy had signed up for today was some outdoor fun and country fair entertainment.

"We've been over this, Son. You gotta let it go."

"Maybe it's not that easy."

"Why not?"

"Because I didn't put in thirty years on the force like you, Pop, that's why. Couple years ago, the closest I came to death was taking the occasional tombstone piledriver in the ring. Now, well, let's just say they don't exactly cover the kind of stuff I've had to do as a PI in professional wrestling school."

"Fair enough. But it doesn't change the fact that you've got what it takes."

Before I could respond I heard Flo blast the high-pitched horn on her ZooMe scooter. An attractive, but snooty-looking group of twenty-something cleavage bombs all decked out in halter tops and cut-off jeans shorts looked up from their phones and scoffed.

"Uh, like tell your grandma to chill or whatever," snapped the blonde-haired leader, before the mean girls started sneering and giggling among themselves. One of them even tried to snap a picture of Flo and Declan.

My cousin was not having any of that. He crushed the empty can of Hell's Gate Lager in his hands and chucked it at Blondie, pinging her right in the middle of the forehead. She squealed in horror, while her friends gasped and rallied around her like a PR team for a Hollywood star who had just broken a heel on a red carpet.

"What is wrong with you, Asshole?!" screamed one of Blondie's buddies.

"Don' ya dare be disrespectin' this here blue-haired angel, ya manky brassers! Now sod off with the lot o'ya!"

The traumatized girls scooped up their fallen comrade and scurried off while Flo grabbed my cousin by the crew collar of his sleeveless shirt, pulled his head down, and planted a kiss on his cheek. I tried not to wince when I saw her use her tongue to tickle his earlobe.

"For shite's sake, they'll be time for that later. Floor it, Flo!"

The zesty octogenarian didn't need to be told twice. She cranked on the hand throttle of her scooter, and plowed forward into the masses while honking her horn to create a bit of space ahead. I picked up my speed and kept pace.

"What in the blue hell is all that racket?" asked my father, still on the line.

"Nothing. Just Declan, well, being Declan."

"Say no more. Since this lumber jackass is in the wind, can I assume you're headed to talk to this Lewis character then?"

"Exactly. And even if he's still on site, he's likely already in custody. Whether it's here at the rodeo or at the nearest local detachment, I need to talk to this guy."

"I hear you, Boy. And a good friend of mine, Garry Bashum, is the OIC of the District Four Community Policing Bureau out there."

"District Four?"

"Cloverdale."

"Perfect," I said, relieved.

"I got this. You may need to sweet talk the clown into signing a waiver if he's in a secure interview room, but you'll definitely be met with some blue friendlies. That I promise."

"Thanks, Pop."

"One more thing."

"What's that?"

"Sit on what you know about the bribe. I don't anticipate any problems, but there's no harm in keeping that bargaining chip in your back pocket for now."

"Roger that."

I went to end the call when I heard my old man's voice again.

"John," he said, staying true to form and referring to me by my given name as opposed to the shorthand for John Edward my mom had nicknamed me and I went by exclusively.

"Yes, Sir?" I responded automatically, as if I was a teenager again answering the call of my strict-but-loving father.

"I just want you to know ... I'm damn proud of you."

A welcome feeling of warmth flowed through me as I absorbed my old man's praise. Frank Ounstead wasn't exactly known to be a softie, and for him to say something like that, meant more to me than I realized until I heard the words.

"Now go get'em," he said, with authority.

"Yes, Sir," I replied, dutifully.

I clicked off my phone. Flo and Declan had emerged from the amusement park and were now driving along a much less congested paved path that slowly veered to the left and away from the crowded Stetson Bowl. I throttled up to maximum speed in order to close the gap between us. I wasn't sure if it was my somewhat spiritual encounter with Kooty, the breakthrough I had made with the case, assurances I would get a chance to confront Kelly Lewis once more, or my father's surprisingly supportive words. All I knew was things were finally starting to not look so dire.

That was until my phone, still in my hand, vibrated and chirped with an *"Ooooohhhhh Yeeeeaaaaaah!"* "Macho Man" Randy Savage text tone alert.

My heart skipped a beat when I saw who the message was from.

Annie.

I swiped with my thumb and an image popped up on my screen that confused me at first. But there was no denying who it was.

Kelly Lewis.

Face down.

Limp on a table.

I tried to make sense of what I was looking at when three dots below the picture started moving before being replaced with three words.

He's dead, Jed.

TWENTY-NINE
"CATAWAMPUS"

When we rolled up on our scooters to the portable that served as the *Cloverdale Rodeo's* Agri-Zone security station, there were already two RCMP SUVs out front. The lights atop the vehicles were flashing red and blue and while it was enough to keep back bystanders, it did little to dissuade the looky-loos from milling about thirty feet away as their collective curiosity grew.

The small building was half the size of the one in the Home Depot parking lot, where Declan and I had met with the Seven Heads of the Rodeo. A horse-drawn carriage being pulled by two Clydesdales lumbered by as I dismounted my three-wheeler to approach the lone officer standing between the cruisers. The horses' hairy, snow-white feet clip-clopped on the pavement while the passengers and even the coach's driver craned their necks attempting to see why so much law enforcement was present at such a family-friendly venue.

I nodded at Declan who understood and silently acknowledged my gesture, leaving me to approach the cop alone, while he turned his attention to his scooter companion and moved to assist her from the driver's seat.

"I don't need your help, goddamn it," she barked, as she hopped off the ZooMe. Her shock-absorbing orthopedic sneakers hit the pavement with ease.

"Jaysus, Flo, take it easy," said my cousin. "I was just tryin' to be a gentleman."

"Where were those manners earlier when my carpal tunnel was flaring up?"

"I told ya not to take off yer brace."

"Can you two give it a rest?" I snapped, in the hopes they would pipe down as I approached the well-built man in uniform in front of me.

"Aye," grumbled Declan, before tapping two cigarettes out of his pack and proffering one as a peace offering to our cantankerous but resourceful aged ally.

I turned my attention to the cop. "Officer," I said, by way of greeting.

"We're asking everyone to stay back, Sir," he said, his arms crossed across his chest.

"I can see that. I was hoping perhaps for a bit of professional courtesy."

I reached into a pouch on my everyday carry sheath and took out my PI license. "I'm a private investigator and—"

"Ounstead," he said, cutting me off. "I was told you were coming."

Son of a gun, my father had worked fast.

"Is it true?" I asked. "Lewis is dead?"

"Yes."

"How?"

The officer shrugged.

"Have you seen the body?"

He nodded. "My partner and I are assigned. She's inside right now taking statements from security and a witness."

"Cowgirl?"

"Yep. Friend of yours?"

"You could say that. Have you got a working theory?"

The officer looked back and forth, ensuring we were alone. "Apparently the guy was pretty upset while in custody before we arrived. Something to do with that lumberjack who was murdered here earlier."

"Jasper Adams."

"That's right. Top brass says you're working the case, but …"

"But what?"

"That dude's body probably still has an axe in the back of its head. Kind of weird a private dick would have been hired so quickly."

"I'm not your typical PI."

"Kind of figured that. And while I'm no wrestling fan, I do know of your old man."

"Even though he wasn't RCMP?"

"Are you kidding? A cop like him, it doesn't matter he's not 'E' Division. Your dad is blue through and through. Respect."

"Much obliged, Constable—"

I checked his nametag before continuing.

"—Capps."

"Ben," he said, offering a hand, which I shook firmly.

"Jed," I replied.

"Anyway, all I know is apparently the guy was sobbing, then he put his head down on a table to rest. Next thing security knew he was dead."

I nodded as I tried to envision the scene playing out in my head. "Look, Ben, since we're friendly and all, what say you let us in for a quick peek at the deceased?"

"Us?" said Capps, before tipping his head to the side and looking behind me. I followed his gaze to see Declan, still wearing his Stetson cowboy hat and amber-tinted aviators, who had managed to connect his phone's Bluetooth into the speaker of

Flo's medical alert necklace. They both bopped their heads to the beat of a Dropkick Murphys song in-between drags of cigarettes.

"How about just me?" I said, quickly.

Capps pursed his lips and scratched the back of his head. "Look, Jed, I wish I could. But the coroner is just a couple minutes out. Maybe I can make something happen after he's done, but until then, the scene's gotta remain pristine."

I opened my mouth to try and contest when the door to the portable swung open and Annie strode out. Her face lit up as soon as she saw me.

"Jed!" she exclaimed.

She darted down the steps and the next thing I knew was in my arms. I squeezed her tight as we embraced. After a moment, she pulled her head back, and I instinctively brushed a few strands of her strawberry-blonde hair out of her face.

"Are you okay?" I asked.

"That's the first thing you ask?"

"It's the first thing I want to know."

Annie smiled softly. "Still sweeter than a banana cream pie," she said, before tapping an index finger against my nose. "This whole Kelly thing is catawampus as all hell, but I suppose otherwise I'm all right."

I glanced up, only then realizing that Constable Capps had given Annie and me some privacy. "I tried to get a look at the body, but they won't let me. At least not until the coroner has finished."

"Not really much to see," said Annie.

"Were you with him when he died?"

"Yep. Me and them security fellas."

"How long was he conscious before …?"

"Not long. I tried calling you when he came to, but—"

"Yeah, I was, uh, a bit preoccupied," I replied, suddenly feeling the sting of the goose egg that Harland McGraw's axe had left behind. "Can you tell me what happened?"

"He was pretty groggy. Just kind of woke up and started crying, really. Kept saying *'I'm sorry, Jasper, I'm so sorry,'* over and over. Then he put his head down on the table. Next thing we knew the cops showed up and he wasn't breathing."

I nodded sympathetically, yet couldn't help but feel Kelly Lewis's last words made my attempt to connect "Hot Saw" McGraw to Jasper's murder pretty thin, regardless of a bribe gone bad and a bump to the brain.

"Still, it's weird, right? I mean, how did he die? An aneurysm?"

"Oh, Jed," said Annie, before cupping my cheek ever-so-gently. "It wasn't that."

"You sound like you know something that I don't."

Annie looked down and avoided my gaze. After a moment, she met my eyes with hers. "He said his throat was hurting," she said. "And that it felt swollen."

"His throat?" I replied, my voice croaking as I spat out the last word and the memory hit me like another blow to the head.

I tried to avoid it, but it was no use. All I could see in my mind's eye was me blocking Kelly Lewis's arm as he swung his Bowie knife wildly, before delivering an uppercut to his Adam's apple, where the vulnerable thyroid cartilage met his jawline. I could almost hear Lewis's hacking again as he had stumbled backwards and clutched his throat.

"I killed him," I finally said.

6:08 P.M.

THIRTY
"SEARCHING FOR THE ELEPHANT"

"Hush your mouth!" scolded Annie, as she pulled me close into an embrace. "You did no such thing."

"Yeah, Annie. I think I did."

She looked around furtively, to ensure we were still alone and out of earshot of everyone including Capps, the crowd of onlookers, as well as my blood-related Celtic boozehound and his golden girl.

"Even if that's the case, it was self-defence. And let's wait and see what the coroner determines first," she implored me.

Only then did I notice the black van arriving on site, and Constable Capps jogging over to the vehicle's window to direct the driver where to park.

"What's the point? The security guards are just going to tell them what Lewis said."

"I don't think they heard anything."

"What do you mean?"

Annie took a deep breath and exhaled before continuing.

"Look at those chumps," she said, nodding toward the two pot-bellied, out-of-shape men in ill-fitting and cheap-looking security guard uniforms by the door to the portable, still chatting with the female cop with a notepad, whom I assumed was Capps's partner. "They're just a couple of backcountry bubbas trying to pick up a few extra bucks. There ain't no protocol that they've been following. I told them I wanted a word with Kelly before the cops came and they didn't even hesitate letting me have a go at him."

I took a good look at both men and based on first impressions, they definitely didn't appear to be the cream of the crop. While Annie had a point, I found myself more curious about something else that had just come to light with her revelations.

"Why did you want to talk with Kelly?"

"What do you mean?"

"I mean, why speak to him? And what about?"

Annie scoffed and pulled back from me. "To see if he'd confess to Jasper's murder, of course."

"Did he?"

Annie shook her head. "He was pretty out of it. Just kind of ignored me and started cryin' like a tore up yaller dog."

"Yaller dog?"

"A coward, Jed. He knew what he had done, and it was eating him up inside. It was clear as day. I'm telling you, even if it was some kind of fluke accident caused by a swollen throat that caused him to die, I don't think Kelly was gonna be long for this world."

"Are you talking about suicide?"

Annie shrugged. "You only know the tip of the iceberg when it comes to his mental problems. And if you ask my daddy Gus or any of the other Seven Heads, they'll all tell you the same. The guy was highly unstable."

I lowered my head as I tried to absorb everything Annie was telling me while Capps escorted the coroner and his team past us and into the portable. The appearance of the official investigators also put a damper on Declan and Flo's jubilance, as they were now leaning against one of the two scooters while quietly puffing on their cigarettes.

"No," I said, with a sudden degree of resolve that surprised even me. "There has to be more to it than that."

"I don't think so, Sugar. C'mon, now. Let's go for a walk or get a drink, just you and me. I promise you'll feel better."

"I'd like that, Annie, but something's not right."

"Like what? Seems to me you're just searching for the elephant."

Annie and I just stared at each other for a few moments. Eventually, I had no choice but to prod her. "Do I really need to ask?"

"Sorry," she said, clueing in to my lack of familiarity with her country colloquialisms. "I just mean you should quit looking for something that ain't there."

"I'd say a hundred-thousand-dollar bribe gone bad qualifies as something."

"What?" she said, shocked.

I recapped how, after a little creative entry, Declan and I had found a bag of cash in Jasper's locker, before I discovered Kelly Lewis's involvement and his role in facilitating a payoff with Harland McGraw. Then I filled her in on all the other events that had occurred up until my recent attack courtesy of "Hot Saw" while in axe-throwing alley.

Annie listened intently, and was still shaking her head when I had finished.

"Son of a bitch."

"Yeah."

"Now it totally makes sense."

"What does?"

"The last thing Kelly said."

"I thought you already told me that."

Annie leaned in and gave me a gentle peck on the cheek. "Jed, despite all that muscle and what your shirt says, let's face it—you're just a big ol' softie."

I looked down at my prototype wrestling attire and reminded myself of Dylan Thomas's nuanced words—*Do Not Go Gentle*—and realized that only now was I starting to see the subtle layers in their meaning. Maybe the significance of the statement was more than just an adopted credo to aspire to as a grappling gumshoe. Maybe after everything that happened over the last couple of years, I had been trying to tell myself something. And maybe the message was that I no longer had what it took to be a PI.

"What aren't you telling me, Annie?"

She took a deep breath and exhaled. "He let slip one more thing while he was talking to Jasper's spirit or whatever, apologizing over and over before he put his head down on the table and passed."

"Which was?"

"I can't live without you."

I could almost hear the door slam shut on the case. That was it. Kelly Lewis had killed Jasper Adams. It all made sense. In his desperation he saw an opportunity for a windfall for himself and his lover. He just underestimated the integrity of the man he loved so much. Which led him to a crime of passion, in the heat of the moment, after an argument, by a man prone to mood swings and suffering from mental illness.

The Mounties could see it. So could Annie and everyone else. But why couldn't I?

I almost smacked myself upside the head. It was all right there in front of me. Yet here I was making a fool of myself while trying to connect the dots between Harland McGraw's Timbersports skills, axes, and jagger wires, when in reality, those were all around the loggersports pit like items in a lumberjack scavenger hunt. I had seen it myself. Of course Lewis could have simply grabbed a wire to choke out Jasper in a fit of rage before giving into his worst impulses and driving a hatchet into the back of his head. And so what if there was a washer necklace of Kooty's on the bottom of the log boom pool? I had established that the Doukhobor guru's unique trinket and style of self-help was wildly popular at the *Cloverdale Rodeo*. Was it really such a stretch that a chain simply broke off the neck of one of the many competitors who ran on the floating logs? And that the cheap jewelry probably snapped loose from all the herky-jerky action during such a vigorous event before sinking in the water?

Annie was right. I *was* searching for the elephant. I guess on some level I thought solving Jasper's murder could have been some kind of second chance for me, an opportunity to make peace with my past and get myself back on track. But now I saw that was nothing but a pipe dream. And even though he was a murderer, that delusion may still have very well cost a troubled individual his life because if I hadn't been so doggedly on the hunt for a killer then Kelly Lewis would not only be in custody but also most likely alive. Despite what I had previously accomplished as a private detective, and regardless of the encouragement and pep talks given to me by my cousin and father, I could see now that I had to face the cold hard truth—I just wasn't that guy anymore. Not the one they wanted me to be.

I was about to take Annie up on her offer to go for a walk and grab that drink when I heard stirring spaghetti-western chimes again. I scooped my iPhone out of my hip pouch to see an image of Brutus the yoga goat underneath my bookmaker buddy's name.

"Sykes," I said, answering the call.

"Mr. Ounstead," he replied, with an unusual amount of urgency in his voice. "I am most relieved you answered so quickly."

"Is everything okay?"

"I am afraid not."

"What's wrong?"

"It is Bartholomew."

"Buffalo?"

"Yes. It appears word of the death of his cousin reached him. He ... did not take it well."

"What happened?"

"The unfortunate news has put him in an incredibly volatile and enraged state."

"Can't you calm him down?"

"I cannot even get near him. The entire area is in disarray and people everywhere are panicking."

"What area?"

"My Agri-Zone."

I glanced at Annie, who seemed quite worried. "Is Buffalo okay?" she mouthed. I held up a finger as I continued talking with Sykes.

"Damn it," I muttered. The mess that I had already made was having an even greater domino effect.

"Are you able to provide assistance?" pleaded Sykes.

"Yes, of course. I mean, he's probably just blowing off a little steam, right? Buffalo might be a big boy, but he would never hurt any animals or people or anything."

"He has utterly run amok, Mr. Ounstead. And given his intellectual challenges, there is no telling what he is capable of. I fear the worst."

I turned to face the Agri-Zone. The huge, helium-filled parade balloons of cows, sheep, pigs, and roosters tethered to ropes were swaying in a gust of wind in the distance as they hovered above the indoor ice arena that had been temporarily converted for the country fair. I turned around to see Declan and Flo had joined Annie, and they all shared expressions of concern. I looked them each in the eyes before responding to Sykes.

"I'm on my way."

THIRTY-ONE
"HIGGLEDY-PIGGLEDY"

"Poor Buffalo," bemoaned Annie. "That boy may be about half a bubble off plumb, but God love him, he's got a heart of gold."

"Unfortunately, I don't think many people are going to see past all six-foot-six and three hundred plus pounds of him demolishing everything around him in order to consider that."

"Good point," she replied.

Annie matched me stride-for-stride as I picked up the pace. She was certainly in shape and her cardiovascular endurance showed no sign of waning as we ran in tandem well above a jog but just below a sprint. A long line of patrons waiting for entrance into the Longhorn Saloon wrapped around the popular drinking hole and spilled out into the street, congesting the paved road that was lined with carnival games on one side and attractions like a house of mirrors on the other. I caught a glimpse of my reflection mid-run only to see a creepy elongated nine-foot version of myself that made me look like the Slenderman if the urban legend had beefed up in the weight room. A moment later the visage was gone, replaced with a contrasting mirror image in which I was more stout, stubby, and hairier than a clawless yet comic-book-accurate Wolverine.

The distorted reflections were disconcerting. And while they left me unsettled, somehow given what I had gone through so far that afternoon at the *Colossal Cloverdale Rodeo and Country Fair*—not to mention the eight months since my complicity in Cassian Cullen's death—the warped likenesses felt like oddly accurate representations of what I had become.

"Hurry up, Jed!" barked Annie, having noticed my speed had reduced during my melancholic self-reflection.

I shook it off and accelerated, catching up to my cowgirl companion just as she cleared the last of the sideshow kiosks and ran by the pony ride station where we had been only hours before. Now that we had entered the Agri-Zone it occurred to me I had yet to check on my cousin, so I stole a glance back over my shoulder. Sure enough, there were Declan and Flo bringing up the rear, their ZooMe scooters struggling to maintain their top speed as they jumped the concrete curb and adjusted to the patchy burnt yellow grass and dirt ground of the outdoor animal exhibit.

Chaos reigned as we entered the area. Panicked families and shrieking children scrambled about in all directions. Banners, signs, and decorations had been ripped down and scattered across the grounds. Wooden benches and barrels serving as markers had been overturned and tossed aside. And several ticket booths had been completely smashed to pieces. Instead of feeling warm and welcoming, the family-friendly landscape looked instead like a small cyclone had torn through the area and left a swath of devastation in its wake.

"Snap my garters!" exclaimed Annie, and for a moment I had to catch myself from thinking it was a literal request. "I've been around a ruckus or two in my day, Jed," she continued, "but I ain't never seen any higgledy-piggledy like this before."

We slowed to a stop as we reached the epicentre of the petting zoo pandemonium. I tried my best to focus among the shouts, screams, and cries from both humans and animals alike, but it was clear the only common denominator between folks and beasties was that of palpable fear. The same beefy team of security meatheads in their too-tight, red T-shirts who had given Declan and me trouble earlier and denied us access to the rodeo arena went racing by, and they seemed almost giddy at the sight of all of the mayhem as they plowed through the panicked crowds. Given their haste, they must have known something that we didn't. And after taking a closer look, it was also evident Buffalo was nowhere in sight. He must have taken his warpath into the indoor arena portion of the Agri-Zone to continue his onslaught.

But why? Was he simply out of control and enraged? Or was there something in particular he was trying to get to while seething from the soul-crushing news that his beloved cousin and caretaker had died?

I turned to say something of the sort to Annie, but before I could even form the words the gate to the large pigsty swung open violently as a sounder of swine escaped. The entryway had been utterly destroyed, with sharp shafts of wood hanging off broken metal hinges at dangerous angles, making it appear as if a Mack truck had driven straight through the barrier and into the muddy pit. Startled hogs squealed and oinked as they ran around in frenzy, spooking the other animals in the open-air area surrounding the inside portion of the zoo.

The ponies in particular were thoroughly frightened, and despite the best efforts of their handlers, the little horses were bucking, kicking, and causing one hell of a commotion. An adjacent wire-fenced stockade, while still intact, contained dozens of nervous sheep, goats, and rabbits, with pretty much every animal in the enclosure acting up, clearly unsettled by the tumult given all the bleating, wailing, and hopping of the distressed creatures.

One young girl, who couldn't have been older than five or six, sat alone, crying, on a hay bale in the middle of the pen, abandoned in the bedlam among surrounding critters that continued to act up. I jumped over the fence and darted into the corral, dodging rams, ewes, and lambs coming from one direction and goats from the other. One particularly frisky, horn-headed, black-and-white kid bounded right toward me and either tried to leap into my arms or attack me. I instinctively turned away and the varmint let out a yelp as it bounced off my meaty deltoid and spun around, landing on its rump before limping away.

I hoped it wasn't one of Sykes's prized yoga goats, because the furry little bastard wasn't going to be vaulting on and off any practitioners in plank positions anytime soon. I reached the sobbing child, scooped her up in my arms, and held her tight as we made our escape. Annie was waiting for us with outstretched arms. The child nuzzled up to Annie, who shushed and rocked her. I gave them space as the little one's sobs turned into softer stifled cries.

Declan and Flo rolled up a few moments later, providing a welcome distraction.

"Is the wee lassie all right?" he asked.

I nodded. "Just a bit rattled is all."

"I don't blame her. What an arseways kip and a half this is!"

As if on cue, a familiar-looking black-and-white Holstein cow with a halter and rope around its head and neck wandered by in front of us.

A moment later Flo yelped as an especially aggressive goat started biting at one of the straps that dangled from the bright blue fanny pack that hung off her hip. She didn't give up without a fight, however, and blasted the horn on her ZooMe scooter.

BRRRRREEEEEEEEEEEEE!!!!!!!!

Sykes's prized heifer responded to the horn by halting in its tracks, letting out a very loud moo, then reflexively defecating on the spot. Declan leapt backwards as some of the wet manure splattered on the ground and sent droplets near his feet.

"Jaysus Christ, Flo! Ya just made the thing shite itself!"

Flo was engaged in her tug-of-war with the goat nibbling at her fanny pack, when I heard an alert from my own hip, and pulled out my phone to see I had another message from Sykes.

The message was an emoticon of a buffalo followed by the words *IN THE ARENA MR OUNSTEAD! SOS!*

"Holy hell," I said.

"What?" asked Declan and Annie in unison.

"Sykes is inside," I said, nodding toward the rest of the Agri-Zone's zoo.

"That's what's got ya worked up?"

"He's using emojis, acronyms, and exclamation points. Things must be bad."

I grabbed the rope hanging from the cow's neck and wrapped the slack around my hand.

"Yer gonna bring the bloody cow?" asked Declan.

"It's Sykes's and it ... has value, okay? Trust me."

Declan shrugged and started to light a cigarette while I turned to Annie, who still had one hand cupped behind the back of the little girl's head while she bounced her gently in her arms.

"Go on, Handsome," she said. "Help Buffalo. I'll stay here and find her parents."

Declan turned to say something to Flo, but thought better of it when he saw her cussing up a storm while yanking on her fanny pack with one hand and smacking the head of the thieving goat with the other.

"Looks like it's just us, Boyo. Besides, them security apes from before headed in there," said Declan deviously, "an' I certainly wouldn't mind sayin' hello."

I nodded in agreement. And with that, Declan, a cow that crapped on command, and I hurried inside the Agri-Zone arena.

THIRTY-TWO
"WAKE SNAKES"

The beads on the end of the rattlesnake's tail shook so loudly they drowned out the frightened chatter of the people remaining in the arena, most of whom were hell-bent on exiting the place as quickly as possible. Hockey season was over so there was no ice beneath our feet, and although the sound of Sykes's cow's hooves clomping on the concrete floor was amplified, it too was muted by the reptile's warning to potential aggressors to back off.

I towered over the low-sided terrarium, as did the healthy-looking heifer we had in tow. But Declan just had to flick the butt of his smoke against the glass-fronted case, and that caused a puff of orange embers to burst and reflect in the snake's black elliptical pupils. Its head thrust forward lightning fast, sharp fangs banging against the transparent barrier as it lunged in an unsuccessful attempt to bite Sykes's prized pooping cow.

The serpent was just one of the many reptiles and amphibians present in the aptly named "*HERPETOLOGY HABITAT*" that was on our left, housing additional terrariums and above-ground pools filled with water, lily pads, rocks, snakes, frogs, turtles, and other slimy or scaly critters. The rest of the near empty sportsplex was occupied with tables, kiosks, and displays, all displaying facts about guinea pigs, mice, spawning salmon, and other local fish and wildlife.

As we neared the end of the arena, I spotted Sykes next to a particularly large snake pit and lizard lounge. He was standing in a section below where the blue line on a hockey rink would have been, an area cordoned off with large, lime-green and white-striped draperies suspended from strategically placed scaffoldings, to create an excluded area that concealed what lay behind.

Ever the cool cucumber, Sykes stood calmly by the entrance to the tarped sector, and I couldn't be sure what remained hidden because all the banners and signs had been knocked down, save for one—an oversized placard mounted on a large easel that read "*THE AVION CAFÉ.*"

The four red-shirted, rodeo security goons fanned out as they slowly surrounded Sykes, who, despite having both of his hands up in the air submissively, stood his ground, blocking access to the café. His jet-black hair and Versace sunglasses only made him more difficult to read, but given his text message, I knew that beneath his trademark composure my atypical ally was more distressed than I had ever seen him before.

"Step aside, Wolf of Wall Street," snapped Ripplechest, the same powerhouse punk with the puffed-up pectorals who had gone toe-to-toe with Declan.

"I am unable to do so," replied Sykes, calmly. "And I strongly suggest you gentlemen leave at once. The situation is now under control."

"The fuck it is!" shouted one of Ripplechest's colleagues, another juicehead gym rat who had traps so thick, coiled, and V-tapered they may as well have been holding up a suspension bridge. "Where's that giant retard? He's getting a beatdown for what he's done!"

V-Traps rolled his shoulders forward aggressively as I caught Declan's eye. He tipped the brim of his cowboy hat downwards, understanding my intention, before we started to slowly flank the brawny red shirts from behind. It was hard to read Sykes and tell if he knew what we were doing, but I saw the bookmaker nod in our direction, and I realized he was wise to our plan.

"What is it that has caused such a formidable foursome like yourselves to seek out my associate with such indignation?" inquired Sykes, carefully drawing out his question in order to buy Declan and me more time.

The meatheads glanced back and forth between one another, perplexed.

"Ain't nobody said nothin' about no fucking Natives, Fancy Pants!" barked a third member of the quartet who had legs so thick and muscular it looked as if his thighs could burst out of his John Cena-style denim jorts at any moment.

This time my cousin caught my eye and shook his head in exasperation at their sheer ignorance, but we weren't ready to intercede just yet.

"That giant farm boy fuckwit just knocked my nephew into the back of a pony and the goddamn thing up and kicked him in the belly so hard he puked," continued Quadzilla. "So, we're here to teach him a lesson."

"You tell him, Clay," chimed in the last and least built of the musclemen, who seemed almost slim by comparison to his three beefcake buddies.

Quadzilla (AKA Clay) appeared emboldened by Slim's comment, and, as a result, he, Ripplechest, and V-Traps confidently closed the gap around Sykes, who was now fully surrounded and penned in at the café entrance by what had to have amounted to a cumulative weight of muscle mass totaling at least eight hundred pounds.

Declan and I made the most of the escalating showdown, however, and while he removed his aviators, placed them in his

Stetson, and laid the hat and his beer backpack on the concrete floor, I found a colourful Haida totem pole next to an Aboriginal Harvesting Rights kiosk and hitched Sykes's precious cow around its base.

Seeing Declan and me in readiness, Sykes began to laugh.

"What's so funny?" snapped Ripplechest.

"Curse, bless, me now with your fierce tears, I pray. Do not go gentle into that good night."

All four of the red-shirted security guards looked back and forth at one another, utterly perplexed by the poetry.

"Jesus Christ, is this guy a retard too?" asked Quadzilla.

Sykes continued. *"Rage, rage against the dying of the ...* MIGHT."

"What the fuck are you trying to say?!?" exclaimed Ripplechest in exasperation.

With Sykes's cue clearly received, Declan and I made our move.

"He's saying 'walk away'," I commanded, causing all four men to snap their heads around.

"You get one chance," I warned.

Recognizing me, Ripplechest couldn't help but smirk. "Well, look who it is. *Sher-The-Rock-Holmes*. Where's your little leprechaun sidekick?"

I shook my head and smiled.

"What's so funny?" snapped Ripplechest.

"He really, really hates being called a *'sidekick.'*"

As if on cue, Declan emerged from the shadows of the snake pit, flying through the air to deliver a crushing fist to Ripplechest's cheekbone, which I could only describe as a hybrid, Irish bare-knuckle, *Dornálaíocht*-style Superman punch. By the time my cousin landed on his feet like a cat, Ripplechest had nearly spun around on the spot three hundred and sixty degrees, his eyes rolling back in his head, before he crumpled to the ground like a car lot inflatable tube man with its air flow supply cut off.

"That's for layin' yer greasy mitts on me before, ya geebag!"

Although Slim's jaw nearly hit the floor at the sight of their leader being dropped like a bag of hammers, Quadzilla and V-Traps didn't hesitate and sprang into action. The chunky-thighed brute launched himself forward with enough force to flip a pickup truck. I may have been more shocked than Declan by the bold attack. My cousin planted his feet behind him and did his best to try and stop Quadzilla, but it was no use, and the powerful man pushed him backwards like a tackling dummy being run back ten yards during drills on the gridiron. Eventually, Declan gave up trying to combat Quadzilla's sheer strength and instead started delivering sharp elbows to the back of his skull, the last of which connected with enough of an impact that both men collapsed together into one of the above ground pools filled with serpents.

A couple water snakes spilled onto the ground from the impact while Declan fought against Quadzilla's bear-hug death-grip as they splashed and struggled, with reptiles slithering over and around them. I winced at the cold-blooded combat before I caught movement coming toward me out of the corner of my eye.

"Mr. Ounstead!" shouted Sykes, trying to warn me, but it was too late—V-Traps had grabbed the crewneck of my shirt with both of his hands and pulled me close to his face.

"Nothing gentle about this, Asshole," he snapped, lowering his brow and delivering a head butt.

I reacted instinctively, dropping my head even further, so when his noggin connected with mine, he not only bypassed the bump left behind from "Hot Saw" McGraw's axe attack, but also unintentionally cracked his forehead against the top of my skull and hardest part of the human body. It was an old wrestler's trick to ensure you or your opponent never made contact with this section of the cranium, and I knew firsthand just how excruciating it could be. As V-Traps recoiled clutching both of his hands to his crown, I took advantage of him being stunned and speared him, driving my shoulder into his solar plexus so hard all of the air exhaled out of his body. By the time I heard his head crack against the concrete as he hit the floor, the only question remaining was how bad would his concussion be.

As I stood up over the dazed goon writhing and moaning on the ground, I caught sight of Declan, who had managed to gain the upper hand in his battle with Quadzilla. Although he had been taken down, my cousin utilized his wiry strength to his advantage. Despite being flat on his back in the artificial pond of snakes, Declan had turned his vulnerable position into an attack, by wrapping his lean and lithe legs around his aggressor's neck in a triangle choke. For all of his lower body strength, Quadzilla was essentially helpless, frantically pedaling his feet trying to gain traction against and grip the slippery bottom of the pool to no avail. Like a fly caught in a spiderweb, the more he struggled, the deeper he became entangled in the hold as Declan continued tightening the grip of his legs around the thug's neck. By gripping the back of the ornery security guard's head and pulling downwards, cutting off the blood flow from the carotid arteries to the brain while lifting his hips and squeezing even harder, Quadzilla's body quickly went limp. Declan released the hold and rolled the man off of him, who flopped onto his side. A particularly large boa constrictor then slowly slithered over the defeated goon's body as my victorious kin climbed to his feet, dripping wet, head-to-toe.

"All the muscle in the world ain't worth a shite if ya can't use yer hip flexors, ya brawny eejit," he sniped, as he pulled a wet cigarette out of his pocket. "Bollocks," he muttered, breaking it in two and tossing it away in frustration.

"Ahem," Sykes interjected, clearing his throat. I glanced at my upscale associate to see him pointing at Slim, the only red shirt remaining. Having witnessed each of his three pals being put out of commission, the last of whom now served as a new playmate for the snakes to slip and slide on, Slim looked like he had seen a ghost. An awkward moment of Slim, Sykes, Declan, and me all staring at one another followed and was so rife with tension and side-glances it felt like the showdown of a Sergio Leone spaghetti western, but without the revolvers. Slim made a wise call and bolted toward the exit, and neither Sykes, Declan, nor I made any attempt to prevent his escape.

I stepped around V-Traps, who was still barely conscious and moaning on the floor, and approached my animal-loving ally. Despite all of the action, Sykes seemed remarkably composed. He smiled broadly as we came together, basking in triumph over three of our four defeated attackers, who were still incapacitated.

"Well done, Mr. Ounstead. I must say, while well aware of how formidable you and your cousin are, observing the two of you in action is most impressive."

"You're going to make me blush, Sykes."

At that point Declan sauntered over to us, however, he was not alone—draped around his shoulders was a five-foot-long, black-and-brown, ball python.

"Look at what a beauty this fella is," my cousin declared, showing off the scaly, nonvenomous constrictor like Hulk Hogan strutting to the ring with a red-and-yellow, fashionable feather boa. "He's kind o'cute, eh? Now I get why yer ol' pal Jimmy Mimbo used to wrassle with one."

"Johnny Mamba," I said, correcting him, thinking of my former tag-team partner whose kidnapped pet snake first put me on the path to becoming a private investigator.

Son of a gun, I thought. All of the over-the-top in-ring theatrics of my professional wrestling career suddenly didn't seem so absurd by comparison.

"Buffalo is a big boy, D. I'm going to need you focused and not distracted in order to subdue him."

"Aye. Whadda ya say, Sykesy? Keep an eye on me new mate here while we save the day then, yeah?" Declan lifted the python off of his shoulders and held him out like an offering.

"While I am most appreciative of your timely intervention Mr. Saint James, I believe the habitat from whence that creature came will suffice."

"Feckin' fun sponge," griped Declan, before returning the python to a nearby terrarium.

"What do you think Buffalo is doing inside this Avion Café, anyway?" I asked.

"Returning to a calmer state, I hope," replied Sykes, "as he was utterly devastated upon learning of the death of his beloved cousin."

"Then we better get in there before he starts pulling off bird heads like champagne corks."

"I think perhaps it might be best if you first attempted to mollify Bartholomew on your own. He was quite thrilled by your encounter earlier and could not stop discussing how excited he was to have met a bona fide celebrity."

"Wrestling fan, eh?"

"Indeed."

I nodded as Declan re-appeared at my side. We started toward the green-and-white striped drapes when Sykes held up a hand.

"There is one more thing I should warn you about, Gentlemen."

"Ya got a giant croc back there or somethin'?"

"It is about the nature of the café."

"Aye, Avion. 'Tis sponsored by RBC Visa or some shite, yeah?"

"Avion is the French and Spanish name for airplane, from the Latin word *avis*."

"So, it's a car rental coffee shop then?" asked Declan.

"It's a bird café," I said, connecting the dots between my language history and Sykes's penchant for bizarre business ventures.

"Correct, Mr. Ounstead. Modeled after the very popular trend of such bistros in Japan."

"What are ya sayin', Sykesy? Yer makin' a buck off o' folks sippin' lattes next to canaries on katanas?"

"Not exactly, Mr. Saint James. You see, one of the conditions I had before accepting the managerial position for the *Colossal Cloverdale Rodeo and Country Fair* Agri-Zone was the opportunity to draw upon my colleague's many wildlife resources, including those he has through the Calgary Zoological Society and the Zoo itself, which are quite vast since the park remains one of the top tourist attractions in Canada. Needless to say, you may rest assured that all of the birds themselves are of impeccable pedigree and most docile."

"Any idea why Buffalo would have made his way here?" I asked.

"He enjoys the company of his feathered friends and is fond of hand-feeding them. You should take this with you," he said, pulling a mini Ziploc bag from the inside pocket of his dapper suit jacket and offering it to me.

"Thanks," I said, taking the birdseed.

Sykes pulled back one of the striped green-and-white curtains for us to enter, but before we even took a step, a large, royal blue-necked and dark orange-bellied peacock emerged. The large bird let out a loud squawk before its brilliantly-coloured tail expanded vibrantly.

"JAYSUS MOTHER MARY AND JOSEPH!" screamed Declan in a terrified voice.

He turned on a dime and sprinted off in the other direction, and by the time Sykes had processed this sudden turn of events, he was already out the door of the arena.

"I do not understand. Your cousin has no issues with reptiles but fears birds?"

"Just peacocks," I replied. "It's a long story."

"I see."

"Looks like it's up to me then."

"Good luck, Mr. Ounstead."

The peacock shook its tail again before losing interest in us and returning to the inside of the Avion Café. I gave Sykes a pat on the arm of his crisp white blazer, then followed the blue and emerald plumaged bird through the curtains, only to have something even more unusual waiting for me on the other side.

THIRTY-THREE
"DE-HORNING BUFFALO"

"Hammerhead! Hammerhead!"

I looked around in all directions, but for the life of me had no idea who had announced my entry into the bird café. The small space was filled with a handful of tables and chairs, as well as several comfy-looking loungers and sofas. Colourful tapestries, paintings, and area rugs—all depicting tasteful and beautiful avifauna artwork—were hung around the café in-between various wooden poles, each with thin horizontal dowels jutting out with dozens of brightly-coloured birds perched upon them. A blue jay and a budgie frolicked together in a bird bath near a small display case that featured pastries and baked goods, and I couldn't help but chuckle at a few of the items listed on the chalkboard above the counter, which included *Cuckoo Cold Brewed Coffee*, *Osprey-ssos*, *Tropical Toucan Tea*, and *Macaw-iattos*. I had to give it to Sykes, the man was nothing if not consistent with his trademark peculiar panache.

"*Hammerhead! Hammerhead!*"

There it was again.

I scanned my surroundings, and with the non-stop chirping, tweeting, and trilling, it felt like I was walking across the wooden foot bridge in the aviary at the Vancouver Aquarium.

It took a few moments, but I located the source speaking my squared circle nickname—a small, white-faced, black-beaked grey parrot. However, unlike all of the other birds in the Avion Café, this particular winged warbler wasn't resting atop a perch. Instead, the feathered chatterbox had its talons partially wrapped around one of Buffalo's beefy extended forearms.

The giant of a man sat with his back to me at a table in the rear of the café. He kept his upper arm elevated for the parrot to give it a full view of its surroundings, while Buffalo himself sat slouched forward with his head hanging. I approached them, then pulled back a chair, which dragged loudly across the floor.

SQUAWK!

"Hammerhead! Hammerhead!"

"I taught him your name," said Buffalo, with his leviathan-like lats still facing me. "He likes to say it."

"I can see that," I replied, before taking a seat.

"Mister Sykes talked to me through the curtain. He said if I stopped smashing that the 'Hammerhead' come visit."

"He did, eh?"

"Yep. I stopped smashing. For now."

"That's good, Buffalo. That way no one can get hurt."

"I no hurt anyone. I'm just so angry about cousin."

"I know."

"But now ... now I'm feeling the sad."

I didn't know how to respond. A few moments went by before Buffalo's head started bobbing up and down, and while they were far from quiet, I imagined for a guy his size they were his equivalent of soft cries.

"I feel the sad so bad, Mister 'Hammerhead.'"

I let him shed some more tears for a while, saying nothing. Even the parrot seemed a bit unnerved by his huge pal's emotional outburst, scuttling up and down his arm a couple times before flapping its wings once and shaking its head. When the time felt right, I spoke.

"I'm very sorry for your loss."

Buffalo nodded and sniffed, wiping his nose on his other massive arm. The table shook as his feet thumped on the ground and he turned around to face me. The goliath's nose was red, his cheeks were streaked with tears, and his eyes were puffy from crying. When I realized he couldn't yet bring himself to look at me, I reached across the table and gently patted his shoulder. Buffalo nodded, then forced a smile and lifted his head.

"Thank you, Mister 'Hammerhead.'"

"You can call me Jed."

"Does that mean we can be friends?"

"Sure, Buffalo. We can be friends."

The behemoth nodded and although it was only for a moment, the smallest of smiles appeared on his face.

"Here," I said, offering the bag of birdseed to Buffalo.

He ripped open the bag effortlessly with his thumb and index finger.

"We feed him together," declared Buffalo.

I nodded and we spent the next couple minutes pouring handfuls of birdseed onto our palms and taking turns feeding the parrot, who seemed delighted and moved back and forth between us. A couple of times the bird's black beak nipped both my hand and Buffalo's, but while I winced in momentary pain, Buffalo only giggled.

"Silly bird," he said. "That tickles."

If that tickled the thick hide of the man, then I sure as hell was glad we were having a calm conversation and sharing a quiet moment with a friendly bird as opposed to any alternative measures that might have been required to settle him down and ensure his one-man riot ceased.

"Mister 'Hamm—' ... I mean, Mister Jed?"

"Yes, Buffalo?"

"I gots so angry I stills don't know."

"Don't know what?"

"How cousin died."

I looked up at Buffalo and am not exactly sure what it was that made me say what I did next. Maybe it was that his marble-sized doe eyes were filled with more innocence than a deer in the forest. Or perhaps it was his oversized blue denim overalls and how they made him look like a ten-foot toddler. Hell, maybe it was the fact that one might just be more willing to trust a person who has a friendly parrot nestled on his arm. All I know was that in that moment, amidst more birds than I could count, and after the longest day of my life, I simply didn't have the heart to lie to the hulking, heartbroken, and now seemingly harmless man.

"I think it may have been my fault."

THIRTY-FOUR
"FEATHER PLUCKING"

"That's crazy talk, Mister Jed."

"I wish it were."

"But ... I don't get it."

"Kelly's death. It might have occurred because of me."

Buffalo shook his head aggressively, as if doing so would rid his simple mind of the very thought. "No, no, no. That can't be true."

"I'm sorry."

"You wouldn't hurt cousin. You're my friend."

"I am, Buffalo. But right before we met, your cousin and I, well, we had a fight."

Buffalo pinched the last remaining bit of birdseed Sykes had given me out of the plastic Ziploc bag with his sausage-like digits. However, when he went to feed the parrot, he shoved it so hard into his grey-feathered friend's beak that the bird's head snapped back and it let out a distressed squawk.

"What kind of fight?" he asked.

"A tough one."

"But just a yelling fight, right Mister Jed? Me and cousin have those sometimes. Everybody does."

I tried to choose my words carefully, but there was no turning back now. "It started off as a yelling fight, sure. But then things … escalated."

"You were on a bum mud potato?"

"Bum mud potato?"

"You know. The rides at the mall. I call them 'bum mud potatoes.'"

"I don't know what those are."

"Yes you do. They're everywhere. You probably just use a different name like cousin does. He calls them '*Ass Clay Taters.*'"

I hesitated before responding, only now gaining more insight into the specifics of Buffalo's intellectual disabilities.

"Are you telling me you had a yelling fight with Kelly at a mall while on an escalator?"

"Yep. Cousin was real mad after I tooted. It was so loud it scared an old lady in front of us. She dropped her purse and the bum mud potato's silver mouth at the bottom almost ate it."

I leaned back in my chair and gritted my teeth. I didn't have a lot of experience with developmentally disabled people and was definitely struggling in my efforts to explain things clearly to Buffalo. I also got the impression that, whether he knew it or not, the gentle giant was doing everything he could to prevent me from sharing the details of my knife fight with his cousin.

"We weren't at the mall, Buffalo. We got into a fight by the pony rides."

"I like ponies."

"And it wasn't a yelling fight. We were hitting each other."

"Cousin smacks me sometimes. But only when—"

"Kelly pulled a knife. He tried to kill me."

"No …"

"He was having one of his mood swings from his bipolar condition—"

"I know all about cousin's handicap! He's like me kind of. But different. And he takes his polar bear medicine, Mister Jed! It makes his brain work good."

"I don't think he's been taking his 'polar bear' medicine. He was also very upset over Jasper's murder."

I realized a moment too late what I had done by sharing the last piece of information, and although I instantly regretted it, I couldn't take it back. Buffalo's shoulders slumped downwards so much the parrot made a clicking sound with its tongue before scrambling further up one of his huge arms.

"M—m—murder?" stuttered Buffalo, more tears welling in his eyes. "Jasper is dead too?"

"Yes," I said, realizing at this point that I had no choice but to rip the Band-Aid off completely.

"But what about the farm?" he finally asked, meekly.

"What farm?"

"Cousin said extra money was coming and me and Jasper and him were going to buy farm land with the house in hundred miles."

"The house in hundred miles?"

"Yes."

I paused for a moment, processing what Buffalo had just said but also keeping in mind his particularly challenging vocabulary.

"Do you mean 100 Mile House?"

Buffalo nodded softly.

That was it. The missing piece of the puzzle and the reason Kelly Lewis had concocted a bribery scheme with "Hot Saw" McGraw. In exchange for a hefty payout, Lewis thought he could convince Jasper to drop out of the STIHL sponsorship race and planned to use the money to buy land up in 100 Mile House, a district located in the South Cariboo region of central British Columbia. Although it only had a population of a couple thousand, the primary industries were forestry and ranching—just the kind of place where a lumberjack and a rodeo lifer with a bonus hundred-grand in cash could drop a solid down payment on much lower priced property than any available in the greater Vancouver area, and live a nice, quiet life with the developmentally disabled man in their care.

That was the "dream" Randy Pippen had heard Lewis screaming about Jasper giving up when the lovers had their last known confrontation in the loggersports pit, less than an hour before my friend was found dead with an axe in the back of his head. All of Kelly's ensuing erratic behaviour, having Buffalo choke me out with a flank strap for asking questions about Jasper and mentioning that I was a PI, his attack on me with the Bowie knife, not to mention his well-established struggles with a manic-depressive disorder—it all made total sense.

"Mister Jed?"

I wasn't sure how long I had been connecting the dots in my head when Buffalo's question snapped me back to the present.

"Yes, Buffalo?"

"You said cousin being dead might be your fault."

"I did."

"How?"

"During our fight, I, uh … struck him. In the throat. And I'm afraid it's likely that is why he died."

"You punched cousin in the throat?"

"He was trying to stab me with a knife."

"You punched cousin in the *throat*."

"It was self-defence."

"*You. Punched. Cousin. In. The. Throat!*"

"Easy now, Buff—"

My words were cut off when the colossus slammed both of his fists down on the table and snapped it in half. The parrot squawked, flapped its wings frantically, then flew away as the broken table between us collapsed to the ground. The next thing I knew a hand rivaling the size of Andre the Giant's wrapped around my throat and lifted me up and into the air as if I weighed less than a kitten.

I clawed at Buffalo's monstrous mitt, but it was no use, and his vice-like grip only tightened as he carried me with one arm toward the wall behind us, then slammed me hard against the green-and-white striped drapes which hid the boards from the iceless rink behind it. The Plexiglass rumbled as it sent off a vibration in both directions like a jackhammer drilling into the concrete. Dozens of birds screeched and cheeped nervously, and many flew off their perches and around in circles inside the Avion Café as the tension mounted.

I could feel my face turning bright red as I gasped for air, and as much as I tried to pry his hand off of my neck it was no use—Buffalo was choking me out for the second time in a matter of hours. The difference was this time I fully acknowledged the man's primal power, which made me realize the flank strap he had used on me earlier was a much more merciful way to be rendered unconscious.

I managed to look into Buffalo's eyes one last time, and whatever childlike wonder and innocence had been there before was gone, replaced by pure anger. The longer I was unable to breathe, the more I realized that, just like the last time I tried to solve a murder, my efforts only managed to bring pain and devastation to everyone around me. In that moment I gave up struggling and resigned myself to my fate, waiting for the sweet release from passing out or that inevitable visit from the Grim Reaper himself.

All I could think was that I deserved my fate.

THIRTY-FIVE
"COW PUNCHER'S CHANCE"

The mind can play tricks on you when it's deprived of oxygen.

Between thirty and one-hundred-and-eighty seconds you lose consciousness.

At the one-minute mark brain cells begin dying.

At five minutes death is imminent.

The longer Buffalo kept me hoisted in the air with one arm, pressed against the Plexiglas of the hockey rink boards, the more images from my past began to flash before my eyes. I saw the many long road trips and endless venues I visited during my travels back in my indie and WWE professional wrestling days. All the laughing, beer drinking, raising hell, and fighting side-by-side with Declan, hugging it out through the good times and bad. Visions of my pop and me working cases as father-and-son private investigators and celebrating jobs well done with Dairy Queen treats. And my beautiful mother during my childhood weekend afternoons at the Granville Island Market, where we would shop for groceries and produce together, before she would treat me to a banana milkshake and allow me to watch as much professional wrestling as I wanted upon returning home.

But the final, fleeting glimpses that appeared in my mind's eye were of all the women who had captured my heart. Laughing with Stormy in the parking lot just hours earlier, having a cooler and reminiscing, holding hands as we walked along the Vancouver Seawall, so infatuated we ignored the picturesque view and incoming tide.

To my surprise, I saw myself with Annie, despite only just meeting her that day. Her strawberry-blonde hair was shining in the sunlight, and she looked up at me with an interest and admiration I had not felt in a long time.

But the last image as the darkness began to creep in was of Rya busting my chops as we butted heads on overlapping cases, or the private time where we had given into our mutual attraction and even shared a forbidden kiss. It made us forget that we had both been in relationships—we had a special connection and both knew it could not be denied—and that last memory of Rya sent a jolt of energy throughout my body.

No, I chastised myself.

I refused to go out like this. I had too much more left to live for.

My eyes opened wide as adrenaline coursed through my veins. Buffalo still had me by the throat, his face contorted in a mixture of rage and hurt, but his eyebrows went up in surprise when he saw me grip his bear paw with both my hands, grunt loudly as I exerted every last ounce of strength I had in my body, and rip his massive meathook away from my neck, freeing myself from his death grip. He took a step back, as if he was shocked by my strength and ability to free myself.

"Back off, Buffalo!" I managed to croak, in-between hacks and coughs as I struggled to catch my breath.

"You ... how did you do that, Mister Jed?"

"How did I do what?" I rasped.

"How did you be stronger than me?"

I stood up tall, embracing the surge of vitality shooting through me. "Because I had to be. There are people who still need me. And I owe it to them to be here."

"But you're a bad guy. You killed cousin."

"Yeah, I did. And maybe I am a bad guy. Or maybe sometimes I've just had to do bad things for the right reasons."

Buffalo stared at me intently. I could see he was only thinking of the role I played in Kelly Lewis's death, but for me, it was more than that. I was speaking to him as much as I was to myself, given the grief I had carried around for nine months. I had foolishly hoped I could ignore the emotional fallout after arranging a hit on Cassian Cullen, a murderous psychopath who would have continued leaving bodies in his wake while never being brought to conventional justice.

"How can you be a good guy if you do bad things, Mister Jed?"

"I'm still figuring that part out."

"I don't get it."

"I'm just trying to say life ain't all rainbows and milkshakes. As you found out today, things can get ugly. And it can leave you feeling broken inside. I know what that feels like."

"You had people you love die?"

"Yes," I replied. "Or get hurt real bad," I continued, remembering my former tag-team partner "Mad Max" Conkin, tragically paralyzed during one of our in-ring rehearsals.

Max.

He had been there for me during my battle with Cassian, and told me that while I couldn't change the past, I could still make a difference in people's lives. Here I was, feeling sorry for myself, when the only thing he had ever asked of me since the accident was that I keep on going, helping those who couldn't be helped by anyone else. I made Max a promise, one that I had forgotten for the better part of a year.

"I'm not perfect, Buffalo. But even the difficult decisions I've had to make—and the action I've had to take—it's always been in service of me trying to do the right thing. I may not be the good guy. But I'm sure as hell trying to be."

Buffalo stood still for a few moments before sitting down on a wooden chair. His huge frame dwarfed the seat so completely it looked like he was floating in a seated position.

"I've done bad things too. Like when I gots so mad. I smash everything. I don't even remember."

I walked over to the big man and stood next to him for a moment, then put a hand on his shoulder. He sighed and sniffed, but managed to fight off the tears.

"I know you lost a lot today. But it's going to be okay. You're going to be okay."

Buffalo slapped a monstrous mitt down on top of mine and squeezed so hard I thought my hand might snap off at the wrist. I winced and said nothing, not wanting to ruin the moment.

"Thank you, Mister Jed."

"You're welcome, Bub."

Buffalo let go of my hand and took a deep breath.

"I know something that might cheer you up."

"What?"

I took a few steps back toward the entrance to the Avion Café and hollered. "Sykes! Come on in here. And bring Buffalo's pal."

Buffalo looked at me quizzically as we heard some rustling on the other side of the curtains. After a few moments, Sykes entered the bird bistro with his prized bovine in tow. Buffalo's face lit up the moment he saw the animal.

"Cow!" he exclaimed excitedly, then jumped to his feet and lumbered toward the dependable defecator.

Buffalo's thunderous steps reverberated throughout the coffee shop and every single bird in the place either squawked, chirped, or flapped their wings as a result. The gentle giant reached the cow and gave it a hug, before petting its snout over and over again as he had done on the cow-pie bingo field.

I joined Sykes as he stepped away from Buffalo and the cow, and we shook hands.

"It seems I am indebted to you yet again, Mr. Ounstead."

"No debts between friends, Sykes."

"You are smiling and seem in better spirits than I have seen you in quite some time. If I may ask, what exactly transpired between you and Bartholomew as you succeeded in diffusing the situation?"

I glanced back at Buffalo, who continued happily stroking and talking to the cow.

"Buffalo and I ... let's just say we worked some stuff out."

"I am delighted to hear that. So, Mr. Ounstead. What now?"

"I finally go home."

THIRTY-SIX
"STRINGING A WHIZZER"

Declan, Flo, and Annie were all waiting for me outside when I left the Avion Café, and the rodeo staff had begun swiftly cleaning up the mess Buffalo had left in his path of destruction. The Agri-Zone itself had been more or less shut down for the time being.

The sun was slowly descending behind the snowcapped mountains in the distance, its blood-orange light bleeding out across the lush, verdant Fraser Valley landscape. With a twenty-ounce plastic cup of beer in one hand, and a lit cigarette in the other, Declan was in the midst of retelling our showdown with the security guards to one woman who was old enough to be his grandmother and another who could have been his daughter.

Although I offered to assist, Sykes stated that he would not only deal efficiently with the security men when they regained consciousness, but also assured me that any news of our reptile rumble would remain confidential and avoid any law enforcement entanglements. I had witnessed firsthand enough of his seemingly endless connections, to not doubt for a second he was a man of his word. What had just gone down would never be made public. How he planned to pull that off was just one of the enduring mysteries about my enigmatic friend.

"Then I put the eejit in a triangle choke while the snakes were swimmin' all over us!" Declan proudly boasted.

"Ewww!" said Flo, sipping on a raspberry-flavoured, White Claw Hard Seltzer.

"I'm with you, Flo," said Annie, before making an "ick" face.

"I kind o'became mates with a python too. Scaly bastard fit right 'round me neck like a St. Paddy's Day scarf. No flute needed for that lad, he was grand."

"Jed!" exclaimed Annie, upon noticing me. She jumped into my arms and we exchanged a warm embrace and even warmer smiles before she gave me soft kiss on the cheek.

"Howdy, Darlin'."

"Look at you," she chuckled. "Maybe there's still a chance I can make a real cowboy out of you yet."

"I was chasin' the gobshite that ran off," interjected my cousin, falsely and defensively.

I turned my attention to Declan, handing him his cowboy hat, sunglasses, and beloved near-empty beer backpack that he had left behind due to his frantic retreat after encountering the colourful fowl that so frightened him. "Did you catch him?" I asked, with a smirk.

"'Fraid not, Boyo."

"You just gave up?"

"He's a brisk bugger and I just stopped to wet me whistle is all."

"I don't know, D. Seems to me you're *peacocking* a bit for the ladies."

Declan's face started to turn a crimson hue. He immediately chugged back the rest of his beer and tossed the cup aside.

"In all my born days, Declan! I should give you a lash with my bullwhip for being such a nasty litterbug."

"Ah, them rodeo blokes'll get to it. They're already cleanin' this place up from King Kong's rampage. How is that huge bastard, anyway?"

"He's inside with Sykes petting the cow."

"Pettin' the cow?"

"I told you it had value."

"Deadly, cuz we gotta move *tits sweet* if we want to catch that 'Hot Saw' hooligan an' get even with him givin' yer noggin a crack. To the Bat-Scooters, Flo!"

Declan's gal pal moved quickly for a woman her age and was pulling the keys out of her fanny pack when I held up a hand.

"I'm not going, D."

"What do ya mean, yer not goin'?"

"I mean I'm done. Kelly Lewis was off his meds and he killed Jasper in a jealous rage. Now he's dead too. I'll probably have to come back out here and give a statement to the Mounties at some point, or maybe Pop can run interference, or mediate thanks to his pull with the boys in blue. All I know is it's been one hell of a day and I'm toast. I'm going home."

I noticed the disappointment on Annie's face, but she said nothing. Declan whispered back and forth with Flo for a moment before responding.

"Fair enough, Mate. Ya don't mind if I stick around here with Flo, do ya? We'll see if we can dig up a lead on that lumberjack in the wind who beaned ya with the axe, but even if we don't, I have a feelin' I'll be bunkin' out this way tonight."

"You bet your sweet ass you will," declared Flo, before slapping my cousin on the butt.

"Settle down, ya frisky tart. Let's go then, eh?"

Flo started trudging off toward the scooters. Declan turned and enveloped me in a big hug, before looking me in the eye.

"Ya okay, Jed?"

"Ya, D. I'm actually pretty good. Thanks."

He patted me on the cheek and smiled. "I love ya, *Deartháir*."

"I love you too, Brother."

I watched as Declan trotted off after Flo, then took a knee. The spry octogenarian climbed onto his back and he gave her a piggyback ride the rest of the way to the ZooMe scooters. I turned to face Annie, who was smiling sweetly.

"Gosh darn it, Jed. I might need to get myself a handkerchief."

"Oh, stop it."

"You sure that's your cousin? Because you know, if you guys have got some kind of *Brokeback Mountain* thing going on you can just tell me—"

I slipped a hand around Annie's waist and pulled her toward me, removed her Stetson with the other, before silencing her with a kiss. And what a kiss it was. Soft and sweet, just like her. She kissed me back, and my entire body tingled with excitement. After five or ten seconds, we pulled apart. Annie's cheeks were rosy red and flushed, and she took a moment to compose herself before speaking.

"Wowzers. I guess not."

"I want to see you again soon, Annie," I said, brushing back her strawberry-blonde hair.

"I suppose that could be arranged. But I have to admit, I'm still a bit miffed."

"About what?"

"That dad and his kid who interrupted what should have been our first kiss earlier."

"I thought we just rectified that."

"Yes, but …"

"But what?"

"Well, they got a selfie with the famous 'Hammerhead' Jed Ounstead. I never did."

"What happened to the Hemsworth brothers?"

"I'll take a homegrown Canadian wrestler over an Aussie any day of the week, thank you very much. It was your poster I always wanted. I was just stringing a whizzer before. Didn't want to come on too strong, I guess."

"No time like the present."

Annie twirled into my arms, until her back was pressed against my chest. She wrapped my hand tightly around her taut tummy and whipped out her phone.

"Dangnabbit, Jed, do you think you can duck down or something?" she said as the camera on her phone cut off my head and the top of my shoulders. "If I wanted a pic of me with muscular pectoral muscles, I could have just stayed at the stables with Rosco."

"Rosco?"

"My bronc."

"Right. How about this?" I said, before slouching down and popping her Stetson onto my head, which given that it was a few sizes too small, made me look like I was wearing the cowboy hat that came with a Western Ken Mattel doll.

Annie burst into giggles as she took a series of snaps. "You are such a dweeb!" she said, before turning and planting a big kiss on my cheek while taking the last pic. With our photoshoot finished, I handed Annie her hat as she spun back around into my arms, kissing me on the lips one more time.

Not long after, while driving away from the *Colossal Cloverdale Rodeo and Country Fair* toward the nearest Dairy Queen programmed into my phone's GPS, I recognized the sensation that had my skin tingling from head-to-toe. I smiled when I realized that, in one frenetic day, I had managed to harness the very thing Kooty preached during his motivational speeches.

Happiness.

THIRTY-SEVEN
"AFTERCLAPS"

The little boy stood in front of me staring, one finger up his nose, the other on his crotch as he held such a secure grip on his private parts it was obvious that he needed to relieve himself. I tried to ignore the kid as I sat by myself in the booth and instead focused on the two large banana milkshakes, held in my hands, while I took alternating sips from both.

"That's a lotta desserts," the kid said, finally.

"Yep," I replied curtly, not letting him ruin the moment as my taste buds were treated to what they had been desperately craving for the better part of the afternoon.

"Is that a map?" he asked, pointing to my detective's notebook which was wide open on the table before me. I had killed what felt like an eternity waiting for my banana milkshakes by digging the pen and pad out of my EDC sheath and sketching a layout of the chaotic fairgrounds.

"Tommy!" snapped the kid's mother, before running over and grabbing him by both of his hands. "Stop doing that," she admonished, before giving me a leery look as she noticed the two-hundred-and-forty-pound man all by his lonesome double-fisting milkshakes with a look of pure bliss on his face.

I ignored Tommy's mom and slurped back the rest of one of my shakes, silently thanking Declan for insisting I take a PI retainer by sticking some bills from the duffel bag in Jasper's locker into my pocket earlier, because the Cloverdale Dairy Queen's debit and credit card machines were down and the store was only accepting cash. I also said a little prayer in my head for Jasper, and couldn't help but feel sad that while my actions that afternoon had helped reveal the truth, they had done very little to lessen the sting of my lumberjack pal's murder.

Having emptied the first milkshake cup, I shifted my focus to the remaining one when the epic instrumental theme "Head Of The Table"—better known as the entrance music for WWE Superstar Roman Reigns—began to boom from my iPhone's speakers.

I knew who was calling by the personalized ringtone and picked up right away.

"Hey Pop."

"How's it going, Boy?"

"Coroner was on scene by the time I got there," I said, referring to my efforts to get to Kelly Lewis ASAP while he was still in custody of the country fair security.

"The coroner?!?"

"Yeah. Turns out Lewis expired right before we arrived."

"Jesus."

"There's more."

I told him about Lewis's complaint about his throat being sore and the punch I had delivered during our knife fight.

"Could still be something else and just a coincidence," he said, matter-of-factly. "And even if not, we're talking an open and shut act of self-defence. Guy came at you with a knife in front of a hundred witnesses, so you won't even get as much as a slap on the wrist."

"I suppose you're right."

"Of course I am. Plus, with headcases like that, you never know what kind of drugs—legal or illegal—they're pumping into their systems. Seems more likely that it could have been an accidental OD, or something in response to his crime of passion."

"Maybe. Either way, I thought you could get a jump on things for me with your OIC buddy."

"You're not sticking around to give a statement?"

"Not after the day I had."

I filled in my old man on everything that transpired after discovering Lewis had died. When I got to the part about Declan and the peacock, my father was laughing heartily.

"What I would have given to have been there for that!" he said, still cackling. "All these years and he's still scared of those damn birds."

"Petrified."

Eventually my old man's laughter faded and he cleared his throat. "Where are you headed now?"

"Home to crash. I'm going to need a good night's rest before I come into the office tomorrow."

There were a few moments of silence on the other end of the line.

"You mean the Shillelagh."

"No, Pop. I mean Ounstead & Son Investigations," referring to our private investigators' office on the second floor above our family pub. "Unless you don't have any work for me?"

I heard the sound of frantic hands on a desktop followed by the phone receiver dropping, before it was picked up and my father got back on the line. "Oh, I've got work for you, don't you worry about that."

"Then I guess I'll see you tomorrow."

"Roger that."

I was about to end the call when I heard my father speak once more. "I'm proud of you, John."

"Thanks, Pop."

I placed my phone down on the table and took a deep breath. By the time I exhaled something inside of me had started to shift. It felt good.

I took a long sip of my shake, and was enjoying the treat and the solitude, only to have my moment of peace interrupted by a text message alert on my phone.

I put my DQ cup down and checked my screen, expecting to see a follow up from my father. Instead, the name *Grasby* was there.

"Shit."

I opened the text and read the message.

What the fuck, Ounstead?!? I heard you left the rodeo? You're supposed to headline tonight's show—we had a deal!

I started to type an apology, explaining that I was unable to make it and would find a way to make it up to my pro-wrestling boss when another message came through.

Annie.

I abandoned the draft I had been writing for Grasby and checked what she had sent. It was one of the selfies we had just taken, where we were cheek-to-cheek, her smiling like a beautiful country gal, and me looking like an overgrown and exhausted goof wearing her too-small Stetson. Nevertheless, there was no denying that I had a lightness in my eyes and playful expression I had not seen in a long time.

I grabbed my DQ cup with my other hand and pulled it close for another sip. But it never made it to my lips, because that's when I first noticed it. I put down my shake and rubbed my face with my free hand. *I was just tired*, I thought to myself. My eyes were playing tricks on me. I scrolled up and took a closer look at the pic Annie had sent me earlier, the one of Kelly Lewis, dead, lying face down on the table in the portable while in custody with the country fair security guards. I clicked on the photo and made it full screen.

It was still there.

I couldn't believe it. Holding my phone with my left hand, I used my thumb and index finger to zoom in even further on the image. There was no denying it. What I thought I saw was there. My pulse quickened. My mind raced. And ten-minutes later, I was back at the rodeo.

THIRTY-EIGHT
"CLASH WITH THE CLYDESDALES"

I called Declan as I sped back toward the country fair and filled him in on what happened at the Dairy Queen. He was skeptical at first, but when I mentioned I was in such a rush to return to the western exhibition that I had forgotten my banana milkshake and left it on the table in my booth, he fell silent and I could tell even he was a bit rattled. We agreed to meet at the stables behind the Stetson Bowl rodeo arena not far from where Declan had choked out the clown and I stole the poor bastard's clothes.

Damn it, I thought. If I ever got out of this mess, I owed that jester VIP tickets or signed wrestling merch or something after what my buzzed cousin had put him through. I parked in a disabled spot at the nearby casino, given its proximity to the stables, but barely gave it another thought. I suppose the fact I had talked an intellectually disabled man out of causing any more damage left me feeling like my cowboy karma offset the small parking violation.

I was hit by a now-familiar nasal punch, the odour of animal dung, as I entered the stables. It was a more formidable stench than I had encountered at the cow-pie bingo station, or from any excrement left behind by Sykes's strategic stinker of a heifer. Weathered, yellow, stomped-on hay was strewn about messily between two rows of stalls. It was a far cry from the quality of the organic bales Sykes had been using for his Bovine Game of Manure Chance.

There was a deep and guttural neigh and then a whinny, followed by an ample amount of snorting. I realized that the stalls to my left were housing two giant Clydesdales. I had seen them pulling a carriage earlier when rolling up to the security portable where Kelly Lewis was held in custody before he had suddenly died. The other stalls contained average-size horses. As I walked alone through the stables, I spotted a placard on the first stall opposite the Clydesdales, which read ROSCO.

Annie's bronco.

I noticed a half-eaten apple on the ground outside of Rosco's enclosure. I picked it up and dusted it off, then fed it to the horse, who gobbled it up greedily.

"There you go, Boy," I said, while petting the side of his long face. "Where's your mama?"

That's when I heard a hushed male voice from outside call her name.

"Annie!" the man said with urgency. "Annie, are you here?"

I ducked behind the end of Rosco's stall, doing my best to shrink my bulk behind the wooden wall so I wouldn't be noticed. The rusted metal hinges creaked as the door at the other end of the stables swung open and I heard heavy footsteps enter.

"Annie!" he chastised. "Quit playing around!"

At that moment, I realized Declan had snuck into the stables himself, and like me, was tucked behind the first stall on the other side of the animal shack. While I didn't know how or when he had joined me, I wasn't at all surprised. His IRA operative training made him stealthier than a jaguar in gym shoes. My cousin gave me a wink, and I nodded in return. United and ready, we held our positions as the person took slow, deliberate steps into the stables, the entire area silent save for the movement and occasional rustling of horses.

I sprung forward from around the corner of the stall, seeing Declan doing the same in my peripheral vision. A moment later we found ourselves face-to-face with the man who was looking for Annie.

Harland "Hot Saw" McGraw.

He was wearing the same sleeveless grey-and-white camouflage track suit he wore when I first encountered him in the axe-throwing alley of the loggersports pit, except this time he wasn't wielding a hatchet.

"You!" he said, recognizing me.

"Hello, 'Hot Saw,'" I replied. "Why are you looking for Annie?"

"Look, I'm sorry about before, okay?" he said, holding up his hands defensively. "I shouldn't have hit you like that and run. I just panicked."

"And why would you do that?" I asked, slowly closing the gap between us with Declan by my side.

McGraw let out an exasperated sigh. "This whole thing with Jasper and Kelly has gone haywire. It was just supposed to be a simple payoff so I could claim the STIHL sponsorship."

"And now both of them are dead."

"I had nothing to do with any of it. Come on, Man. You know my deal. My family is loaded. It's not like I needed the money that comes with the backing from the Krauts. I just want to be the top guy and the face of loggersports in the Pacific Northwest."

"Let's stay focused here, Fellas," interjected Declan, before pointing an accusatory finger toward McGraw. "Ya got one chance to tell the truth, ya understand? Or else I'm gonna beat yer arse senseless for what ya did to me cuz. Aye, they may call him 'Hammerhead,' and he's got a skull like a stone, but if and when this bloody bastard takes one too many cracks to the noggin an' winds up pissin' into diapers while droolin' in his wheelchair, I'm gonna be the one spoon-feedin' him his mashed bananas."

I shot Declan a curious look, unsure if what he said was a testament of our brotherly love or an insult.

"What do you want to know?" said McGraw.

Declan continued his interrogation before I could get a word in edgewise.

"The answer to the million-dollar question, Boyo."

Both McGraw and I waited with baited breath as Declan lit a cigarette and took a drag before continuing.

"It's true that ya lumberjokers call yer willies 'hot saws,' ain't it?"

"What?" replied McGraw, confused.

"For crying out loud, Declan," I scolded, having had enough of his drunken investigative line of thinking for one day. "Leave the sleuthing to me, will you?" Declan scoffed and threw his arms up in the air, but remained silent. I turned my attention back to McGraw.

"Why are you looking for Annie?" I asked.

"Because I thought she might know what's going on."

"How could she know?"

"Because this whole thing was her goddamn idea."

I felt like I had been punched in the gut, but after my epiphany back at the Dairy Queen, McGraw was only confirming what I had already suspected.

"Explain," I growled.

"Annie came to me first. Said she could grease the wheels and, along with Jasper's boyfriend Kelly Lewis, they could convince him to drop out of the competition for the STIHL sponsorship if I dipped into my trust fund and paid him off."

"Why would she do that?"

"To save their rodeo."

"What do you mean?"

"She and her daddy Gus. They're broke. And about to lose their business. So, in exchange for helping me secure the sponsorship, I promised I would use my new clout to ensure I remained with Pippen's loggersports outfit and keep touring with their traveling rodeo. I even agreed to lend them some money to keep things afloat if need be, but with me as the new STIHL superstar working exclusively with them and Pippen, they'll probably make out well enough."

"Ya mean she just wanted to save her family business?" asked Declan.

I shot him a look and he shrugged his shoulders. "What? It's just not that bad o'a move on her part, is all I'm sayin'. I'd probably do somethin' similar if the Shillelagh was on the line."

Declan had a point. While not exactly above board, if all Annie was trying to do was protect her and her father's best interests, it wasn't the most egregious transgression. And after what went down between me, the late Cassian Cullen, and his underground fight club, I was hardly in a position to take the moral high ground.

But I knew there was more to it than that. And I had to talk to Annie herself to get the answers I needed. "I bet I know where she is, D."

"Then get after it, Mate. I'll see what else I can get out o'this eejit," he said, motioning toward McGraw.

"What if he tries to take off again?" I asked.

Declan took another puff of his cigarette and grinned ear-to-ear as he exhaled a stream of smoke. "Oh, don' ya worry 'bout that."

Declan nodded toward McGraw. Only then did I see half a dozen seniors on scooters roll into the stables behind the axe-thrower, who, just like the horses around us, was now penned in himself. McGraw noticed the stern-looking octogenarians behind him, led by Flo, who had her old-school, leather motorcycle goggles on and her mouth formed into a thin line as she gritted her dentures.

"Aye, that's right, ya sack o'shite. Didn't expect me to have a loyal mobile army o'the elderly, did ya?"

McGraw just glanced back and forth between us and the angry-looking geriatric gang on their ZooMe and Rascal machines.

"Go on, now," said Declan. "Find Annie."

I gave him a pat on the shoulder and left the stables, heading toward the one place I could think of where she might be.

THIRTY-NINE
"BARREL RACE"

Fireworks exploded overhead, lighting up the night sky as I sprinted across the country fairgrounds. With Canada Day just around the corner, endless amounts of red-and-white sparks showered down from above, and I could hear the enthusiastic *ooohs* and *ahhhs* of the dazzled spectators seated and spread out across the open grass area Annie and I had run through earlier when racing toward the Agri-Zone in response to Buffalo's rampage.

Annie.

What the hell was she doing? She was such a sweetheart, yet her involvement in Jasper's bribe betrayed a more cunning and strategic side. I think what bothered me the most was the way she had played dumb and gone along with everything, despite sitting on a crucial part of the equation that had led to Jasper's death.

What else had she been faking? Were her feelings for me phony too? They sure as hell felt genuine. Then again, maybe I had been so burned by Stormy and Rya that at this point any interest from a lovely lady would have me seeing stars and not what was right in front of me. I shook off the thoughts as I continued to run away from the still crackling fireworks booming in the sky, with intermittent rounds of applause and cheering from the country fair patrons, who were loving every moment of the evening's big Saturday night festivities.

I reached the pavement area I had spent the better part of the day traveling back-and-forth across as I pursued the truth about Jasper's murder. I caught myself yearning for the simplicity of my life just a day earlier, when Jasper and I were just a couple of down-on-our-luck chumps drowning our sorrows and commiserating over our affairs of the heart. I zig-zagged around packs of teenagers drinking beer and smoking weed and in-between stacked barrels, scattered throughout the pop-up parkland serving as markers for both the walkway and the numerous carnival games that had shut down for the pyrotechnics show. By the time I passed the ring toss and water gun squirt station I was close to my destination.

I went to the same entrance that had been locked earlier, when I was desperately trying to get out of sight while looking like a beat-up, sweaty, and shit-kicked Krusty the Clown, thanks to my altercation with Kelly Lewis and Buffalo. This time the door was ajar.

I opened it slowly and stepped into the darkened hallway. Inside there was total silence, save for the echoing of fireworks continuing to explode in the distance. I slowed my breathing and crept forward until I reached the locker room. I quickly checked the EDC sheath on my hip, ensured my phone was on silent and other items were where they needed to be, then slipped inside.

The change room was even darker than the hallway, and for a moment, the only noise was the slow drip of water from one of the shower heads I had used to clean myself up, before almost calling it quits and walking away from the *Cloverdale Rodeo* and any efforts on my part to try and find Jasper's killer.

Suddenly, there was the clang of metal, followed by the pounding sound of fists striking a locker and muffled swearing. I slinked along the wall until I could see the silhouette of someone in front of Jasper's locker. They had a crowbar and were using it to pry open the upper part of the same door that Declan and I had locked after we stashed the bribe money inside of *my* locker—something it was clear the man in front of me was unaware of.

I slid my hand along the wall until I found the light switch, then flicked it on. The person in front of Jasper's locker whirled around, caught red-handed, an expression of total shock on his face. He was a balding, mustached, and slender fellow dressed in a black T-shirt and blue dungarees, whose sweaty brow was furrowed into a nasty glare as his eyes adjusted to the light. He gripped the crowbar tightly in one hand.

We stared at each other for a few moments before I spoke.

"Gus Tibbs," I said, finding myself face-to-face with Annie's father.

8:56 P.M.

FORTY
"HAMMERED AND HOG-TIED"

"Here's a tip. Lock picks work better than a crowbar."

"What?"

"I'm just saying."

"Who the fuck are you?"

"Friend of your daughter's."

Gus didn't like that one bit. "Right. The 'Hammertime' wrestler guy, I reckon?"

"You know, it's really quite simple. 'Hammerhead.' Not 'Hammerman,' not 'Hammertime.' Although I will say this, Gus. I've been told the rapper and I do have one thing in common."

"Oh yeah? What's that?"

"We're both too legit to quit."

Gus didn't respond, but his scowl made it clear he did not appreciate my taunts. I took a step toward him but he didn't even flinch. If he was at all intimidated, he certainly didn't show it. Instead, he just kept squeezing his crowbar, waiting for me to make my next move.

"That money doesn't belong to you."

"It does now."

"Is that why you killed Jasper?"

"That stupid son of a bitch had it coming," he replied, without hesitation. "And after all we did to help him out."

"Axe to the back of the head doesn't seem very generous."

"That—it wasn't supposed to go down that way."

"Right. I turn down bribes and accidentally split my head open on blades all the time."

"You got a real mouth on you, don't you?"

"Yeah, well, unlike Jasper, at least mine still works."

"All he had to do was take the money and run off with his faggot friend and that overgrown, stupid knuckle-dragger!" snapped Gus. "Could have had a nice little life on a farm suckin' dick whenever he wanted with enough money to eat fried chicken all week long. I wasn't trying to be greedy. I just wanted to keep my rodeo. McGraw gets the STIHL sponsorship, and one way or the other he ensures we stay in business. Everybody wins. But, oh no, that wasn't good enough for Jasper. Not Mr. *My-Granddaddy-worked-on-the-green-chain*. He was too honourable for that, and had to go make things harder than putting socks on a rooster. Which is why he got what was coming to him."

I stood there for a long moment, glaring at this pathetic excuse of a man. I realized that my cousin and father were right. There was evil out there. Men like Cassian Cullen and Gus Tibbs who not only evaded the law, but almost certainly would have gotten away with snuffing out the lives of innocents—unless there was intervention by somebody who could stop them after they slipped through the cracks of the traditional justice system.

Somebody willing to pay the price that others wouldn't.

Somebody like me.

"Save your sad story for the cops," I said, before lunging forward, closing the gap between us.

Gus swung the crowbar, but was too slow. I blocked his strike with my left forearm, then delivered a thunderous blow to his stomach. He lurched forward, gasping and wheezing, but still held onto the crowbar in his right hand.

"It's over, Gus," I said with certainty.

I reached out for the iron bar in his grip when suddenly the noose from a lasso encircled my hands. Before I knew what was happening, it was cinched tight around my wrists and yanked me forward so hard I fell to my knees. By the time I had realized what had happened to me I looked up, only to see Annie standing over me with a frown on her face.

"I told you I could lasso just about anything, Sugar."

Just then I caught a glimpse of Gus standing up behind me. A moment later searing pain shot through my back as the crowbar connected so hard across my shoulder blades I hit the floor of the locker room., my cheek pressed against the cold concrete.

FORTY-ONE
"ACE IN THE HOLE"

"Why, Annie?" I croaked, as I sat up slowly and shuffled back-wards until I was resting against one of the lockers next to Jasper's.

Although the blow to the back hurt like hell and left me dazed for a few minutes, it hadn't knocked me out completely, something for which I was grateful given all the bumps to the cranium I had already taken that day. Despite my moniker, even a guy who was known for having a thick skull could only take so much head trauma. However, I realized my noggin *not* being cracked open by a crowbar was not an act of generosity. It was exactly how Gus and Annie Tibbs had wanted it.

"How did you know, Jed?" she asked.

I looked around the change room and saw we were alone. Annie had the crowbar in her hands and sat across from me on the long bench between the rows of lockers. I tried to wrestle my arms free but had no luck. Annie had secured my hands behind my back even faster than she had Lewis's, although as I began to rotate my wrists I realized in her haste she had not hog-tied them as securely as she had his by the pony ride station. I kept working my wrists behind my back as I realized my EDC pouch had been removed from the belt of my cargo shorts and placed flat on the bench beside Annie. The lock-picking kit had been taken out and sat atop the sheath, and when I glanced upwards and to the right, I saw that Jasper's half broken-into locker was still secure enough that it had not yet been revealed that the bag of cash was not inside. Annie and Gus still had no idea I had moved the windfall to my adjacent locker earlier.

"Where's your dad?"

"Don't worry, he'll be right back. How did you know, Jed?"

"Any chance he's hitting a drive-thru? Because as far as last meals go, I'd like it to be a DQ banana milkshake."

"How did you know!" she screamed, leaping to her feet and banging the crowbar against the metal of the locker room doors behind her.

I looked at the woman who I had spent the day falling for, her softness and sweetness now replaced by scowling and seething rage.

"The necklace," I said, finally.

"The one at the bottom of the pool? It proves nothing. Could have come from anyone. You know how popular Kooty is at his country fair."

"Just like I know you are a big believer in his teachings. That necklace was yours, Annie."

"Unfortunately for you, big guy, there's no actual proof of that."

"Are you sure? I mean, things happened kind of fast, didn't they?"

That caught Annie's attention. She tried to recover but I knew had hit a nerve. I kept pressing her.

"I figure your dad is the one who drove the axe into the back of Jasper's skull. You just don't have the strength. But the only way a guy like Gus could get the jump on a good ol' burly lumberjack like Jasper was with a little help—like when you lassoed him around the neck with a jagger wire and started choking him to death until your father finished the job."

Annie paced back and forth in front of the lockers like a jungle cat. "But how did you know the necklace was *mine*?"

"Because when I fought Lewis by the pony ride station, he wasn't wearing a necklace, Annie. You screwed up when you sent me that photo of him dead and slumped forward on the table. I didn't see it at first. But there it was, a shiny metallic washer on a silver chain around his neck. Which means somebody planted it on his body after we subdued him, I guess to try and make it look like he was a true believer of Kooty's teachings—*just like you*. Whatever the logic, like you said, the country fair security is a joke. There was no protocol for them to follow before the Mounties showed up. Which easily allowed you to slip a necklace around Lewis's neck undetected, making it look like he must have replaced the one he must have lost when he murdered Jasper in the log boom pool. And this wouldn't be considered at all unusual, as after talking with Kooty, the Doukhobor made it very clear that many of his 'pupils of positivity' often buy multiple totems as reminders of his self-help philosophies."

Annie continued to stride around as she listened, but was moving more slowly, never taking her eyes off of me. The tension between us was palpable and mounting. Eventually, she stopped and crossed her arms across her chest. After a few moments, she started to chuckle.

"Well, swat my hind with a melon rind! You really are a good detective, ain't ya, Jed?"

"You seem surprised."

Annie shrugged. "You're just a lot smarter than you look."

"I thought you liked the way I looked."

"I do. That's what makes this so difficult."

"What are you waiting for? If you're going to kill me, Annie, just do it."

"Right. Like having you turn up beaten to death with a crowbar in front of a locker full of cash isn't suspicious. No, you're going to go out the same way Kelly Lewis did."

"No offence, but I don't think even your strongest punch to my throat could kill me."

"Who said anything about a punch to the throat?"

I stared at her for a moment, not understanding. Then I thought of my fight with Kelly Lewis. How Annie had lassoed his hands, then jumped on him and tied his arms behind his back. She moved so lightning quick with her calf-roping skills I must not have seen it. And because he was face down in the mud, Kelly Lewis didn't see it either. But he sure as hell felt it. I remembered the last words Lewis screamed after he yelped in pain, but before Annie had knocked him unconscious with a sharp elbow to the back of the head.

"Ow! What the fuck—what are you doing?!?"

The realization hit me. Annie did something to Lewis—something he wasn't expecting—when hog-tying his wrists. Which meant he didn't die from a—MY—punch to the throat.

I glanced up at Annie to find her smirking.

"You poisoned Lewis, didn't you?"

"I didn't poison him. I euthanized him. Same medley of drugs we use on our old and sick horses. And don't act like I wasn't doing him a favour. What I said was true. Sooner or later, a bipolar headcase as bad as him was gonna bite the dust. Instead, he got to just put his head down on a table and go to sleep peacefully before his heart slowly stopped beating."

"Toxicology will reveal that, you know."

"Of course, it will. And as a longtime rodeo hand and clown with a history of mental instability, it makes sense that he would take his own life in such a peaceful and painless way after murdering his gay lover in a fit of rage."

Annie wasn't wrong. It made sense.

"In the meantime, you were fine with me running around the rodeo sick to my stomach believing I had killed an innocent man?"

"I warned you," she said, before pointing at the DO NOT GO GENTLE text on my prototype pro-wrestling attire. "Doesn't matter what kind of T-shirt you wear trying to convince yourself what a tough guy you are. You're just a big softie. Which is why once Daddy gets back with the needle, you're going to go to sleep too. It's not going to hurt, Jed."

I rolled my shoulders back against the locker and held my head high. Annie wasn't taking any chances. She jumped back a step, gripped the crowbar tightly, and raised it up to her shoulders, at the ready to strike me at any moment.

"And what's my reason for suicide?"

She shrugged. "Guilt over accidentally killing Kelly Lewis? And maybe also over whatever other stuff you've been pining about all day? I'm not stupid, Jed. You've been in a funk about something. Everybody around you sees it."

"You're right."

"It ain't perfect as far as plans go, I'll give you that. But it's the best we could come up with given the circumstances."

I took a deep breath and exhaled, slowly sliding my hands over to the right side of my cargo shorts. "Well, Annie, I guess if I've got to go, I'm glad it's you. The truth is, if things turned out different, I really think I could have loved you."

Annie lowered the crowbar and the sweet and delightful woman who had charmed me suddenly returned. She took a step toward me and knelt down slightly, then reached out the index finger of her left hand and tapped me on the nose.

"'Hammerhead' Jed,' she said softly. "Still sweeter than a banana cream pie."

In a flash I reached into my cargo shorts pocket, grabbed the necklace Kooty had given me, and threw the loop around her wrist. I twisted the chain and yanked, causing Annie to stumble forward. With my wrists still bound, I sprung to my feet, grabbed her by the collar of her pink button-down shirt, and threw her behind me against the metal lockers with all my strength. She slammed face first into a metal door and collapsed to the ground, the crowbar clattering to the concrete beside her.

"Annie!" screamed Gus, as he charged toward us with a large syringe in his hand. His face was a mixture of fear and fury as he looked between his daughter and me, but I still had enough time to pick the crowbar up off of the floor. Even with my wrists secured, I was able to get a good grip of the iron bar and swung it—hitting Jasper's murderer flush across the cheekbone. Gus flopped on top of his daughter, knocked out cold. Annie, however, was still conscious and groaned as she writhed in pain while pinned underneath her father.

I placed the crowbar down on the bench and out-of-reach, then dug around in my EDC sheath until I found my tactical knife. I snapped the blade open and began cutting the ropes binding my hands, slowly but surely.

Five minutes later my hands were free, my PI pouch was back on my hip, and both Annie and Gus had *their* wrists zip-tied behind their backs as they sat propped up against the lockers just as I had been only minutes before.

Gus was still completely unconscious, but Annie had managed to come out of her dazed state. This time I was the one who crouched down in front of her. She met my eyes but said nothing, although they did widen when I held up Kooty's necklace in front of her and swung it back and forth like a pendulum, just the way she had shown me.

"*Wish it. Will it. Wield it,*" I said.

FORTY-TWO
"HELLS BELLS"

By the time Declan and the RCMP charged into the change room I had already opened my locker. I had removed the bag of money intended to bribe my slain woodcutter chum into withdrawing from the STIHL Timbersports sponsorship and send him off to 100 Mile House to live a quiet life with Kelly Lewis and Buffalo. After zipping open the duffel to confirm the cash was still there, I left it in on the bench in front of both Annie and Gus Tibbs ... just out of their reach.

I suppose I could have secured the bag elsewhere and out of sight, but part of me must have wanted to torture them both a little by allowing the father-daughter murder tag team to see how close they came to getting their greedy hands on what to them was worth the lives of two decent men.

I had also lined up the crowbar and the syringe filled with the medley of horse-euthanizing agents next to the satchel filled with stacks and stacks of bills, using a fifty-dollar note as a makeshift handkerchief in an effort to do as little as possible to disturb the fingerprints that were all over both crucial pieces of evidence of Gus and Annie's guilt.

Declan had prepped the officers as per my request in the text message I sent him, so they went right to work taking my statement. I made it known that I had no interest in going down to some Mountie detachment to talk more about my involvement in the day's events. I'm not sure if it was because they found my request reasonable, or because I had, for lack of a better word, peacocked a bit myself while making it known I was the son of retired VPD legend Frank Ounstead—who just happened to be very tight with their Mountie Superintendent Bashum—but either way they didn't seem to have a problem with getting what they needed from me on site and moving things along swiftly so I could hurry up and be on my way.

At one point while giving my statement to a female RCMP member, Gus, who had to be removed on a stretcher by EMTs, was wheeled past me. He was followed shortly by Annie, who was escorted out of the locker room in handcuffs with several officers flanking her.

I tried my best to not get into it with her, but when I saw her shooting daggers at me with her eyes, I couldn't help myself. As a result, I raised my fingertips to my lips, then blew her a long kiss as she left the building, albeit not before she unleashed a string of expletives so vicious and vile I momentarily considered taking another shower before leaving the locker room.

Once outside with Declan, I saw Harland "Hot Saw" McGraw speaking with two Mounties by a police cruiser, and he was so busy gesticulating wildly while spilling his guts to the cops it was clear that the RCMP were going to have all the evidence and witness testimony they needed in order to provide the Crown Counsel with one damning case against Gus and Annie.

The fireworks show had ended, and the flow of hundreds of country fair patrons walking away from the outdoor sitting area on the field bottlenecked as their pace slowed to a crawl past the entrance to the locker room. They were buzzing among themselves about what might have caused such a commotion. There was an even bigger police presence than the earlier one outside of the security portable, where Kelly Lewis had died from the deadly cocktail of equine drugs Annie injected him with after our knife fight by the pony rides.

Still wearing his Stetson cowboy hat and amber-tinted aviators despite the dark of night, Declan pulled two silver cans of Hell's Gate Lager from his insulated cooler backpack and handed me one. We walked by multiple RCMP patrol units with their lights silently flashing red and blue, stepped around a rookie officer struggling to use a roll of yellow crime scene tape to cordon off the area from the looky-loos, and merged with the slow flow of pedestrians.

"'Tis a tragedy, Mate," said Declan.

"Death is never easy, D. But at least we helped Jasper get some justice. I think that's what all this mayhem has made me realize. There will always be things beyond our control, and events that occur whether we like it or not. But we always have a choice."

I thumped a fist on the T-shirt on my chest. "We don't have to go gentle into that good night. We can rage. *Rage, rage, against the dying of the light.*"

Declan looked at me quizzically for a few moments, then popped the top of his brew. "Aye, that all sounds well an' good. But I just meant that I'm out o'beer," he said, before shaking his empty backpack up and down in front of me.

I sighed and opened my drink as well, and we stopped by the entrance to the bumper boats area of the carnival, then tapped our cans together and raised our suds in a toast.

"To Jasper," I said.

"An' his Chop-Chop Pop Pop," replied Declan.

We drank our lagers in silence, until an announcer's voice boomed over the country fair's PA system.

"All right, country fans, that concludes our fireworks show for the evening—but the fun ain't over just yet! Pull up your bootstraps, grab yourselves a bite and beer, and saddle up for all of the evening fun as our Rodeo After Dark attractions kick into gear!"

There was an accidental high-pitched squeal as the microphone switched off, before the steady, ominous, funeral tolling of a two-thousand-pound bronze bell rang out across the speakers. Declan closed his eyes and inhaled, as if he could almost smell Angus Young's epic guitar riff as it kicked in and one of the greatest rock anthems of all time began.

"And there's one o'me favourite jams to celebrate!" he crowed, before miming a little air guitar. "This is a sign, Mate. Let's hit a pub an' have ourselves a proper piss-up for Jasper."

"Wait," I said, looking around. "Where's Flo and her scooter squad?"

"Are ya right bolloxed? It's after eight, Jed. *Waaaaay* past her bedtime. She's back at the nursin' flat waitin' for me to join her at 4 a.m."

"4 a.m.?"

"Aye, she said she wanted to have another go at breakfast."

I don't know if it was the relief after the day's misadventures, our last beer, or my cousin's ongoing geriatric lust, but I suddenly burst out laughing. Declan joined me, and we stood there in the crowd for I don't know how long, chuckling so heartily my abdominal muscles started to hurt.

"I'll have to take a rain check on the pub, D," I said, finally.

"Why's that, Boyo?" he asked, taking off his glasses and wiping the tears from his eyes.

"Because I have one last thing I need to do."

FORTY-THREE
"BABYFACE GOLD"

My opponent was grinding his spandex covered crotch into my face when I first heard the raucous cheers and laughter from the audience.

Current XCCW Heavyweight Champion "Cousin Pappy" Vinny McKinney had put on a few pounds since his prime, and, as a result, had switched up his ring gear in recent years. I myself had gone back to wearing my traditional stretchy, black, polyurethane pants emblazoned with blue lightning bolts—since it was much cooler for the evening show than it had been for the matinee—while Vinny sported a snug, bright green singlet, which made his junk ride high and his muffin top hang low, creating for an especially sweaty and suffocating melding of man meat.

And impair my breathing it did. Although the crowd was loving his use of a bronco buster, it was clear Vinny had very little experience executing the move correctly, especially to ensure his opponent did not suffer too much discomfort.

"C'mon, Bro! Punch him in the nuts!"

My dwarf friend and sometimes squared circle ally, Pocket, stood on the apron of the ring in my corner, his tiny feet level with the titanic tummy of his tag-team partner Tubbs, a four-hundred pound Polynesian man who wore a Tommy Bahama shirt so large it could have been used as the sail for a boat. Although not sporting their straps, the duo were also the current XCCW Tag-Team Champs and went by "*Pocket and Tubbs*"—a gimmick that inspired their colourful pastel suits and sockless loafers ring wear in the style of *Miami Vice*. The sizeable Samoan and miniature mouthpiece were just two of the dozen professional wrestlers surrounding the ring as Vinny and I duked it out for XCCW's top prize during a lumberjack match.

The rules for such a match are simple—a group of wrestlers not directly involved in the contest are known as *"lumberjacks,"* and their presence and sole purpose for being outside the ring is to prevent the competitors from escaping. The problem for me was that the majority of the grapplers serving as enforcers were heels associated with "Cousin Pappy," which is why, when he mercifully kicked me out of the ring after what felt like the hundredth time of his musty loins smothering my nose and mouth, I almost broke kayfabe and thanked him.

The three-hundred plus crowd booed loudly as the "Cousin Pappy" aligned heels took turns whaling on me with fists and kicks, before a piercing shriek cut through the night air faster than a chainsaw could cut a log.

"Here comes the '*Hot Pocket,*' Bitches!" squealed my diminutive ally, before Tubbs, who had lifted up and tucked his little buddy behind his ear, launched him through the air like a shotput.

Pocket spread his arms and legs and splashed onto several of the villainous lumberjacks, allowing me the chance to climb to my feet, compose myself, and roll back into the ring. Vinny charged at me with an attempted clothesline which I ducked underneath. He turned around and tried the move again, but this time I grabbed him by the wrist, used his momentum against him, and threw him across the ring and into the ropes with an Irish whip.

"There it bloody is, ya wankers!" hollered Declan from the front row. "The best bloody move in all o'wrasslin'!"

"Cousin Pappy" bounced off of the ropes and rebounded back toward me. His greasy pomade had sweated off, leaving the wispy black strings of hair that usually covered his bald spot disheveled and flapping about in all directions. I picked him up by the waist, tucked him under my arm, and dropped him hard to the mat with a sidewalk slam. The spectators cheered as they could sense my imminent victory. However, rather than launch into my Five Moves of Doom, I went with a different finish. As soon as the crowd clued into my intention they went wild with anticipation.

I grabbed Vinny by his boots, rolled him over onto his side, then turned my back to him. I slid one of my feet in-between his legs and folded them across my waist, before finally leveraging his weight until he flopped onto his stomach and I sat backwards into a sharpshooter, the submission move made famous by my all-time favourite pro-wrestler and childhood hero Bret "The Hitman" Hart.

While I had never performed his move before, after our charity exhibition match arranged by Sykes had ended in a joint in-ring celebration of mutual respect, *The Best There Is, The Best There Was, And The Best There Ever Will Be* himself had given me his blessing to use his iconic technique in future matches.

"Cousin Pappy" sold the pain like a true ring veteran, clawing at his hair, contorting his face, and screaming in agony. He taunted the audience by holding his hand above the mat, hinting at tapping out, but shaking it wildly, trying with all of his might not to give into the crippling submission hold. At this point the fans were on their feet, and the energy in the outdoor venue was electric. Men, women, and children all whooped and clapped in a frenzy, and just when the collective zeal reached a fever pitch,

"Cousin Pappy" Vinny McKinney gave in and pounded his palm down on the canvas repeatedly.

With that, the bell rang and the referee called the match in my favour. The crowd went nuts, and I dropped Vinny's feet to the mat and stumbled around a bit, selling the exhaustion from my barnburner of a match. My part-time boss and the owner of X-Treme Canadian Championship Wrestling, Bert Grasby, having changed into a more upscale purple velour track suit for the main event, climbed into the ring bearing the big, gold XCCW Heavyweight Championship belt. Pocket and Tubbs joined us in the middle of the squared circle as I accepted the title, before holding it up in the air in victory.

"Well done, Boyo!" shouted my cousin, who was ringside with a fresh twenty-ounce plastic tumbler of beer and seated next to none other than the big-bellied clown he had jumped earlier that afternoon. How he was able to find—let alone get the man to accept an invitation to—my match I had no idea. However, given the way Declan and the jester were enthusiastically celebrating my win together, whatever lingering guilt I had about us stealing the fellow's costume for undercover work had dissipated. Instead, the rotund entertainer and my cousin had their arms around each other while drunkenly singing Queen's "We Are The Champions" off-key and toasting their brews to my victory.

The cheering continued, and I was even more surprised when I spotted Sykes, whom I knew did not care at all for professional wrestling, sitting ringside in the front row. He nodded at me coolly, but approvingly. Only then did I notice Buffalo, next to Sykes, feeding birdseed to his grey parrot pal from the Avion Café while it sat perched on his boulder of a shoulder, while the gentle-hearted giant applauded excitedly, looking as content as I had ever seen him.

All in all, after the day that I had just had, it was pretty much a perfect moment in time.

There was just one thing missing.

EPILOGUE
"PIPE BOMB"

The Saturday night traffic was light, so once I merged my Ford F-150 onto the Trans-Canada Highway West it was a straight shot from the Fraser Valley to Vancouver.

I drove most of the way in silence with a smile on my face. Between sips of the large, Dairy Queen banana milkshake held between my legs I stole glances at the XCCW big gold belt resting on the passenger seat riding shotgun. It was a far cry from the WWE Intercontinental Championship I once held, but I'd be lying if I said it didn't feel amazing to be able to call myself *"Champ"* again.

The driveway was full of cars when I pulled up, and from the lights and silhouettes in the townhouse window, it was clear some kind of party was going on inside. I marched up to the front door anyway, the gold belt over one shoulder, and the DQ banana milkshake in my hand.

I rang the doorbell and waited. A few moments later I heard the deadbolt unlock and she answered.

"Jed," she said, clearly surprised.

She didn't seem irritated or angry, just confused. She looked between my new hardware and my frozen treat and smirked ever-so-slightly.

"Looks like you've had a busy night."

"Yeah," I replied. "I have."

"You look good," she said. "A bit tired, but good."

"And you look more beautiful than the first day I met you," I replied.

She smiled softly, shifting uncomfortably on her feet, her cheeks beginning to turn the slightest bit scarlet as she blushed from the compliment. She pulled an elastic off of her wrist and tied her wavy dark brunette hair back in a ponytail.

"Hon! Get in here," a familiar male voice called out from within the townhouse. "Game night is about to start."

She half-turned around, then closed the door behind her. We stared at one another for I don't know how long, looking deep into each other's eyes. Finally, she spoke.

"What are you doing here, Jed?"

"I had to tell you something."

"Okay. What?"

"I love you, Rya."

ACKNOWLEDGEMENTS

GIDDYUP! To say I was excited to write the acknowledge-ments of the fourth "Hammerhead" Jed mystery-comedy is an understatement—the path to bring this book to the page was in some ways the most challenging, unique, and incredibly satisfying journey I have ever taken.

Thank you to THE best publisher in Canada—*NeWest Press*—because after having had the honour and privilege of putting out FOUR novels with this awesome team (books made so much better due to their virtuoso and tireless efforts) I'm pretty much done pretending any other company in the country comes close to the creative artist constructive Candyland thinktank sanctuary that has been my author home since "Hammerhead" Jed's debut in *Cobra Clutch*.

Thank you to the delightful Christine Kohler, an accomplished artist and potent presence of positivity at NeWest Press, who ensures that regardless of whether she is shipping books, or sending out tax forms, she still manages to always put her authors first. Thank you to the always effervescent NeWest Marketing Coordinator Carolina Ortiz, who not only is endlessly patient with her more enthusiastic authors (*ahem*) but also never ceases to both impress me and expand my knowledge of all things promotion and press-related. Thank you to the lovely and multi-talented NeWest Production Coordinator Meredith Thompson who kicked off her career with NeWest by working on *Five Moves of Doom* ("Hammerhead" Jed Mystery #3) and managed to outdo that stellar performance this time around. Meredith also pulled double duty as the official "rodeo consultant and resident country fair expert" for *Bronco Buster* thanks to her equestrian youth and vast experience. Meredith's keen eye ensured everything from the words inside the book to the images on the front cover truly captured both the accuracy and essence of rodeo and country fair life. When it comes to my editor, the epically erudite Merrill Distad, at this point all I can say is you can read the many words I've already written about how amazing this gentleman is in my previous acknowledgements, and that being gifted the chance to work so closely four separate times with such an incomparable literary mind has benefited my writing career immeasurably. And that unbelievable gratitude extends directly to the bold and brilliant General Manager of NeWest Press Matt Bowes, a true visionary whose integrity, insight, and business acumen is only occasionally outshined by his hilariously savvy suggestions (if you enjoyed the character of Sykes and his *"Bovine Game of Manure Chance"* venture in the novel you just read you can thank my GM who doubles as a true Albertan Son of the Soil). And of course, thank you to NeWest President Leslie Vermeer, whose stalwart leadership and rock-solid support of her authors continues to carry on this truly unique publisher's preeminent mission statement of giving a voice to Western Canadian authors telling Western Canadian stories.

This audacious purpose NeWest Press has set forth and maintained for over forty years is so vitally important to the continued growth of the literary arts in this truly special part of Canada and the world, which is why I would also like to pay my respects to the late NeWest Press co-founders Douglas Barbour (who I was fortunate enough to meet at my first Edmonton book launch) and the recently passed Diane Bessai. Due to the efforts of people like Doug and Diane decades ago, aspiring authors like myself continue to have their lives forever changed in so many positive ways by having the opportunity to be traditionally published.

I would also be remiss if I didn't do a roll call for my NeWest Press crime writing bros JT Siemens, Niall Howell, DB Carew, and Randy Nikkel Schroeder for all of their support both on and off the page, as well as a tip of my hat to my wordsmith sisters Frances Peck, Margie Taylor, Meaghan Marie Hackinen, and future NeWest Press star poet Sarain Frank Soonias. A huge thank you to *New York Times* bestselling authors and two of my comedic crime-writing heroes Steve Hockensmith and Andrew Shaffer, the incomparable and national bestselling author of the outstanding Lane Winslow historical mystery series Iona Whishaw, Crime Writers of Canada Award of Excellence nominees MH Callway and SM Freedman, and all the talented authors who read advanced copies and / or took the time to write a blurb or review.

I remain blessed with wildly supportive family, friends, fellow authors, podcasters, pals, local business owners, and fans of "Hammerhead" Jed, and while I wish I could thank each one (I already ramble on too long in these things), I must give a special shout out to Kathy Findlay, Ben Capps, Jim and Margaret Gillis, Dan Copeland, Ariel Pastorek, Derek Cheng, Mac Daly, my buds Mickey, Juju, and Taylor, Marvin Wildimube, my book launch bros (Darren "The Rocket" Stein, Scott Shoemaker, Steve O'Brien), Greg Rhyno, Sam Wiebe, Rich Ehisen, Claire Booth, Bruce and Gillian Johnson, Bob Harris, Jeanne "Hollywood" Basone, MN Grenside, Kent and Erin Lockhart, Doug and Sue Binns, Russ and Debbie Grist, Joel and Nancy Johnston, Kim Sawatzky, Jack Donohue, Owen and Kathy James, Magnus Skallagrimsson, Winona Kent, Erik D'Souza, and Ludvica Boota of Crime Writers of Canada, Garrick Webster of CrimeFictionLover.com, Andrew Gulli of Strand Magazine, Tamara Gorin of Western Sky Books, Sara Martin and Geoff Boyd of Parkside Brewery in Port Moody, Jaime and Yvette Cuthbert of Rocky Point Ice Cream, Sadie Henchel and the Port Moody Public Library, and my pals at the Port Moody Fire Department.

Thank you to my bestie Shoshana, one of the kindest and most wonderful people I have ever known, and someone who gave me the gift of her beautiful friendship during a particularly challenging time in my life while this novel was on its path to publication.

They aren't blood but they are my brothers, and without "Mr. Bronco Buster" himself Sean O'Brien and Seamus Heffernan in my life I wouldn't be half the man I am today let alone be able to continue "Hammerhead" Jed's story—*I love you guys and can never thank you both enough for all that you have done and continue to do for me and my family.*

Thank you to my mother Dianne, a wickedly funny yet benevolent woman who remains my biggest supporter despite her near constant irritation with my reluctance to trim my hair or beard. And I saved the biggest thank you of all to the two most special people in my life—my budding beefcake of a son Jack and the light of my life and daughter Scarlett, to whom I promise to never stop trying to be her *#DreamDad* (even though it seems I still have a ways to go!)

Finally, I wish to thank anyone discovering "Hammerhead" Jed for the first time—especially if it is with *Bronco Buster*. Writing this pro wrestler detective character has not only been one of the most exciting, thrilling, and rewarding experiences of my life, but knowing that my piledriving PI is still being found by new readers gives me an endless amount of inspiration to continue channeling my love for old school action-adventure escapist entertainment into further adventures for this hopefully loveable and definitely larger-than-life unusual sleuth.

—AJD

A.J. Devlin grew up in Greater Vancouver before moving to Southern California where he earned a Bachelor of Fine Arts in Screenwriting from Chapman University and a Master of Fine Arts in Screenwriting from The American Film Institute. After working as a screenwriter in Hollywood, he moved back home to Port Moody, BC, where he now lives with his family.

Cobra Clutch, the first book in the "Hammerhead" Jed professional wrestling mystery-comedy series, was released in spring 2018 and nominated for a Lefty Award for Best Debut Mystery and won the 2019 Crime Writers of Canada Arthur Ellis Award for Best First Novel.

The highly acclaimed sequel, *Rolling Thunder*, was released in spring 2020 and featured in the *Vancouver Sun*, *The Province*, *Globe and Mail*, *Kirkus Reviews*, *Library Journal*, *Mystery Tribune Magazine*, *Punk Noir Magazine*, *CrimeFictionLover.com*, and on CBC Radio's The Next Chapter with Shelagh Rogers.

The third book in the series, *Five Moves of Doom*, was published in September 2022 by NeWest Press and featured on The House of Mystery Radio Show on NBC. It won the 2022 *Crime Fiction Lover* Editor's Choice Award for Best Indie Crime Novel, was selected by the *Globe and Mail* as one of the Best Books of 2022, nominated for the 2023 Lefty Award for Best Humorous Mystery, and shortlisted for the 2023 Crime Writers of Canada Howard Engel Award of Excellence for Best Novel Set in Canada.